THE NURSE

Claire Allan is a former journalist from Derry in Northern Ireland, where she still lives with her husband, two teenage children, two cats and a dog who thinks she is a human child. In her eighteen years as a journalist she covered a wide range of stories from attempted murders, to court sessions, to the Saville Inquiry into the events of Bloody Sunday and countless human interest features. Claire has been writing crime fiction since 2018. *The Nurse* is her sixth thriller. She has also worked as a story consultant on forthcoming BBC drama *Blue Lights* and is currently working on a TV adaptation of her novel *The Liar's Daughter*.

When she's not writing, she'll more than likely be found dog walking or on Twitter @claireallan.

Also by Claire Allan:

THE
NURSE

CLAIRE ALLAN

avon.

Published by AVON
A division of HarperCollins*Publishers* Ltd
1 London Bridge Street
London SE1 9GF

www.harpercollins.co.uk

HarperCollins*Publishers*
1st Floor, Watermarque Building, Ringsend Road
Dublin 4, Ireland

This paperback edition 2022

1

First published in Great Britain by HarperCollins*Publishers* 2022

ISBN: 978-0-00-838356-5

Typeset in Bembo by Palimpsest Book Production Limited,
Falkirk, Stirlingshire
Printed and Bound in the UK using 100% Renewable
Electricity at CPI Group (UK) Ltd

MIX
Paper from
responsible sources

FSC
www.fsc.org

FSC™ C007454

This book is produced from independently certified FSC™ paper to ensure responsible forest management.

For more information visit: www.harpercollins.co.uk/green

Acknowledgements

Thanks first of all to my editor Helen Huthwaite, who got behind this book from day one and who helped iron out the creases so beautifully. Your support for this book has been incredible, Helen and your faith in it (and me) has meant the world.

To the rest of the incredible team at Avon, HarperCollins for being so great to work with and so passionate about what you do. Special mention goes to Becci Mansell and Ellie Pilcher for helping me get the word out, but thanks to the sales team, production, management and all the other people who keep the wheels turning. Thanks also to Helena Newton for her excellent copy-editing skills.

Thanks to HarperCollins, Ireland for continuing to be so supportive. Hopefully those M50 days will be back soon. Your help and support is so appreciated.

An incredible debt of thanks goes to my agent, Ger Nichol, who has championed this book with incredible passion and who is always there for the good, the bad and the occasional ugly cry from me!

Huge thanks to my writer pals, who understand all about this crazy business and who have provided support, laughs, and inappropriate Gifs at all the right times. In particular, thank you to Louise Beech, John Marrs, CJ Cooke, Cally Taylor, and Brian McGilloway. Extra special thanks to my author pal who I also consider to be a true soul sister, Fionnuala Kearney who has read, laughed, cried and sworn with me over FaceTime for the last two years when we've been unable to meet for a giant hug. FK, you are a blessing in my life.

To my non-author pals – the fact that you put up with me means the world. Especially when I'm lost in makey-uppy worlds or boring you senseless with my latest research on incel forums. This pandemic has made me realise more than ever just how important you all are to me. Thank you Julie-Anne, Marie-Louise, Erin, Fiona and Catherine.

To my family – I love you. I could not love you more and we are so blessed to have each other – and a lock of dogs between us. To my husband – thanks for encouraging me to keep going. To my wonderful, amazing, talented children – thank you for spurring me on, and for teaching me to think and feel outside of the box.

Writing a novel during a global pandemic was not easy. Doing anything during the global pandemic is a struggle, if we are honest. 2020-2021 was a challenge on a number of levels. It would be remiss of me not to include the staff of St Cecilia's College in Derry in these acknowledgements, and in particular the support of principal Martine Mulhern, and art teacher, Lesley-Ann McGrory. You ladies are the epitome of strong women and you pass that ethos, caring and great sense of humour on to all you meet. This book may not have been written at all without you both supporting our family through this challenging year.

Thank you to the book-bloggers, reviewers and media for your continued support, and to booksellers for working tirelessly on behalf of us authors. Special thanks for supporting my writing goes to Jenni Doherty at Little Acorns in Derry and Lesley Price at Bridge Books, Dromore.

The character of Heather Williams (the Family Liaison Officer) in this novel is named after the very generous lady who supported the Books For Vaccines fundraiser which helped bring the Covid 19 vaccine to those who struggled to get access. Thank you for your support for both me and for this very important cause.

Lastly, thank you to all who read this book and who support my work. I am exceptionally privileged to be able to do this, and I am forever grateful to you all.

For my sisters, my soul sisters, my youngest child, my nieces

And for all the women who never made it home

'. . .the feeling when you follow a girl and she notices you, and she tries to loose (sic) you or picks up the pace. That is kind of a good feeling. You become important to her. You are no longer some random insignificant face in the crowd.

'I know it is kind of low-level behaviour. But I do enjoy doing that. I go to another city, look for a girl who is walking by herself and start following her. After a while they notice you. After dark, after sunset it may suffice to just walk in the same general direction as a girl who is walking in front of you. They become paranoid.

'I recommend you lonely incels try it some time. Just to make her afraid. If you know your limits and don't actually harass − let alone rape − that girl, it should be harmless psychological fun.'

Genuine post from an incel forum,
February 14, 2018

Prologue

The petal drifts to the cold stone floor, its landing cushioned by its brothers and sisters already discarded as the game creeps towards its climax. The ending changes with each petal. She loves me. She loves me not. She lives. She dies.

He can hear her move around in the bathroom upstairs. Can hear the floorboards creak under her step. The pipes rattle and fizz to life as she turns on the taps over the sink.

She thinks it has been a good night. He's sure of it. He has cooked them dinner of fillet steak, served with potatoes dauphinoise, green beans and seared asparagus. He thanks God for M&S and their idiot-proof ready-prepared dishes. He'd opened a bottle of Châteauneuf-du-Pape. He doesn't consider himself a wine connoisseur, but it had cost more than £20 so it must be a good one. It is more than she deserves, but he has to play the game properly.

The goal, he knows, is fear. And fear is always most pronounced when it comes as a surprise. When it comes at a moment when his pawn is relaxed. Happy. Hopeful.

There is no rush like seeing realisation dawn on the face of his prey. When they realise they aren't invincible. That they aren't as safe as they thought they were.

But it all depends on the petals. Once he sets the rules, he abides by them. He plucks one more petal, tries not to guess how many more are left. Patience, he thinks. The moment is sweeter for the wait.

A floorboard creaks overhead and his eyes glance upwards. She has been gone a while now and he's starting to get antsy. The adrenaline is already pumping in his veins, making him jittery. The fight-or-flight reflex is primed and ready to go. He thinks, if the petals dictate it, it will be a fight this time. She strikes him as a fighter.

The pipes stop rattling and if he's not sure, and if he listens really intently, he thinks he might hear her talk. It throws him for a moment until he looks across at the empty chair opposite him. The bag that she had hung on the back of it – the bag which contains her phone. No. No, she isn't supposed to do that. That breaks the rules. When they are together, he expects her full attention. It's a matter of manners. Of respect.

His hand tightens around the stem of the rose, the thorns piercing his skin. There are three petals left. He knows what way this would have fallen for her. But she broke the rules. She has brought this on herself. He has no choice.

Getting up, he walks across the room to the small wooden box on his bookshelves. He takes out a tablet, breaks it in half and pours the powder into the remains of her glass of expensive wine. He stirs it around with his finger as he hears the bathroom door open and her footsteps on the stairs, then he plasters a smile on his face.

Chapter One

Marian

Monday, November 1

Missing four days

Nell didn't come home after work on Thursday. That was four days ago. Four days. And this is the first time I've heard about it.

I'm unpacking the shopping, swearing over a busted yoghurt carton, when my phone rings and my daughter's housemate – a terminally timid nurse called Clodagh – asks me if I know where Nell might be.

I look at the clock. It's 7.15 p.m. Nell normally finishes work at 7. Sometimes she works later. Whatever, it's a strange time for Clodagh to be expressing concern for her whereabouts.

It's strange for Clodagh to be calling me at all. I'm not known for my helicopter parenting and Nell has been fiercely independent since she first moved out four years ago. It's not unusual for us to go a week or more without speaking. It's just how it is.

'I imagine she's working late, or just called into Tesco,' I say, grabbing some kitchen paper and mopping up a dollop of M&S

Greek yoghurt before it congeals on my worktop or Harry Styles – the very fluffy tortoiseshell cat Nell named after her teenage crush – arrives to lap it up.

I'm annoyed that I'll have to rethink tomorrow's breakfast. I have all those fresh berries waiting to be eaten . . .

I become aware of Clodagh replying, stumbling over her words. There's something in the pitch of her voice that catches my attention. I blink, as if the act of that alone will bring her words into focus.

Did she say Nell hadn't gone to work? I shoo Harry Styles away, put the kitchen paper down and turn my back to the worktop. Looking at the clock on the wall, I see that it's now 7.17.

'Is she sick?' I ask. The last time I'd spoken to Nell, she'd told me she was afflicted with that most common of all afflictions: Tired-All-The-Time. I'd told her she really should make an appointment to go and see her doctor. Being permanently exhausted at my age was one thing, but no twenty-two-year-old should feel that way.

She'd laughed. 'Mum,' she'd said, 'I see doctors every day at work. I'm fine. Just tired. It's winter. We're incredibly busy and there's always someone off sick. But I'm okay, honest. Or as okay as any nurse is these days. I need a week in the sun, is all.'

'No. No. Well, I don't know,' Clodagh says, cutting through my thoughts, and the urgency in her voice seems to increase. 'So you haven't seen her today?'

'No,' I reply. 'I've not seen her since, maybe, this day last week? She called in to pick something up from her room. Shoes or something.'

It comes to me. It was those awful clumpy platform boots. She'll break her ankle in those one of these days. I'm sure of it.

'But have you spoken to her? Or heard from her even? A text or a WhatsApp?'

I shake my head as if she can see me. 'No. Not in a few days. Why?'

'How many days is a few days?' Clodagh asks and I start to realise something is clearly wrong.

'I don't know. I can't think. I don't think I've spoken to her since she visited. What's going on, Clodagh?' I ask and I notice a sharpness in my voice. It's enough to make Harry Styles arch his back and glare at me in disgust.

'So you've not seen her since Thursday? Shit!'

'Clodagh,' I say as if I were trying to get through to a preschool child. 'Tell me what's going on.'

I can feel the hairs on the back of my neck rise up, a cold shiver creeping from the base of my spine up towards my neck.

'She, well, she didn't come home from work on Thursday. And I thought, well, maybe she was still with Rob.'

'Who's Rob?' I ask, immediately feeling like the worst mother in the world for not knowing who this person in my daughter's life is.

'Rob. She met him a few weeks ago. On Tinder. It's been going well between them. So I thought maybe she was just, you know, with him. You know what it's like when you start seeing someone.'

It has been a long, long time since I'd started seeing someone but I know enough to know what she means. I don't particularly enjoy thinking of my daughter in that situation. Consumed by lust. I shake the thought from my head, and shiver. I should put the heating on. The temperature is dropping quickly. It will be another frost-filled night.

Is my daughter out there in the cold somewhere?

'So, she isn't with this Rob?' I say, which is a stupid question. Clodagh would hardly call me if she was.

'No, or I assume not because Jenny in work had a date with him on Saturday night and he stayed over at hers,' Clodagh says, and I wonder do I hear a trace of a sob in her voice. 'I've called everyone I can think of and no one has seen her or heard from her. And she didn't go to work today – or call in sick . . .'

My head starts to swim. I grasp the edge of the worktop to get a hold of something real. Tangible. I hope my hand will float right through it. That this is all part of a dream.

But I feel the cold granite on my skin.

This is real.

'Since Thursday?' I blurt, my throat tight.

'And she hasn't been on any of her social media,' Clodagh says, and there is no mistaking the crying for anything else any more.

I look at my keys, my bag, thrown on the worktop. I look at the half-empty shopping bags. The discarded kitchen paper. I look at it all and, without listening to what else Clodagh is saying, I tell her to call the police and that I will be right round.

Harry Styles meows loudly as I leave without putting out his dinner. He can have the bloody Greek yoghurt. Everything else will have to wait. I curse as I wait for my phone to connect with my car's Bluetooth system. It never normally takes so long and yet today, of course, it does.

I jab the 'voice control' button, order the car to call Nell. Listen to the automated voice tell me it's calling her. I want to scream at it to shut up, because I want to hear my daughter's voice. No. I need to hear my daughter's voice. And there it is, the 'hello' I need to hear and I exhale until it's followed immediately by 'sorry, I can't take your call right now'.

I stifle a sob, slam my car into reverse, my leg shaking as I release the clutch.

I call my husband. Maybe he'll have spoken to her. He should be driving home from work. I wonder how much I should say knowing he has to drive from Belfast, in worsening conditions. I don't want him so panicked he makes a stupid mistake.

'Stephen,' I say, forcing my voice to remain calm. 'I'm just wondering if you heard from Nell today or over the weekend?'

'Over the weekend?' I hear the ticktock of his indicator light, the swish and thump of his windscreen wipers.

'Yes,' I say, trying not to be impatient even though I want to scream.

'No. I'm not sure I did. I can't think. I would check my phone if I wasn't driving. Why? Is everything okay?'

I make the decision to lie to him. To my husband. To my partner of twenty-seven years. He won't like it. He'll hate it, in fact, but I'm thinking of him behind the wheel of his car. His eyes tired. The salt and pepper of his hair increasingly erring on the side of salt. The crinkles in the corners of his eyes. The commute is starting to take a toll on him. But he won't admit it. Nell describes him as a stubborn old goat.

'Yes,' I blurt. 'I was just wondering. Nothing urgent. I'm going to call round to hers. Just have a need to see her. Why don't you call in on your way home?'

It's a ridiculous lie. A cruel lie, I think, as I imagine him arriving at her house and her not being there. Maybe the police being there instead. But as bad as things are, I need him with me. She is as much a part of him as she is of me. We are tied together by her.

'God, Marian, I'm tired and this is going to be a bastard of a drive. I just want to go home.'

'Please,' I say, and how I keep the wobble from my voice I don't know.

'For goodness' sake,' he sighs. 'If it'll get you off my back, I'll call in. But it'll be a flying visit.'

My stomach tightens at his tone. I can feel the pulse of a headache behind my eyes.

'Thank you,' I say and tell him we'll see him soon. We. As if I'm sure Nell will be there, which of course I'm not.

To my surprise, I find that I'm tearful. I'm never tearful. It's not the kind of person I am. I'm not the kind of mother who dabs away tears of pride at school concerts, or who weeps over baby pictures. I have an ability to remain focused and logical in my approach. I had to be that way when Nell was little.

But now? It's as if something in my very core knows something is wrong.

The emotional umbilical cord I thought I didn't have is connected to my child after all, and it floods me with all the emotions, all the moments that are now just memories. A feeling there may be no more memories – not good ones anyway – to be made.

I put my hand to my stomach. I don't know why. It's as if I hope to feel a movement. To feel a kick. To feel a sign of life. But of course, I think, shaking my head and trying to focus on the drive ahead of me, that's absurd. It's not going to happen. It was never going to happen.

I will my logical self to kick back in. To focus on what I can do. What I can change. Feelings won't help me now. For now, all I need to do is get to Nell's house as quickly as I can to talk to Clodagh and the police.

God love her, but Clodagh isn't to be relied on to start a search on her own. She's a lovely girl but prone to hysteria. Could this just be hysteria? Will she remember that she did in fact speak to Nell yesterday and slap her head in a 'stupid me!' move?

No. I'm clutching at straws. And I don't, as a rule, clutch at straws. But this is different. This is my child. My stomach twists again.

I call Nell's number once more. Listen to her voice tell me she'll get back to me. Her sing-song, youthful, full-of-promise voice. I contemplate leaving a message. Pleading with her to call me. Pleading with her to pick up. Ordering her to do what she is told.

But I don't plead or cry. I end the call and concentrate on driving, finding each change of gear, each brake and acceleration, requiring more effort than usual. This can't be happening.

Chapter Two

Marian

Monday, November 1

Missing four days

It seems so incredibly odd when I arrive at my daughter's three-bedroom semi-detached house and it looks just as it normally does. There is nothing different. No sense of anything being out of place. The pampas grass in the corner of her front garden is still an overgrown monster of a thing that I want her landlord to tear up. One of the panes of glass in the lantern outside her front door is still cracked.

But there are signs that this is a home she has pride in. The winter wreath on the door. The collection of glazed pots on the doorstep, plants well-tended and pruned to survive the frosty mornings. Pot plants she can do. Large pampas grass monsters she cannot.

I reach for the doorbell and startle when the door opens in front of me before I have the chance to press it. Clodagh is in her nurse's uniform, with a thick cream cardigan wrapped tightly around her. Her eyes are red-rimmed, and she is clutching a tissue.

'I'm really sorry, Mrs Sweeney. I just thought . . . I was working all weekend and you know, sometimes we're like ships that pass in the night and then I thought it was unusual we still had milk left in the fridge. And I checked her room but it was just like it was on Thursday morning and I remember that because I sat on her bed while she was getting ready for work and she'd borrowed my black dress to try on and it was still there, where she left it, over her bed. And I called her. Like five or six times. And then I called our friends. And work. And then you.'

I walk into the house and look around, as if Nell might just appear out of the ether and surprise us both.

'You called the police?' I ask, while still looking around. I stick my head through the door into the living room. It's tidy, warm. Lit by two lamps on either side of the room. Nell's oversized knitted throw folded over the sofa. I fight the urge to lift it, to try and get a sense of her from it. The scent of her. I close my eyes and a dozen different scents come to mind. Baby powder. The smell of Vosene shampoo on her hair when she was a child. That overpowering body spray she used when she was a teenager. The soft scent of her favourite perfume now – Wood Sage and Sea Salt by Jo Malone. I've just ordered her a new bottle for Christmas.

'I did,' Clodagh says and I blink, focus on what she is saying. 'They said they'd send someone out but, she's an adult and . . .'

'She's an adult who hasn't been seen or heard from since Thursday,' I bark, then immediately regret my tone. It's not Clodagh's fault. She's only the messenger.

'I told them,' she says, her voice meek.

'And this Rob guy? What do you know about him?'

'Erm, I don't know a lot about him,' she said. 'She'd only been seeing him a few weeks and we've both been working stupid hours so we haven't really talked.'

'She must've told you something?' I plead, finding it hard to believe that there was anything in Nell's life that she wouldn't have told her best friend.

'Yes, well. He's older. Like late twenties. He works in one of those starter businesses down at the offices at Fort George. You know, the new ones? I don't know what he does exactly. New media or something.'

'And do you know his surname? Or what he looks like?'

'I'll check her friends list to see if I can find him,' Clodagh says, pulling her phone from her pocket and scrolling through the screen. She taps a few buttons and swears. 'Damn it. She has her friends list set to only share mutuals.'

'Jenny!' I say and Clodagh looks at me as if I've lost the plot.

'You said your friend Jenny from work went on a date with him. Call her. Ask her what she knows about him. I assume she'll have his number, or his last name at least?'

Clodagh nods, scrolls through her phone and listens as the call rings out. She leaves a short message, asking Jenny to call her back as soon as possible and that it's really, really important. When she ends the call, she looks at me as if she expects me to have the answers to everything. I suppose I'm the mother figure. I'm supposed to know what to do next. Who to talk to. She has no clue that every single solitary fibre of my body is pulsing with dread. That if I could I would run to my own mother. That it's taking all my strength just to keep breathing in and out, never mind trying to formulate some strategy, or find it in myself to offer her some comfort.

I need some space, so I make my excuses and go to Nell's room. Her space has a visceral effect on me. This may not be the room she grew up in. This may not be the room I nagged her to clean, or the colour scheme we clashed over. The chest of drawers isn't the same one where I found a tobacco tin containing one perfectly rolled joint hiding in her knickers drawer.

There are no grooves in the doorframe marking her age and height. But she is there all the same. It smells of her. Her perfume. Her hairspray. I see her Po doll, the fabric bobbly and threadbare, grinning down from the top of her wardrobe. A testimony to the Teletubbies obsession she had as a toddler. I can see clothes that are her size. I see those stupid bloody platform boots and my stomach twists again, so tightly that I don't think I can bear it any more. I'd be sick if there was anything in my stomach, but there isn't, so I bend and break and bow in the middle.

I have never been so scared in my entire life. I know I can't give in to it. Not yet. There is much to do and maybe, just maybe, this is a big menopausal overreaction to something with a perfectly reasonable explanation.

The flashing blue lights of an arriving police car, which illuminate my daughter's room through the open curtains, tell me my fears are justified.

A petite blonde woman in a tailored grey trouser suit extends her hand and introduces herself as Detective Sergeant Eve King. I'm unnerved by her presence. It seems strange that someone so senior would come out for a call that police don't think is too much of a cause for concern.

I introduce myself, and Clodagh, as a tall, gangly man in an ill-fitting suit appears at the doorstep – the sight of him making me jump.

'This is my colleague, Detective Constable Mark Black,' DS King says. 'You don't mind if he comes in too?'

I shake my head, even though this is not my house and I've no right to allow or stop anyone coming in.

'Of course not. Come in,' Clodagh says, her voice shaky. 'Can I get you a tea or a coffee or a glass of water or anything?'

'We're fine, thank you,' DS King says. 'Maybe we could have a sit-down and a chat about your housemate. Nell Sweeney?'

15

Clodagh nods but she seems frozen in shock, or fear, or something at the situation she is faced with. I wait for her to direct the officers to the living room but she doesn't move, so I step in, guiding them to the sofa while Clodagh and I take an armchair each, and sit down, our backs rigid, our faces taut.

'Okay,' DS King begins, taking from her pocket a notebook and a biro, the lid of which had been chewed. I notice little things like that. Nell is forever telling me to chill out. 'Clodagh, you told dispatch that Nell hasn't been seen since Thursday. Is that right?'

Clodagh nods. I can see her bottom lip wobble and I want to shake her. She needs to keep it together, because we need as much information as possible, as quickly as possible, if we are to have any chance at all of finding Nell. Don't they say with a missing person the first forty-eight hours are crucial?

But of course, I realise, Nell has been missing for a lot longer than forty-eight hours already. My own lip wobbles.

'I saw her on Thursday morning before work. We're both nurses, you see, up at Altnagelvin. But we work in different places. I work on the paeds ward, and Nell is on the surgical ward. I know she was in work that day. She had leave on Friday and over the weekend, so wasn't expected in until today. But she didn't show up.'

'And you didn't see her, or register her absence at all over the weekend?' DS King asks.

Clodagh sniffs. 'I was really busy. I was working nights and that always knocks me a bit stupid, and then we were short-staffed so I worked some overtime. Nell has been seeing this guy, Rob, I don't know his surname but I'm finding out, and to be honest, I thought she was probably with him. You know, a long weekend kind of a thing.'

DS King probes a little more. Finds out about Jenny and her own Tinder date with Rob. Asks about Nell's frame of mind.

'She wasn't depressed or anything,' I say, unable to hide the defensiveness in my voice. 'Don't be thinking she took herself off somewhere and did herself an injury because that's not her. Nell isn't depressed. If she was, she'd have spoken to me about it. I'm sure of that.'

'Are the two of you very close?' DS King asks, her eyes, bright and blue, staring at me. She looks as if she is the kind of police officer who wouldn't need a lie detector test to figure out if a person is telling the truth or not.

'She's my daughter. My only child as it happens. We don't live in each other's pockets, if that's what you're asking. But we are close. She knows I'm there for her if she needs me.'

'Erm . . . Mrs Sweeney is right,' Clodagh says, her voice small. 'Nell isn't depressed. Or if she is, she does a really good job of hiding it.'

'Is she a very sociable young woman?' DS King asks.

'Well, I suppose. She's twenty-two. She's as sociable as any twenty-two-year-old to be honest with you,' I say. DS King shifts her gaze to Clodagh as if all my answers should be taken with a pinch of salt. She clearly thinks I don't know my daughter at all.

Clodagh shrugs. 'Yeah. I mean she went out a couple of nights a week, maybe. But she liked to chill out here too. You know, get into her jammies and watch a movie or a boxset. We liked detective dramas.'

'Is that her?' the man, Mark Black, asks, his head nodding towards a framed picture on the sideboard. It's a selfie of Nell and Clodagh – grinning at the camera. It looks like it was taken on their holiday last year. The sea is bluer than any you'd expect to see on the Donegal coast. They have that slightly red-faced, too much sun look about them. Nell looks so young. So full of life. I can't speak.

'Yes,' Clodagh says. 'That was us, in Kos during the summer.'

'Do you mind if I take this for a moment?' he asks, standing up and already lifting the frame. I have to hold back from telling him not to touch it. I know what he wants it for. To put it online, on posters, in the news. He is turning her into Nell the victim and I don't want any of this to be happening. I close my eyes tight for a moment just so I don't see him take it from the room.

I glance at my watch and wonder when on earth Stephen will get here. I'm starting to fall apart and I need him to tell me everything will be okay.

I watch, afraid to ask what is going on, as DC Black takes the frame from the room and out to their unmarked car. It's only then I notice they didn't arrive in the blue-lighted car. That's still outside, and a uniformed officer is leaning against it, looking for all the world as if he would rather be somewhere else.

'Does Nell drive?' DS King asks.

I shake my head. 'No. She's taking lessons but no. I can give you the name of her instructor if you want.'

'That might be helpful, but can I ask, if she doesn't drive how does she normally get to work? Does she take a taxi, or the bus, or bike, or . . .'

'She walks everywhere,' I say. 'Says it clears her mind before the day starts and then again when it ends. And with living so close to the hospital . . . it's easy for her.'

DS King nods. 'Oh, okay. And do you know what route she normally takes?'

'Erm, not for sure. I mean I think she walks down past the big Tesco and then on down Rossdowney Road. It's fairly well lit.'

Clodagh says, 'Mrs Sweeney's right. And she always takes the underpass to avoid crossing in heavy traffic.'

The underpass. I'd pushed that from my mind. I've always

18

hated that she takes that way home, she always argues that it is safer than trying to cross four lanes of traffic and it was so close to the shopping centre nothing dodgy could happen there.

'And she takes that route every night?'

Clodagh nods.

Suddenly, and unbidden, an image of my daughter lying hurt or, God I can't even think about it, worse in the underpass springs to mind. Surely not. It's a busy spot. She would've been found. Everyone would have heard about it by now.

'It's important we know as much as we can,' DS King says. 'So if you can think of any other route she might take, or if she gets a lift with anyone – any detail at all – let us know.'

At that, Stephen arrives, his face a picture of utter confusion. I watch as he looks around Nell's small living room. Takes in the strange woman in the grey suit, taking notes. Spots Clodagh with her red-rimmed eyes. Looks at me. I can only imagine how I look. Fraught. Pale. Terrified.

'Marian,' he says. 'What's going on? Where's Nell?'

I can't speak. I can hardly breathe. How do I say the words to him? Tell him his daughter – our child – is missing. How can I plunge him into the same nightmare I've found myself in?

'Hello. Can I assume you're Mr Sweeney?' DS King says, standing up to address my husband.

'Yes. I'm Stephen Sweeney, Nell's dad. Who are you and what the hell is going on? Where's Nell?' He's terse, angry. I can tell he will be enraged that I let him walk in on this rather than prewarning him of what he would be met with. But I had to get him here safe. He has to see that.

'I'm Detective Sergeant Eve King. We've been called here because your daughter, it seems, is missing.'

He looks at her as if she's speaking a different language. 'Missing?' he says.

19

'According to Miss Clarke here, your daughter hasn't been seen or heard from since Thursday.'

'Thursday?' He blinks. He's trying to process it all. I watch as he folds and bows and sits down on the sofa as if the weight of what he has just been told has flattened him. I want to reach out and take his hand but he is too far away. He is always too far away.

DS King outlines what she's been told while Stephen stares at me, as if this is all my fault.

'So what do we do now? What will you do to find her?' he says. I notice he's clutching his car keys tightly. If only this was as easy as jumping in the car and driving around to find her playing in the park with her friends, having so much fun she missed her curfew. But those days are long gone.

'We'll need to speak to her friends. This Rob guy she was seeing. Her work colleagues, to try and ascertain her demeanour when she left work on Thursday evening. People go missing for all sorts of reasons. It's important we try not to worry too much at this stage.'

He gives a weak laugh and it cuts through me. We are both long past the 'worry too much' stage now.

Stephen looks at me, helpless. As if he needs me to fix all this right now, because that is what I do. I fix things. I oil the wheels and put the money in the meter and I keep things going. Especially when it comes to Nell. She's more 'my job' than any sitting in an office trying to arrange viewings for houses ever was.

It breaks me that I can't, in that moment, do that job. I can't fix this – this that needs to be fixed more than anything else ever has.

The silence is broken by the return of the tall policeman, DC Black. He is carrying the frame and instinctively I reach out to take it from him. As I do I catch something in his expression. Sympathy perhaps. Maybe he knows how these things go. He's probably been around a bit. He's had these conversations with other parents. He has taken photos of smiling faces, frozen in time, and circulated them. Maybe he's delivered sad news a few days later. It suddenly feels all too much. I look at her picture. Her smiling face. The face I have loved more than anything else in my entire life.

I fight the panic that threatens to destroy me. I concentrate on my breathing, on the sound of my own heartbeat echoing in my body. I think of her heartbeat, how it once echoed mine.

Please, I beg, *please be okay.*

Chapter Three

Him

Two months earlier

This first time is an accident. He doesn't even realise what is happening until her breathing becomes more laboured and her body stiffens. Until he feels the fear radiate from her in waves. Until the staccato echo of her heels on the cold stone pavement speed up, the click-clack of them at an unnatural pace.

He almost calls out. Almost tells her not to worry. It's not like he is going to hurt her. He isn't a rapist or anything. Shame nips at him. The collective shame all men share. The knowledge that they all have the potential to be predators. The potential to overpower. And control. And hurt.

He realises quickly that his shouting would only be likely to scare her further. He imagines her hand gripped tight around her car keys, ready to strike out, score her fear into his face as she simultaneously raises her knee to his groin.

By the speed of her step, the purpose in her walk, he knows she has already judged him a risk. Without even knowing him. He is a threat because he is a man walking down the same street as she is, at night.

That's when he starts to get angry. He's had a shit day at work. His boss was on his back all day – treating him as if he were stupid. She hasn't been in the job much longer than he has, but the power of her promotion has gone to her head. His boss makes such a big thing about her 'doing so well in a male-dominated field' – so much so that it sometimes feels as if she holds him personally responsible for the patriarchy.

And she's not alone. Everywhere he looks now there are feminists accusing men of 'mansplaining' or describing what used to be called flirting as some sort of sexual assault. This nonsense, where this woman is speeding up in front of him – considering him a potential rapist when that couldn't be further from the truth – is just another example of a world going mad. When, he wonders, did it become the case that men can't walk the streets at night without being prejudged as sex pests? When did it become criminal to have a penis?

His growing anger and frustration at an unfair world quickens his step until his pace matches hers. He stays still a few steps behind, of course. He doesn't want to hurt her and it's not his fault if he scares her just by walking the same path. That's on her. On her judgement of him and all men. He realises, his heartbeat has increased and not just because of his increased pace. There is something driving him on. Something that is hitting the very primal part of him. That is channelling his frustration after another day of having tasks he is more than capable of doing being allocated instead to female colleagues, as some sort of affirmative action.

The woman crosses the road without stopping to look for oncoming traffic and he follows her, realising his frustration and anger are morphing into something else. A feeling of power. A sense of control.

The faster he walks, the quicker her step. He can hear an almost imperceptible shake in her every exhalation. Her fear,

23

he realises, is intoxicating. He drinks it in, finding himself smiling, happy to know that while he isn't a threat to her – not now anyway – she doesn't know that. She is just scared. Of him. A man who nobody has ever really taken seriously before.

It doesn't take much for him to reach her. A stretch in his step, a slight increase in speed. Without thinking too much about it, he reaches out and can almost sense her body shrinking away from his touch. She can feel his energy in the air around her. His fingers brush along the bottom of her long, dark hair; his senses so heightened that it feels as if every strand is caressing his nerve endings. The air fizzes and crackles with it. He's shocked to realise there is a stirring in his groin. A reminder of his biology.

She stops, suddenly, and turns to him, her face white with fury and fear. He likes that he can see just how much he has got under her skin. He can see it in the whites of her eyes and the tautness of her jaw.

'Stop it right now or I'll scream as loud as I can,' she says, her words tumbling over each other.

He puts his hands up in mock surrender, his courage dimming. 'Stop what? I'm only walking home.'

'You're following me,' she says. He glances at her closed fist, now raised, and can see the glint of a key poking from between her fingers. 'You fucking bastard. Take one more step and I'll . . .'

'Jesus, I'm sorry,' he says, an automatic response. Always apologise. Always back away. He is surprised to realise that he doesn't mean it. Not at all. He isn't sorry. He's still angry, maybe even more so now that she is swearing at him, but he knows he would be stupid to tell her how he really felt. 'I didn't realise I was freaking you out. Sorry. Why don't you walk on? I'll stay here. Or cross the road.' He takes a step back then. And another one. He fakes shame in his expression and watches as she edges away, afraid to turn her back to him just yet.

24

So he stands and watches. His h[...]
until, finally, she turns and hurrie[...]
sight.

She'll no doubt tell her friends a[...]
her home, he thinks. He's surprise[...]
thrill. He enjoys that thought. H[...]
impact.

By the time he gets home, his ne[...]
feels electrified, fired up. Taking[...]
orders Alexa to start his favourite p[...]
of 'Mr Brightside' by The Killers [...]
Alexa to increase the volume as h[...]
for something for dinner.

No, he decides he won't coo[...]
takeaway Indian. And a few beers. [...]
now. The adrenaline from his wal[...]
it gave him, is exhilarating. It fl[...]
instructs Alexa to crank the volum[...]
food through an app on his phon[...]

He downs the bottle of beer in [...]
the worktop and cracks open a se[...]

He's playing some air guitar, wai[...]
song when he hears it. The thum[...]
over the volume of the music, ov[...]
the thump cuts through. That same[...]
bangs, which signals control. Which[...]
as he thinks. He's feeling hyped up[...]
He shouts louder, ignoring the rep[...]

He pays his rent, the same as [...]
home. If he wants to come in [...]
fucking beer while listening to s[...]
has every right to do so.

or a run. Not everyone wants
he gym. Nothing wrong with
be if you tried it more often
the arse.'

usic again. Turns his back on
e doesn't need to have Cormac
nd her viva guilt-tripping him.
are like. The pressures he is
y don't care.

late that Cormac is reaching
g device and hauling the plug
s bravado ebbing, as Cormac
urtling towards the tiled floor.

e able to process what he has

bellows. 'Or find somewhere

ousemate turn and leave the
en anger and shock. His mood
. The beer, half-empty, in his
ny more. Nor does the Indian
ots with tension and anxiety.
stress returns to where it was

ere. With these people who
ow him to be himself.
is lips again but it tastes sour
his stomach. Looking at the
ing he has been silenced just
his breath and contemplates
too.

But his bravery is gone. His sense of being someone important, someone powerful, has gone. He pours the beer down the sink and puts the bottle in the recycling bin. Then he brushes up the smashed plastic on the floor and puts all the pieces in a plastic bag. He doubts it can be repaired but he'll try.

The doorbell peals and he knows his food has arrived, but his appetite has disappeared. He takes the food from the delivery man and leaves it on the kitchen worktop. Grabbing a pen, he scribbles a quick note, 'Help yourself', and leaves it on top of the sweaty, thin plastic bag.

He's done. He's defeated. And he goes to his room, disappointed in himself and angry at life.

Chapter Four

Him

Two months earlier

He logs onto his computer, loses an hour to YouTube. Another thirty-four minutes to Reddit. Twenty-seven minutes to Pornhub. But not even his favourite porn videos can lift his mood, or his cock for that matter. Fucking Cormac and Jade thinking they have the right to control everything about his house. His environment.

Jade had knocked on his bedroom door shortly after he went to his room. She stood there, her blonde hair tied into a messy bun, wearing her short pyjamas – the ones that showed off her pale, soft thighs not quite enough, and with the top that hung off one of her shoulders flashing a pale pink lacy bra strap. She called them her 'comfies' when she padded around the house in them, or occasionally borrowed one of his oversized sweaters when she felt a bit 'chilly'.

Jade likes to do that. Walk about dressed provocatively, playing the demure but definitely slutty tease. God forbid anyone makes a comment that might be considered sexist. She can look like she has just crawled out of bed, give him that 'fuck me' smile

– but the lines are very firmly drawn in the sand. She wants to be admired for her brain, not for the body she flaunts so relentlessly.

He's not so much in the friendzone as the housemate zone, which was worse, much worse. Actually, it is worse than that. He's in the third-wheel zone, sure that Cormac and Jade have done it. Or they will do it at some stage. He sees the way they move comfortably around each other. There is an intimacy to their interactions that really only comes from knowing someone intimately, and sexually.

It maddens him.

And he was already mad enough when Jade leaned against his doorframe, a plate of Indian food in front of her and thanked him for being so considerate. 'You're so lovely,' she sighed. 'This is just what I need to get me through my study.'

'Would you like me to help you?' he'd asked, the thought of being close to her in those skimpy clothes, maybe in her bedroom suddenly giving him a thrill that ran directly to his dick. 'I can run through some of your questions if you want.'

She smiled, tilted her head to one side, a hint of amusement playing on her lips. 'Oh bless you, but Cormac has been helping me. Academia is more his thing. You'd be bored stupid. And you sounded so stressed earlier. You should just relax.'

He'd not been surprised to hear that Cormac has been in there 'helping'. He resists the urge to ask her to define help. He wished he could just tell her that Cormac was no angel. He wanted into her knickers as much as the next man. Cormac's no more interested in her academic pursuits than he is crocheting. He just wants to get laid.

Just as she left, Jade had turned and blown a kiss in his direction before she walked away, her arse tight in those tiny shorts of hers.

He'd thought of those shorts when he watched his porn,

but he couldn't get there. But now . . . now it's different. He's not thinking so much of her shorts, but thinking of what happened on his walk home. He imagines the woman scared and intimidated by him is Jade and not the mystery woman whose face is already disappearing from his memory.

He thinks of her walking faster, her breath hitching, sweat breaking on her perfectly made-up brow. Now that is something worth fantasising about. The fact that it's so taboo − getting a hit of endorphins from scaring women − makes it even more of a turn-on.

This is a new high. An addictive high. One he will chase again. Maybe with Jade or maybe with another anonymous woman on the street. All those women just like his housemate. They're all the same. They're all dead set on emasculating men like him. Good, decent, hard-working men who women like to tease. To taunt and play with. To play the poor damsel in distress role with and then to turn and laugh at, or to point the jagged end of their keys at, or call perverts and bastards and claim they're intimidated by the very act of a man existing.

It would be different, he muses, if he was muscular and toned like Cormac. If he wasn't so socially awkward. If he could manage to find clothes that looked good on him rather than just hang off him like he's still waiting to grow into them. Maybe if he had hair that behaved instead of sticking up at all angles no matter what. If he drove a flash car or squandered his savings on designer clothes, gaudy jewellery and champagne dinners out. It's not a falsehood that a woman's eye can be turned by possessions and looks. For all the 'beauty is on the inside' crap, very few women he has known have ever taken the chance to get to know him enough to see his inner beauty.

He's feeling angry again. He wants to vent. He wants someone to acknowledge just how incredibly unfair it is. He wants someone to say they understand.

31

But who can he talk to? He scrolls through his phone again, searches out the chatroom he'd stumbled on a week or two before. Men only. The kind of place that he worried would be filled with toxic masculinity, dick measuring, boasts of gym reps and the like. The kind of place that he would find no home in.

But this one is different. There is a board in its collection called 'The Weaker Sex' where men can give out about their partners, or sisters, or friends, or female bosses. Or about those radical feminists who think men are inherently flawed creatures. Or the gold-diggers – those independent women who drop their knickers for anyone with a flash credit card. It's a place he can give out without being accused of being a misogynistic pig. He's not a misogynistic pig. He's a realist.

He scans the current threads. Looks for something that expresses the frustrations he's feeling, or something that connects with the high he felt on his walk home.

There's nothing. So he takes a deep breath. This is a board where he can hide behind an anonymous username. He's working through a VPN and has set up a second email account to try and protect his identity more. Just in case. Because all it would need would be for the wrong person from the wrong place to see what he is writing and it would wreck everything.

He starts to type. Talks of his frustration, and of how he hates that men are seen as either predator, nerd or bank. Talks of how he felt a little bit of control, of power, from his walk home. From knowing he had some power after all. He had made that woman, who had already decided he was a predator, scared. He had controlled her fear until he watched her leave.

With the enthusiasm of someone who has had three beers on an empty stomach, he types 'maybe you might want to try it too'. He adds his self-made hash-tag – one that just comes to him in that very moment. One he laughs at as he remembers a cartoon character of his childhood saying it. #IHaveThePower.

Yes, he thinks, it's a bit wankerish but he feels it in that moment. Empowerment. The kind of empowerment women like to bang on about. If it's good enough for the goose, then it's good enough for the gander.

He clicks the icon to publish the thread – and he sits back. He wonders if people will laugh. He wonders if even in this space he has thought to be safe, people will mock him. Tell him his behaviour is unbecoming or some other such shite.

There's one 'like', then another. Until the trickle of likes becomes a river. Until the replies start, congratulating him. Saying they might try it. Jumping in with #NotAllMen and rants about how all men are lumped together.

He knows he is working the next day. He knows he should go to sleep, but he can't. He's wired now. But in a good way. He has hit a nerve. He has started something.

Chapter Five

Marian

Monday, November 1

Missing four days

'We'll be running checks on her phone, her bank cards that kind of thing. To be honest, the best thing you can do now, Mr and Mrs Sweeney, is go home and get some rest. All being well, Nell will wander in after being on a four-day bender or something, but do rest assured that if that doesn't happen, we're very much on the ball here. We'll be looking into this thoroughly.' DS King is talking. I'm nodding. I can hear the words she's saying but I can't quite believe they are for real. That they are directed at me. That they are about my daughter.

The fear on my face must be obvious because DS King reaches out and takes my hand. 'Mrs Sweeney, I know this is frightening and it's hard not to think the worst, but please bear in mind that Nell is an adult. There is still a chance that she has gone somewhere of her own accord. Sometimes people just need space from others, you know.'

I shake my head. 'Not Nell. She wouldn't do that. She'd know we'd worry.'

She looks at me, sympathy written across her face. I wonder how many other parents have told her they'd know if their child was unhappy but who, in fact, knew nothing about the person their child actually was.

'We'll appoint a Family Liaison Officer to you in due course, someone you can lean on and who'll act as an intermediary between yourselves and those of us investigating the case. But honestly, I'd try and rest if I were you.'

A gruff laugh sounds from Stephen, one that quickly morphs into a sob. 'How under God are we supposed to sleep? Our daughter is missing. Our daughter who would never do something so irresponsible. I've no intention of going to sleep. I'm going to drive around a bit and look for her,' he says.

'Stephen,' I urge. He's tired, pale and broken-looking. He's in no state to drive anywhere, let alone around the town winding himself up. 'It won't do any good. She won't be wandering the streets. She's not sixteen any more. You aren't going to find her up on the City Walls with her friends and a bottle of cider. It would be like looking for a needle in a haystack. Let's just try her friends again. And rest. We can give her more of us tomorrow.'

He stands up, his car keys jangling in his pocket, and glares at me. 'You might be able to rest on your laurels, but I can't just sit and do nothing. DS King, if it's okay with you, I'm going to go now and look for my daughter.'

'We'd urge caution,' DS King tells him, her tone gentle but firm.

'Noted. But I think I'll go anyway,' he says sharply. Dismissively. I feel like apologising for his rudeness but I daren't say anything – when Stephen makes up his mind about something, it doesn't do to question him. Defeated, and embarrassed by how he has just spoken to the police, I watch as he pushes his way past the tall police officer – DC Black, the one who took her picture – and out of the door. I glance down at her beautiful face again. That broad smile. The blue sky bright behind her. She'd loved that holiday. Said it was the 'best ever'. I'd sneaked her some spending money before she left and she had brought me home the most beautiful handcrafted ceramic earrings as a thank you. My hand goes to my ears, half expecting them to be there.

But, just like Nell herself, they are gone. It feels like a horrible omen and panic threatens to suffocate me. I can't breathe. I actually can't breathe. I don't want to. I want to curl up and disappear myself, or wake up and find this is all a nightmare. I wonder how many people who go through hell harbour that hope – that it is just a bad dream. But if it was just a bad dream I would be able to breathe. I wouldn't feel the pain in my chest, in my very core. I wouldn't be so scared. There would be some detail that was just slightly off, slightly bizarre, that would alert me to the fact none of this is real. But there is nothing bizarre in the details here. Horrific? Yes. There is much that is horrific but I know in my bones that this is all too real.

I hear a voice, Clodagh's, come through the haze – drown out the sound of my heartbeat, the first sound that Nell would've heard. 'Mrs Sweeney, it's okay. It's a panic attack. You're safe. You can breathe. Listen to my voice, focus on me.'

With blurry vision, I see her face – young, beautiful, just like my daughter. She guides me in slowing my breathing down. 'That's right, in through your nose for one, two, three and four. Then blow, slowly, out for five, six, seven and eight.'

I do as I'm told as she tells me I'm safe. All the while my heart is aching, not knowing if my daughter is.

Chapter Six

Him

Two months earlier

He's on edge today and finding it really hard to focus on his work. It's not that he doesn't like his work – he docs. The work itself is very rewarding. Helping people. He feels like he makes a valuable contribution to society. That he is not as worthless as his inner voice tells him. Normally he loves the distraction of his job.

But not today. Today he wants to check in on the chatroom. He wants to see how the response to his message is going now. When he looked this morning, before work, it had exploded overnight. There were over 300 replies now. Over 700 'likes', only a handful of 'thumbs down' emojis. He likes that he has struck a chord.

He wants to write something more, to continue the discussion but he wants to read all the responses, take his time to savour them. Time he simply doesn't have in work.

He can't even sneak onto a work computer to check. The powers that be have keystroke trackers and all sorts of spyware to make sure none of the minions look at anything they shouldn't. Some things he can get away with in the name of research. This, however, would be a red flag and he can't risk anyone asking questions. Especially now he has an idea forming in his mind.

He wants to do it again. Find another woman walking on her own and speed up behind her. He wants to know if it was a one-off – that high he felt the night before. Could it be one of those things that never lives up to that first experience again?

It's not that he hates women, he tells himself. He has a healthy respect for them, most of the time. He just thinks there's a dangerous movement out there. One that doesn't look for equality with men but wants to prove they are better. They don't need men. They can mock them and look down on them and cry about misogyny while cackling together in groups, tearing strips off their menfolk and waggling little fingers at each other and laughing. Reducing men to the size of their dicks. Or the money in their bank. Or how much housework they do.

These women have never stopped to think of how things have changed so rapidly for men that it's hard to find their place in the world. Try to be helpful and you get accused of mansplaining. Get emotional and you're told to 'man up'. Try to be friendly and you find yourself slapped with a #MeToo hashtag and your name is blacklisted.

He's seen it. He's seen it time and time again. In his life, in his work. Women who use their status as the 'weaker sex' to get away with murder, but who are more calculating than many of the men he has come across. Men, like him, who are just trying to navigate the changing world.

You'd think they'd have more understanding of what it feels like to be downtrodden. They'd be more empathetic but it's not enough to change things. They have to punish every man on the planet for the sins of his forefathers.

The ringing of his phone pulls him away from his thoughts, and his growing rage. It snaps him back to the moment. He has to concentrate. He has to focus. The reward will come in its own time. After he's tried it again.

He answers the phone, switches into professional mode. No one will question his ability. Or his dedication to his work. He just has to keep his cool for another few hours. He can do that. He knows he can.

Chapter Seven

Marian

Tuesday, November 2

Missing five days

We haven't slept. How could we? For every night of her life until now, we have had some idea of where our child has been. We have known if she has been in this country or on holiday. We have known if she was asleep in her university digs, or at her best friend's house. We have known that she was out there in the world, living her life.

But we don't know that any more. We don't know anything and that nothingness claws at me. I remember my granny telling me, when Nell was a toddler and driving me to near distraction with her clinginess, to enjoy those years. Enjoy the closeness. Enjoy knowing where she was all the time. More sleepless nights come when they aren't under your roof, she'd told me. I'd scoffed at the time. Nell was a notoriously bad sleeper. She had the nickname 'the child who never sleeps'. When I spoke about her with friends, while guzzling as much coffee as I could without giving myself a heart attack, I always had a story about how she would wake in the wee small hours full of beans and ready for the day ahead. Even if it wasn't gone midnight yet.

It was utterly exhausting and yet there was a part of me that lived for that smile in the dark hours. That, when she was a little older, loved the feeling of her little hands stroking my face and begging me to 'wake up, Mummy'. The warmth of her soft breath on my skin as she would crawl in between Stephen and I, and prise my eyes open if I so much as dared to close them for longer than a standard blink.

I didn't realise at the time that there would be a day when I'd miss those middle-of-the-night interruptions or when I would give everything I owned for one more of them.

I'm drinking a coffee that has already gone cold when the doorbell rings and my heart almost stops with the fright of it. Stephen and I look at each other across the kitchen table, eyes wide. It's early still. The sky an inky grey as it chases the night away. It's too early for visitors and besides no one calls here anyway. Not without ringing first.

No one except Nell. For the briefest of moments I feel hope. It floods in, but ebbs away just as quickly. Nell would use her key, of course. I'm frozen to my chair. My legs refuse to work. Even if I wanted to, I don't think I'd be able to stand up.

Stephen moves, and I watch him leave the room, listen to his footsteps as he walks up the hall. I want to listen, but at the same time, I'm so scared.

In my head the 'I'm so very sorry' conversation has already started. My body is already deciding how to react. I can feel the scream in the back of my throat. I can see the blackness start to edge in. I want to scream for it all to stop, as if my words would have any power over whatever is coming next.

His voice, a low thrum of words I can't quite make out.

A higher voice, female, not Nell, replies. The buzzing in my ears makes it impossible to understand what is being said.

I hear footsteps, see Stephen first, and then a uniformed police officer, dark hair, maybe in her thirties, look at me sympathetically.

'Have you found her?' I ask, and it sounds as if my voice is coming from somewhere else.

'Not yet,' the woman says. 'But we're doing everything we can.' She introduces herself as Constable Heather Williams, our newly appointed Family Liaison Officer. She'll be there to help us while police look for Nell. I suspect she's also here to have a sneaky snoop at us in our home environs. See if there is anything about us that screams that we might be responsible for our child's disappearance. Or if we are the kind of folk who make enemies easily.

She'll be sorely disappointed at our ordinariness, I think. Stephen makes her a coffee. I haven't even thought to do that. I'm still sitting, in my dressing gown, my legs unable to move.

She smiles at Stephen, thanks him for the coffee and sits down to better explain her role. She tells us we'll probably see DS King later for a full update on what they are doing and what they plan to do. From what I can see, she doesn't actually have any information to give us other than her name and rank.

She has a nice manner about her though. I appreciate that. It's a comfort. Her voice is softer, less judgemental in tone, than DS King's. She has mastered the sympathetic head tilt, so often employed to show compassion and understanding.

I glance down at the toast in front of me. I don't remember making it, or if Stephen made it and put it in front of me. Regardless, there's no way I can eat it. It would stick in my throat, or I would throw it back up.

I've not eaten since yesterday lunchtime but strangely, I'm not hungry. I don't care about food.

'Nell is your only child?' Heather asks. (She has told us we simply must call her Heather.) She sits at our table and sips her coffee. Her uniform looks so uncomfortable. Bulky. The extra security that's necessary when policing in a place like Northern Ireland. I think, for a moment, about the fact she has a gun with her. A gun, in my house.

'She is,' Stephen answers. 'I think we would've liked more, but it just didn't happen for one reason or another.'

I raise my eyebrow. No, we didn't want more. Or at least I didn't. I didn't do pregnancy well and I'd been violently ill through my pregnancy with Nell – so ill that I'd sworn never again before the first labour pang.

And then, Nell has always been enough. She's completed me in a way I never thought any other human being could. I would not hesitate in telling anyone who asked that despite my more distanced approach to parenting my adult child, Nell is the love of my life. I've long ago given up the notion of Stephen and I ever being in love again. His will not be the face I recall on my death bed. Nell is the greatest love I've ever known.

'She was enough on her own,' I say, and my voice is small. It cracks as I speak but I stop, take a deep breath and settle myself. If I give in to worry and grief now I will simply fall into pieces that I don't think anyone could put together.

'I don't have any myself,' Heather says, even though neither of us have asked. 'One day, maybe. I might have to rethink the job if I do though.'

'I'm sure there are plenty of mothers in the Police Service of Northern Ireland,' Stephen says.

'Oh yes, of course. But it can be harder for women, you know. Add a child into the mix and the security threat . . .'

Silence falls in our kitchen again. We resume our waiting – waiting for news. Waiting for her to walk in the door. Waiting for a dog-walker to come across a horrific sight on the edge of the road. I squeeze my eyes shut. I push the image away. No. I will not allow my brain to go there.

'Has she lived away from home for long?' Heather asks.

'She moved out when she was eighteen,' I tell her. 'At first to Belfast to study nursing and then when she came back to Derry last year she decided to house-share with Clodagh instead of moving back home. They've been friends for years.'

'How did you feel about her moving out?'

I shrug. 'She's an adult. I want her to be happy and independent. To be honest, I was proud of her confidence and how she knew what she wanted. I don't blame her for not wanting to move back in with her mum and dad. We're not exactly hip and happening.' I smile, weakly, twist my earring in my ear. It's my tell, Stephen says. When I'm stressed – or lying.

'She's been very happy sharing with Clodagh. She comes back for the odd night. She stayed over at Christmas, and then when she had the flu she came here so her mum could nurse her,' Stephen says.

Heather gives a small, soft smile. 'Ah sure, don't we all just want our mums when we're feeling rotten?'

My stomach clenches. Is Nell somewhere now calling out for me? Does she want me to make her better? Is she beyond that?

Even though I've not eaten and I haven't taken more than a couple of sips of my cold coffee, I excuse myself and go to the bathroom where I retch and throw up what bile is lying in my stomach.

This is pain unlike anything I have ever felt before and I am powerless.

Chapter Eight

Him

Two months earlier

He did it again. On his way home from work. Not on the same stretch of road, of course. He wants to be careful. He's still finding his way.

It's a cold night – wet, windy. He hadn't been sure he'd pass anyone out walking at that time in those conditions. But there she had been. It was different this time. There was something off-kilter about this woman. She stumbled a little, her steps precarious on her high heels as if she was just wearing them for the first time.

She'd been wearing a short skirt and short puffy jacket. Her hair was flying around her face. The wind and rain whipping around her bare legs. She must have been freezing.

At first she hadn't sped up. He realised that the sound of the wind was probably drowning out the sound of his footsteps. And by the way she walked, he thought she might just be under the influence of alcohol or drugs.

It would've been easy, he'd thought, to escalate things. To get a little closer. He'd probably have been able to reach out and touch her. Grab her and watch her turn around in fright only for him to smile. Make up some excuse about needing directions or something. Once he'd seen the fear in her eyes, his need would've been met.

He'd decided, in the end, not to reach out though. Not yet. He replayed things exactly as they had happened the night before. And it had gone beautifully. Just as he'd hoped.

Until, that is, she had tried to make a hasty escape from his closeness and had toppled from her vertiginous heels. He'd watched as her ankle had twisted under her, and she had put her hand out to block her fall. He'd heard the thud as she landed on the wet tarmac of the footpath.

He'd had to make a decision. He'd had to choose whether to come to her rescue, or walk away. He'd watched her sit up, rub at her ankle as the rain came down in sheets and he'd decided in that moment that he would leave her to it. He hadn't done anything wrong, bar walk a little bit too closely to her for her comfort. She'd made the judgement he'd known she would, to see him as a threat. She could pick herself up and dust herself off.

He'd liked it though, he thinks now as he turns the key in his front door and lets himself in. He'd enjoyed seeing her defenceless like that. It gave him a thrill that she got her comeuppance. She'd been incredibly stupid. Walking home, late at night, dressed like a prostitute. What did she expect?

He doesn't stop at the kitchen or stick his head around the door to the living room to see if Jade and Cormac are watching TV. Chances are they're at it in Jade's room, or possibly, at this hour, asleep. He's tempted to open Jade's door just to see if they are there, together. He's done that once before – opened her door late at night when he knew she'd be asleep. He'd stood and looked at her, in the darkness, her hair splayed on the pillow, the duvet half kicked off, one of her long, toned legs curled over the top of it as she lay on her side. She'd been wearing a vest top, one of those stringy ones, and just her knickers. He'd stood and admired the curve of her arse, the shadow between her legs.

But no, he won't do that tonight. He won't risk waking her, or enraging Cormac. He wants to enjoy the high of what has just happened. So he goes straight to his room, switches on his laptop and logs into his chatroom.

He types in his version of what has happened that night. He doesn't embellish it. He keeps it real. He doesn't need to embellish it, he thinks. He uses his #IHaveThePower hashtag again and presses the enter key to post it. Only then does he grab a shower, thinking of all the replies that will be waiting for him when he's done.

He feels good.

He feels in control.

Dressed in his boxers with an old T-shirt on, he sits down at his desk and looks at his post to read the responses. He's buoyed by the encouragement. By the assertions he's a 'legend'. By the men who say they might give it a go themselves.

But there's one post that gets under his skin. He starts to read it, expecting more of the same praise but instead there is a meme of the *Mastermind* chair. The words: *'And my chosen subject is things that never really happened'* written in white font across it.

He wants to ask the poster why they would doubt him? He wants to tell them to fuck off. He wants to make one hundred and one arguments as to why they are wrong. But he sees their reply get a handful of 'likes'. The mystery poster is not alone in doubting his story.

He'll have to do something, and soon, to prove to them that

he's for real. That he is doing this. That this is as good a high as he says it is.

He'll show them and they won't laugh at him any more. He just has to figure out what.

Chapter Nine

Marian

Tuesday, November 2

Missing five days

There are more questions than answers. I suppose I should've been prepared for that. Heather hovers around, making cups of tea or coffee. At some stage she's nipped out and bought chocolate biscuits. I had to resist the urge to tell her to shove her chocolate biscuits up her arse. They seem too normal for this insane situation. Too much of a treat. All of this feels like a play.

I've managed to shower and dress – something I'm sure Stephen, and everyone else for that matter is happy about. But it's not more than a cat's lick, as my mother would've said. And I don't put on make-up or dry my hair. I'm clean and I'm wearing clean clothes. That is effort enough.

DS King arrived half an hour ago. She looks as though she's wearing the same suit she had on last night. Not that I really remember the details too much. I do note she looks tired. I find that strangely comforting.

They confirm that Nell didn't go to work yesterday. On the

off-chance this has all been a storm in a teacup, they called her work this morning too just in case she had showed up. But no. My daughter is still missing.

They've tracked down this 'Rob' character and someone is on their way to speak to him at his workplace. He doesn't have a criminal record, DS King tells us. He seems to be a fairly unremarkable office worker – civil service. But then predators don't tend to come with a sign above their head advertising the fact. Most of them live fairly unremarkable lives until . . .

They've spoken to her managers. Checked her bank accounts, and the hospital just in case she has been admitted, but no. She hasn't been. I could've told them that. She works in the hospital. She was wearing her uniform when she was last seen. If she had been wheeled in in her nurse's uniform they'd have clocked she was one of their own.

So they start with the questions. Does she have friends or family she might have gone to see elsewhere? Had we rowed the last time we spoke? How was our relationship normally? Had she ever done anything remotely like this before?

Stephen tells them about the time she skipped school and got the bus to Belfast for the day when she was seventeen. How we'd had a call from the school, which had sparked a bit of a panic. I glare at him. That's hardly relevant. It's not the same, and it was five years ago. That's like a lifetime for someone of her age. She was young and foolish and it was the only time she'd ever stepped out of line in her life. Part of me admired her for it. Got pleasure from seeing a rebellious streak in her. But I don't want the police thinking she is the kind of girl who does things like this and then, maybe, decide not to try so hard to find her.

'No,' I cut in. 'No. This is not like her. We don't live in each other's pockets by any means, but no, she has never just disappeared for a few days. It's not like her at all. She just wouldn't.'

So we move on to enemies. Family secrets. Anyone who might bear a grudge against her. Or us. Had there been an incident with a disgruntled patient at the hospital perhaps? Or an old school associate? An angry lover? I shake my head. None of this rings true. Nell just isn't the kind of person who collects enemies and grudges. It's not that she's a saint, but she has led a life that's not all that remarkable. She has done her work, hung out with friends, started on her career and been a good daughter.

I can't think of anyone who would have anything against her at all. In a strange way I wish I could – then at least we would have somewhere to start. As it stands it's like searching for a needle in a haystack and the haystack is infinitely huge.

I hear Stephen clear his throat and I brace myself for what will come next. I am only too familiar with that throat clearing. He starts to speak, clear, just a little too loud. He wants to be heard – to assert his dominance. 'We're sitting here answering all these stupid questions. And you've told me there's little point in me driving around looking for her, but I don't see any evidence *anyone* is actively looking for her. Where are you searching? What are you doing? All this "we have it in hand" nonsense; tell me what does that actually mean?' he rages. I inwardly cringe. I want to tell him to calm down. We don't want to get on the wrong side of the police. We don't want to annoy them.

I don't say anything of course. It wouldn't end well. As much as we don't want to get on the wrong side of the police, I don't want to get on the wrong side of Stephen even more.

'We have a team working on it,' DS King tells him. 'We have to remind you that Nell is an adult and not considered vulnerable. People go missing, all the time, and it's not necessarily a sign a crime has taken place. But we do believe there is enough out-of-character behaviour for us to take this seriously. Mr and

51

Mrs Sweeney, I need you to know, you won't hear about everything we're doing, but you will hear of anything significant. It's important that just as we're trusting that you're giving us a truthful response to these questions, you trust us to do our job in our own way.'

I have to give her her dues, DS King has kept calm, but I'm under no illusion she means business.

'We're just scared,' I mutter and it's the first time I've admitted out loud the fear that is eating at me. This is more than worry. This is more than concern. This is cold, hard, suffocating fear. I am terrified.

'Of course you are,' DS King says softly, while Heather nods sympathetically. 'And we don't mean to be cold with you, but it's important we ask the questions we do, and get the answers we need. I know it might feel a little business-like when it's your daughter we're talking about, but getting as much information as we can helps us target our efforts in a way likely to get her home to you soon.'

Stephen doesn't bite back. He is now subdued and he nods, rubs his chin. I can hear the bristle of his stubble under his fingers. He needs a shave. And a shower. I realise he is wearing the same clothes as he was yesterday. There is a faint whiff of stale sweat from him. I reach across and place my hand on his knee, which he is jiggling up and down. He stills. For a moment I feel like we are truly in this together. That we will be able to put everything else aside now and work as a partnership to get our daughter back.

'So, back to my question. You can't think of anyone who might have a grudge against your daughter?'

'No,' I say. 'She didn't make enemies. If you knew her, you would know that's not her way.'

'Okay,' DS King says.

'Now, what about boyfriends or any kind of romantic

relationships? Is there anyone significant in her past we should know about? Even if it appeared a relationship ended amicably, is there anyone we should talk to?'

I think of my daughter. She's a romantic at heart. Loves soppy movies, Taylor Swift songs, and reading romance novels. But she hasn't found her Mr Right, much to her annoyance. She's had a couple of boyfriends – who she saw for a few weeks, possibly a couple of months. But no one serious enough to register as significant in my mind. I think of how I told her to calm down, and that love will come when it does. She's so very young.

'No serious relationships. I think she's waiting for the big romance,' Stephen says and I think of when I was the same age and throwing myself body and soul into the big romance I felt with him. I startle as he places his hand on my knee squeezing it a little too tightly for comfort.

'She's a good girl,' he says and I bristle. She's not a puppy, for God's sake. She's our child. She's our child who is now a grown woman. I take a deep breath.

'I'm sure she is,' DC Black says. It's the first time he's spoken. For the rest of the time he has been standing by the sink watching us. I imagine that's his job. To read the room. To watch for any clues, any subtle tells. I wonder has he picked up on the tension between Stephen and I? He must have. The room is heavy with it.

Stephen looks at him as if he has forgotten he was there at all. There have been so many faces coming in and out of the room, so many titles and people to get to know, I feel dizzy from it. I imagine he does too.

But DC Black has moved on to something else and is looking at his phone. I watch as his eyes widen a little and he excuses himself. I can read rooms too. I've become an expert at picking up on subtle shifts in mood. I want to follow him. I have a feeling deep in the pit of my stomach that this is about our daughter and it seems absurd that anything to do with her is being discussed without us knowing, no matter what DS King has said. I realise I won't be good at accepting this 'only knowing what's relevant' approach to things.

'We do appreciate how difficult this is for you,' DS King says. 'I'm a mother myself. I can imagine what you are going through. But trust me, we have to come at this from numerous angles. We'll be issuing a press release imminently, with Nell's picture, asking if anyone knows of her whereabouts. We'll be sharing that out over social media as well as to the usual news outlets. What we hope, of course, is that Nell is out there somewhere perfectly safe and sound, maybe having an adventure, and this will make her aware that we're all worried about her and she'll get in touch. But that doesn't mean we won't be doing anything and everything else we can until we have her back.'

The sound of DC Black coming back into the room distracts us. He nods at DS King and she excuses herself.

As if it's a well-worn script, Heather immediately steps in. 'Try not to think too much about what that might mean,' she says, nodding to them.

I am almost tempted to laugh. How on earth are we supposed to not think about it?

I don't have time to laugh, or cry, or even roll my eyes before DS King returns. 'Okay, we've just seen CCTV footage of a car, possibly a taxi, picking Nell up from work on Thursday. We're trying to track down the driver now to find out where he dropped her off. We'll leave you here with Heather while we go and look into this further.'

A flicker of hope ignites in me. The first piece of the puzzle is falling into place.

I look at my husband, wanting to share the connection of

having something tangible to hold on to, but he is looking down at the table, his head in his hands. I jump when he stands up, his chair scraping loudly against the tiled floor.

'I have to go out,' he says.

'Mr Sweeney, it might be wise . . .' Heather begins.

'You can't compel me to stay here. Isn't that right? I can go out if I want to?'

'Stephen,' I implore. 'Heather is just trying to help. What if Nell gets in touch? Don't you want to be here?'

'Oh for God's sake, Marian!' he shouts. 'She's not going to get in touch. She either doesn't want to get in touch or can't get in touch. You're not a stupid woman, Marian. You must know that.'

The tone in his voice is like a slap to my face and I feel my cheeks blaze as if he has indeed just hit me. It's one thing to speak to me like this inside the confines of our perfectly dysfunctional family, but in front of other people?

Surely Heather will sense this tension between us is nothing new. This latest outburst is more than just panic or spur-of-the-moment anger. This is how he feels. This is what he thinks of me. He stalks from the room and once I hear the front door slam shut, I feel tears prick at my eyes.

'Don't underestimate the strain this puts on relationships,' Heather says, her voice soft and full of sympathy. 'I've seen all sorts. I'm not here to judge.'

I look at her, not believing a single word she has said about not judging. I wonder how much of what she sees she reports directly back to her superiors. She can't believe we're naïve enough to think that supporting us is the only reason for her assignment here.

I nod anyway. It seems the appropriate thing to do. I have a headache. It's like a tight band around my head, which is only getting tighter. I wish I could storm out too. Go and get some fresh air. Even being at work would be a distraction from my own thoughts – my own nightmares. I don't imagine Heather would understand though. I'm a bereft mother. And anyway, how could I prioritise the needs of house-hunting clients over the needs of my daughter?

'I think I need to lie down for a bit,' I tell her. 'Is that okay?'

She nods. 'Of course. I'll wake you if I need you. You need to keep your strength up.'

I stand up on wobbling legs. 'Heather,' I say and look at her. 'You've done this before?'

'Yes,' she says.

'In your experience . . . is it likely she's okay? That she'll show up?'

I watch her face closely for a reaction. There's a pause, her face a perfect blank canvas. 'It wouldn't be fair of me to speculate, Mrs Sweeney. Not at this stage.'

I don't have the strength to push her for more. 'I'll just lie down now,' I say and climb the stairs. Nothing about this – nothing at all – is fair.

Chapter Ten

Marian

Tuesday, November 2

Missing five days

The press release has 'gone live'. I know because my fruitless attempts to get some sleep are further hampered by the persistent pinging and ringing of my phone. I should've switched it off, I think, before realising that I probably won't ever switch it off again. Not until Nell is home, safe and sound.

I scroll through my phone, desperate to make sure I've not missed a call or a message from her amid all the 'R u okay?' messages and 'OMGs' blasting my phone to life. As if 'OMG' is a suitable message to send anyone with a missing daughter. This is not a reality show. This is real life. Actual real life.

There are no messages from Nell. I click onto the website of *The Chronicle* – expecting to see her picture beaming from the screen. But it isn't there. I have to scroll and click several times before I see an appeal, just a few lines long, asking for Nell, or anyone who has seen Nell, to get in touch.

A DI David Bradley, who I've not met and didn't know was

assigned to the case, has said that this behaviour is 'out of character' for Nell but there isn't a lot of urgency about his words.

Still, word has got out there. That much is clear. But there can't have been any breakthroughs. Heather hasn't knocked on my door to speak to me. I wonder if Stephen is back. For some reason I feel uncomfortable about going back down my own stairs into my own living room without knowing if he is there or not. Will Heather still be there? With her gun and her baton? Sitting on my sofa, watching *Loose Women* with Harry Styles purring contentedly on her lap perhaps. How must she pass the time when we're not sitting wringing our hands with worry in front of her? Maybe she has a nosy around, taking in everything we have on display.

Would she not be better off sitting with Clodagh in Nell's own house? With Nell's own things. The clues to her life. There is very little here to give them any clue as to what she may have been up to. Maybe I'll suggest that to her when I get up. Tell her I'll come with her to Nell's. Let her have a better look.

My phone beeps again. The tinny sound reverberating around my head, which still feels as if someone has tied a belt around it. I glance down and see Clodagh's name flash up with a notification of a new text message. I think in all the time Clodagh and Nell have been sharing a house I've had maybe two messages from this number before. The first a message to ask me to let Nell know she had forgotten her phone at home, and the second on another occasion actually from Nell letting me know she had left her phone in work but could be reached through Clodagh.

Is it too much to hope that the message now is actually from my child? Maybe she lost her phone in some mad hedonistic and completely out-of-character weekend and now she is back and just mortified at the press release going live.

A quick look at the opener of 'Mrs Sweeney,' lets me know it's not Nell. My heart sinks.

I look at it again. *Mrs Sweeney,* Clodagh has written. *'Could we meet up? I think we need to talk about something.'*

My first reaction is to swear at the phone for not telling me immediately what it is we need to talk about. Is there a more cursed phrase than 'we need to talk' – left hanging out there full of threat and promise and laden with fear?

My second reaction is to type an immediate 'Of course' message back, adding that I'll be round as soon as possible.

I slip my feet into my shoes, glance at the mirror and note I still look as haggard and broken as I did before I came upstairs, and decide not to do anything about it. I quite simply don't have the energy. Instead I pad downstairs and tell Heather that I have to go out.

She raises an eyebrow but stops short of asking me where I need to go.

'That's okay, isn't it?' I ask her.

'Of course. I'm here to support you, not to keep you prisoner. You know the appeal has gone out?'

I nod and tell her about the messages that have flooded my phone.

'Don't forget to let us know if you think there is anything in the messages that might help get us to Nell,' she says and it's my turn to raise my eyebrow. Does she think I'm so stupid or selfish I won't do whatever it takes to get my daughter back?

'Of course,' I say.

'Look,' she says, 'I'll head back to the station and see what's happening there. I'll call round later with an update. Maybe after four? And please if you're contacted directly by the media, do direct them to our press office who will deal with all queries.'

I agree, grab my bag and wait for Heather to leave before I

pull the front door behind me and jump into my car. Maybe I should call Stephen and let him know where I'm going. Then again, he hasn't told me where he is, or who he's with. That's nothing new, I realise, and while it doesn't normally annoy me – not any more anyway – today it does. Then again, today everything he does annoys me. It could be the case that I'm angry with him for not being able to find her. He should be able to fix this. *We* should be able to fix this.

Clodagh looks as if she hasn't slept either. Her eyes are still red-rimmed. Her face is devoid of any make-up, highlighting how naturally pale she is and how her youthful skin still battles against the occasional bout of acne.

She's dressed, just about. In jogging bottoms and an oversized sweater, the cuffs curled into her hands. She starts to cry when she sees me, and I watch as she draws her sleeve across her face to mop her tears and her runny nose.

'Mrs Sweeney,' she says, her voice shaky. 'Come in.'

She leads me to the kitchen, to my daughter's kitchen, where I see two cups of tea, half full, beside the sink. Clodagh nods at them. 'Can't seem to get round to finishing a cup,' she says. 'They just go cold and I make another. Would you like one?'

She switches the kettle on before I can answer. I just want her to tell me why she has brought me here.

'Clodagh, can we just cut to the chase. You said we needed to talk.'

She looks at me, wounded. As if she's a puppy I've just kicked. Maybe my voice was too harsh.

'Sorry,' she mumbles, and I notice her hand is shaking as she pours the hot water from the kettle into a mug and drops a teabag into it. She proffers the mug to me and even though I've not told her if I want one or not, I take it, and put it down on the table. It will probably go cold, just like the others. Sitting down, she twists her hands together and looks up at me. Her big, brown puppy dog eyes have filled with tears.

For a moment she looks just like the geeky twelve-year-old she was when I first met her, when Nell and she had become inseparable in school.

'Clodagh,' I say, forcing my voice to be soft and non-threatening. 'Please, if there's something you want to tell me then please just spit it out.'

'I didn't mean to keep anything from you. I was just scared and the police were here and I didn't want you to think badly of her. But you need to know and the police need to know because I'm really scared,' she said.

One tear, followed by another, runs down her face and she wipes the same sodden sleeve of her sweatshirt across her face to dry it. My heart thuds, my blood whooshing through my veins. I want to know what she's going to say but at the same time, I really don't want to know. It's not good, whatever it is.

'Clodagh . . .' I say.

'Look, I had been going to get in touch with you anyway because I wasn't sure where else to turn. But things with Nell have been off for a little while now.'

'Off?'

'She's not been her usual self. It started with her going out a couple of nights during the week. Said she had new friends she wanted to hang about with. People from the hospital, but she never told me who they were. If I started to ask too many questions she'd tell me I wasn't to be jealous. It wasn't a good look on me, she said.' Clodagh blushes a little. I don't, or can't, speak.

'Then she stayed out overnight a few times. Didn't tell me first. I'd try and call her and it would ring out or go straight to voicemail. She always came home eventually. Maybe mid-morning, or in the afternoon. Or I'd see her in the canteen in work, looking a bit worse for wear. It wasn't usual behaviour, but you know, we're young and I thought she was just outgrowing me and our friendship or having a bit of a mad spell or something. I thought she'd come round.'

'I sense a but?' I say, already trying to marry the picture of Nell that is being painted for me with the young woman I know and love.

'But, well she didn't come round. She started staying out more and missed a few days' work here and there. The week before last she missed two days without letting them know where she'd gone. She got a written warning for that.'

I feel my face colour with referred embarrassment. Shame at my child's behaviour. And the police have already spoken to her bosses, perhaps know that she has had her card marked.

'So when she didn't come home on Thursday, I thought she was just on another bender,' Clodagh continues. 'And to be honest, I'd been really angry with her anyway so I was glad of the break.'

'Why were you so mad at her?'

Clodagh glances down to the kitchen table and then back up at me. I watch as she takes a deep breath and I can see just how uncomfortable she is with this conversation. 'She owed me money,' Clodagh says. 'For the rent. She hadn't paid her full share in two months. In fact she'd hardly paid anything at all and I'd asked her to sort out the electricity bill because it was her turn to pay for it but then I got a final reminder in the post. When I asked her where the money was she just laughed and told me to chill. She'd work it out, she said. Life was for living and she was having fun. I was just acting old before my time. She started to say that a lot,' Clodagh said.

I can tell she's deeply hurt by this. I have to say it doesn't sound like the Nell I know. The Nell I knew. If I ever knew her at all. Until this moment I'd have described her to anyone who asked as 'a sensible wee girl' and I was proud of her quiet and responsible ways. I'd tell everyone how she'd never given me a day's trouble in her life and I was so very lucky to have her.

I couldn't reconcile that with this new version of Nell that Clodagh was telling me about. Being slack with payments, missing work, getting a warning. Going on benders. And all the time I thought she was doing everything as she always had.

'We'd started to fight more and more. Well, argue, you know. She'd even begun to get lazy around the house. Not doing her share. I didn't want to tell you this,' she said. 'But then when she didn't come back, and now with the police looking for her . . . I realised I have to tell you and I have to tell the police.'

'Who has she been going out with?' I ask.

Clodagh shrugged. 'It was a few nurses from work at first, and then friends of theirs. And a couple of Tinder dates. People I didn't know. She didn't talk about them by name. It was "my new friends" this and that. I don't know that they're involved in her not coming home, but maybe they are. Maybe she's with them?'

A moment of hope. Maybe she has just been on the bender to end all benders. I'm cross now, with Clodagh, for not telling me this last night. The police could've spoken to her work friends, maybe found out who Nell had been hanging out with, maybe even found Nell herself.

This might've been over before it began.

'Tell me their names,' I say, fishing my phone from my bag. 'Let's call DS King and get her to look into it.'

'Will I get in trouble?' Clodagh asks. 'If they find her. Will I get in trouble? For wasting police time?'

'If we find her, I'll make sure you don't,' I say, even though I'm well aware that won't be my decision. I tap in the number DS King gave me the night before, and I nod at Clodagh when it starts to ring and connects.

'DS King, it's Marian Sweeney here. I'm with Clodagh, Nell's friend. Look, she has some more information for you. Can I put her on to you?'

'Of course,' DS King replies, and I hand the phone to Clodagh and listen as she tells the police just how much my daughter has gone off the rails in the last couple of months. DS King must think the very worst of me. I'm a mother who does not know her daughter at all.

I don't know what she has done, what she is capable of or what kind of trouble she might have got herself into. I'm floored by a feeling of guilt, mixed with intense disappointment in my child. She has let me down, so badly.

Chapter Eleven

Him

Two months earlier

It came to him as he lay in bed, unable to sleep, the following night. It had nagged at him all the previous day, making him more short-tempered than normal. He'd been told to cheer up on at least two occasions and it had taken all his willpower not to reply 'fuck off' both times. That wouldn't have gone down well. He'd be accused of bullying, or sexual harassment or some other such bullshit.

Before he'd gone to work he'd read through the chat forums, trying to ignore his growing anger with those who accused him of lying. He found the forums fascinating. They were making him think about the world in a whole new way. He felt he was finally able to start putting a name to that nagging feeling of being off-kilter with the world around him. Life was increasingly weighted against men. He was expected to be strong and masculine, but God forbid he be too masculine. God forbid his masculinity would sway into toxic territory.

Except no one really seemed to know where that line was. Cry but don't show emotion. Stand up for yourself but don't be a bully. Be a leader but listen to women. The constant men bashing. Men are useless. Men are stupid. Men start wars. Men don't know how to look after their own children. Men are angry. All men are rapists. All men are sexist.

It fed the anger in him. He wanted to scream Not All Men, but even that would be met with derision.

All this, all those experiences, dance around his head as the idea to prove everyone wrong comes to him.

People want proof. He will be only too happy to provide that proof. He can use the GoPro he normally uses when cycling. He can catch the whole thing. Post it online for them to see. They can't argue with that.

He feels like punching the air. It's so simple he doesn't quite know why it didn't come to him before now. Maybe he just needed a little quiet time. He needed it to come to him in the small hours. If he thought there was half a chance there would be anyone still out and about at this time, he would get up, get dressed and head out on the hunt right now.

But he knows the world is asleep. He'll have to wait until after work. That's frustrating for him but still he can use it as motivation to get through his working day the best he can. It will give him the extra bit of oomph he needs to survive his colleagues. To survive being put in his place. Being ordered around by his female boss, who is only a couple of years older than him and – for his money – not half as good at the job as he is. But of course it would be her who got the promotion to his senior. Quotas have to be met regardless of merit.

He feels his mood drop and takes a deep breath. He's not going to go down the road of this negative thinking. He's going to focus on making his video, uploading it and waiting for the likes to come rolling in. He knows they will. Just as he knows there will be praise. The people who use this website are angry. They are eager to cling on to something that feels like a win.

This, he knows, will feel like a win to them because it already does to him.

He only has to get through the day at work, then he'll be able to show people he's not just some sad case, sitting alone in his room, making up stories. He's someone to be respected.

At just after half past eight the following night, he changes into his black jeans and puts on a charcoal grey sweater. It's cold, so he wraps up in his navy puffa jacket, and pulls on his black beanie hat and gloves. Despite the darkness of his clothes, the shadowy ensemble of the whole outfit, he doesn't think he looks too out of place. A lot of men don't feel the need to dress like the colours of the rainbow to go out for a walk. Most men, he'd bet.

There's a white strip on his Vans, a cursory nod to brightness. He doesn't dress as if it's his goal to lurk in the shadows. He dresses for comfort. To blend in. To keep warm.

He's given a lot of thought to where he will go. It has to be somewhere there's a chance of a woman walking on her own. Possibly even a little tipsy from after-work drinks. That might be a good thing – it might give him the extra advantage. Add a little more fun to the game. If he's being honest, it helps salve his conscience too. If a woman, in this day and age, is going to go out, get drunk and walk home alone, believing men to be awful and predatory then it's sort of her fault, isn't it? Isn't she just asking for trouble? He's well aware it's not considered politically correct to say that, but that doesn't make it untrue.

He decides to wander around Waterloo Street – a street famous in Derry for being lined with numerous pubs. It's even right beside a taxi rank, so really if a woman walks on from there on her own without jumping in a taxi to be safe, he can't be blamed for taking advantage of her stupidity.

After all, he reasons, he isn't actually going to hurt her. Just scare her. Just show her how stupid she has been. If you think about it, you know, really think about it, he's doing her a favour. She might think twice about taking such a stupid risk again. Next time she might not be so lucky.

Knowing that he may have to wait around for a while, until he sees the right person, he decides he might just nip into Peadar O'Donnell's for a pint. He can sit at the bar and maybe look around him, identify someone he might be interested in. Then again, Peadar's is small, and chances are he might be recognised or show up on CCTV.

No, he'll stand outside, out of the sight of any cameras and enjoy the anticipation until it's time. With the GoPro primed and ready to go in his front jacket pocket, the lens peeking over the top, he watches. He takes in a group of girls, perhaps in their early twenties, laughing and clinging to each other as they walk out of the bar, arms looped together. One of them glances in his direction and he wonders if she will smile at him, or perhaps say hello. A quick assessment tells him she's not really his type, but she's not offensively ugly.

She'd look better if her hair wasn't quite so big, and her skirt not quite so short. There's one thing for certain: she carries herself with much more confidence than she should. But she'd do, in a push. Her eyes lock with his and she opens her mouth to talk, stalling her procession down the street with her two laughing hyena friends.

He raises his eyebrows, wonders if he should step out of the shadows. Say hello. Introduce himself. God loves a trier, after all. But no, he can't be distracted from his mission. Whatever hope he has of this big-haired, fake-tanned piece of skirt actually giving him the time of day will never match the high he will feel from proving he wasn't lying to his online community.

His internal debate is soon muted as the woman in his eyeline speaks.

'Oi, you dirty cunt!' she slurs. 'Fuck off and stop being a creepy bastard.' Her voice is harsh, grating. Like fingernails down a blackboard. Nasal. Common. Cheap.

He bites back the urge to tell her he wouldn't touch her with a ten-foot barge pole that had been bleached first. Humiliation starts to burn at him as she walks on, her friends whooping and cheering as if she is some modern-day suffragette who has just defeated the patriarchy with her witty repartee.

But humiliation quickly turns to anger, which in turn fuels his determination to claim his power back. When the door to the bar opens again and a woman walks out on her own, looking nervously in both directions, he feels his senses tingle.

She's mousy-looking in comparison to the tramp who has just called him out. If he had to put money on it he'd say she'd come straight from work. Grey suit trousers and black court heels give away her inner office worker. A sensible black handbag over a woollen coat, a soft pink woollen hat over straight blonde hair. She looks sad, vulnerable. She presents the perfect opportunity.

He switches on his GoPro and starts to follow her down the street, watching as she turns up past the taxi rank at the bottom of William Street and walks on. He keeps a good twenty steps behind her for now, aware his breathing sounds heavy. He's excited. Adrenaline floods his veins and he walks faster, his hands deep in his pockets. He whistles, just loud enough to make sure she will have heard him and he notices, to his pleasure, that she starts walking a little faster too.

So he speeds up, the gap between them closing. She turns to glance behind her, and he sees the fear in her eyes. Even in the dark and the rain it's clear. He looks down, walks on. She crosses the road and he takes a few more steps where he is. He wants to lull her into a false sense of security, make her think he isn't following her after all.

And then he makes his move, crossing the street, almost level with her. Close enough to see her breath misting in front of her, to hear the slight hitch in her breathing, to see how she reaches into that sensible handbag of hers, pulling out keys, which she rattles as if that will be enough to ward him off.

That's when he really wants to laugh. This is playing out exactly as he hoped it would. He hears the smallest yelp from her – an involuntary expression of just how scared she is. He's got what he needs, he thinks. He has done enough.

He steps forward again, so he's almost level with her until she turns to look at him. She isn't angry like the first woman. She isn't ready to come at him with her keys to scratch his eyes out.

'Please,' she says, her voice shaking. 'Don't hurt me!' She is crying.

For a second that stalls him. He wasn't expecting this.

He looks at her, her eyes wide with fear.

'I'm just walking to my car,' he says. 'I didn't mean to frighten you.'

She stares at him and he stops, puts his hand in the air. 'Sorry,' he says. 'I'll go the other way, if that helps.'

She nods but she doesn't speak, just turns and walks on, still fast. Fear has buckled her. Her shoulders are hunched, heaving. He can hear a single sob carried in the night air.

He waits for the guilt to wash over him. He knows he should feel bad for bringing this young woman to tears, but he doesn't.

If anything, he feels more empowered than last time. He feels as if he has more power. This fear was different. It was real. It was inbuilt. It was, and is, intoxicating.

He taps his GoPro, already itching to be home and uploading his catch online. That will show the fuckers, he thinks with a triumphant smile. That will fucking show them!

Chapter Twelve

Marian

Tuesday, November 2

Missing five days

There have been so many questions. Most of them I don't know the answer to. I sit there, shaking my head and shrugging my shoulders like an OAP doing physio to stop her neck from seizing up. With every 'I don't know' I feel the weight of judgement from DS King push down on me. But that's nothing compared to how Stephen is looking at me.

Child-rearing was my responsibility. That much was very clear from the day after I came home from the hospital, leaking and bleeding and trying to figure out how to make it through the day without killing this tiny human being with my ineptitude.

He went back to work without so much as a backwards glance, leaving Nell and I to our own devices. Whoever said babies sleep most of the time had clearly never met Nell. Even as a newborn, she only slept in short fitful bursts. Or that's how it felt. Time lost all meaning as I wandered around, still shell-shocked from the brutality of giving birth. Nothing can prepare you for it – the primal, bloody, shit-stained, wanting-to-die reality of it. The total loss of control over your own body as it twists itself into knots to expel this screaming creature into the world. All you can do is try to process what happened.

'As soon as I held my baby I forgot all about the pain,' is the biggest lie told to women and it should be a criminal offence to utter those words.

Anyway, from that moment on, it was clear Nell was my responsibility. Stephen swooped in and out of her childhood, bestowing treats, affection, and acting as her ally during our teenage clashes. He did none of the hard stuff, the dirty stuff and the downright heartbreaking stuff but he still got to wear the coveted favourite parent crown in those earlier years. She even insisted on saying 'Dada' first, and 'Mama' did not follow for a good six months.

'How on earth did you not know this was going on?' he yells, his face puce, as Heather pretends to concentrate on making a cup of tea. 'You're her mother for God's sake!'

'And you're her father!' I yell back.

'That's not the same,' he says with such conviction that I realise he actually believes it. Wholeheartedly.

'She's an adult, Stephen. She's been living independently for four years. I don't track her every move. The umbilical cord was severed after she was born, you know!'

'Now is not the time for your stupid jokes,' he jibes and I look at him, really look at him, and wonder if I know him at all. This man who I have known for more than half of my life. This man who I have lived with, endured good and bad times with. This man who I vowed to love until death do us part. I look at him, at the way his increasingly bushy and greying eyebrows knit together. At the extra jowls around his chin that have come with his slow decline into middle age. The vein that protrudes above his right eye. The look of . . . of . . . of disappointment on his face. Yes, disappointment with a hint of irritation.

I suppose I should be used to that look by now.

I take a deep breath, listen to the sound of boiling water pouring into the white 'Best Dad Ever' mug that he insists on drinking from. The glaze is cracked, on the inside. I've often wondered if one day he will catch some ungodly bacterial disease from it. I've heard that can happen.

No, I remind myself, it's no use getting angry with him. We have to focus on Nell. Stupid, messed-up Nell who I still feel tethered to despite the severed umbilical cord.

'I'm not making a joke,' I say, and I hear the defeat in my own voice. 'I just don't have answers. I don't know where she is. Christ, I wish I did. I wish I knew everything that had been going on in her life and that I was able to pinpoint her right now. But I can't. And I'm scared shitless, Stephen, so please . . .'

I think it's the calmness in my voice, the beaten-down nature of my words, that finally gets through to him. 'I'm sorry,' he says, his voice cracking. 'I wish I could pinpoint her too.'

He sits down and his cup of tea is placed in front of him by Heather who is maintaining a silent vigil. A second mug, one that declares '#CaffeineQween' in strong black comic sans, with a slightly blurry golden crown dangling off the end of the final n, is placed in front me. Nell both loves and hates that mug, something someone in the office picked up in a pound shop and passed off as a Secret Santa present in my work the previous Christmas. She'd laughed at the awfulness of it. The way the colours bled into the white ceramic. The misspelling, which we thought was an attempt at being down with the kids. (Or 'down with the kidz, with a z, Mum' as Nell said, laughing.) I wrap my hands around it now, around the warmth of the tea that I won't be able to swallow, and I will myself to wake up from this nightmare.

We sit in silence for a minute or two. Stephen doesn't touch his drink either. Heather has made herself a cup and she slurps from it, testing the temperature. She's not even been here a day and I already wish she would get lost.

'What happens now?' Stephen says, quietly, and turns to look at Heather who is pulling a face at the cup.

'I think this milk might be off,' she says, and I glance down to my own cup, see milky flakes of cream floating on top of the tea. I think she might be right. I'll have to go and get more. And more teabags. You need teabags in an emergency, even if you don't normally drink tea.

I watch as she puts the cup down. 'Well, the team are looking at the new information Clodagh provided and speaking to these new friends of your daughter's. The appeal is still out there.'

'Has there been a response to it?' Stephen asks, which seems a stupid question. If anything useful had been discovered we'd surely have been informed.

'I'm not sure,' she says. 'But the team will let us know if anything of significance comes to light.'

'And the car that picked her up on Thursday? The taxi?' Stephen asks.

'I believe the car was picked up on ANPR, that's Automatic Number Plate Recognition, at some stage. I can check for you what's happening there.'

Stephen nods, absent-mindedly lifts his mug to his lips and takes a sip of tea. He grimaces too. 'This milk is off,' he tells me, as if he hadn't heard Heather just moments before.

'I'll go to the shop and get some more,' I say. Truth be told I need the fresh air. My own house has become claustrophobic.

I get a cursory nod of response and he turns his attention back to Heather. 'When do we escalate things?' he asks. 'When will she merit more than a "concerned for the welfare of"? If she's not using her cards, or her phone or hasn't been seen – should you not be doing more?'

'DI Bradley will make that call,' she says. 'He's the chief investigating officer, senior to DS King. I can request he come and speak with you?'

'Yes, can you do that? Because I need to know he has the best people looking for her.' To Heather's credit she never flinches at the tone Stephen uses with her. He speaks to her like she is his lackey, and she hasn't once told him to shut up or to mind his manners.

'This is hell,' I say, to no one in particular. 'Sitting here and doing nothing.'

'I know it's difficult,' Heather says with her tilt of the head and soothing voice. 'But you have a good team working to find her. The extra information from Clodagh today should be a big help. Try to . . .'

She is interrupted by the ringing of her mobile phone and she glances down at it before telling us she really has to take this call and walks out of the room. Stephen and I are left with just each other for company. There is so much that needs to be said, I know that, but neither of us speak. Stephen breaks the silence by standing up, the legs of his chair screeching against the tiled floor, and emptying his mug of tea down the sink. Without speaking, he takes mine from in front of me and does the same.

I notice it as soon as Heather comes back into the room. Her face is pale, almost grey against the unflattering green of her PSNI uniform. There is a hint of panic in her eyes and she reaches for her rotten tea and sips again as if she's forgotten it's off.

'I'll go and get milk,' I say and stand up. I don't want to be here. I know something bad is coming and I want to get the hell out of my house as quickly as possible. I look to the worktop where I threw my keys and purse earlier. I'll grab them. I'm wearing my house slippers but I don't care. I'm only nipping to the Spar shop. I don't give a damn if someone sees me in pink furry slippers. I'd run out of the house naked if I had to. Just to get away.

'Mr and Mrs Sweeney.' Heather's voice is soft, a quick glance lets me know her head is at the sympathetic tilt. I try to stand up but my bastard legs won't work. She walks to the table and sits down while I will my stupid body to move, or to shut down or to drop dead. That buzzing is back in my ears.

I see her lips are moving, her face serious, but I don't take in what she's saying. Her voice is distorted, like the teacher in Charlie Brown. I watch Stephen to see his reaction even though I don't want to see it. But like a car crash, I can't look away.

Colour drains from his features. Everything about him slackens as if he has ceased to be. Heather reaches across and takes his hand. I notice her nails are painted the palest of pinks. The same pale pink as the receiving blanket I brought Nell home in from the hospital. I'm still staring at her hand holding my husband's when I feel her other hand squeeze mine. It pulls me into reality.

'DI Bradley and DS King will be over shortly. I know this isn't what we wanted to hear but we mustn't jump to any conclusions.'

What 'we' wanted to hear? The use of the 'we' grates on me. This isn't her child that 'we're' talking about.

Stephen thumps the table, his closed fist hammering against the wood so loudly both Heather and I jump. He stands up, throwing his chair behind him. It hits the wall and falls on its side as he walks to the kitchen window where he stares out. Harry Styles bolts from his usual spot on the windowsill at the noise and I'm aware of Stephen muttering, crying.

I'm numb. I haven't heard what Heather said. No, that's not

true. I have heard. I've just refused to allow it space in my head. I've been trying to fend off the horror of it by ignoring it and hoping it will go away. But it chips and chips at my consciousness until there's a crack and it squeezes in, wrapping itself tight around my head and my heart.

A body has been discovered.

Chapter Thirteen

Marian

Tuesday, November 2

Missing five days

Heather can't tell us much. It's a body. Female. That's it. That's the limit of what she can, or is willing to tell us. If I was her, I'd wait for the senior officers to do the dirty work too. It has to be above her pay grade.

No matter how many times we ask her where the body was found, or what the body was wearing, or what age the dead woman appeared to be, Heather just says she doesn't know. I know we are annoying her. I know that between us asking the first time and the third time she has had no way of gaining any extra information to report back to us. But that doesn't stop us asking.

I think I have to ask those impossible questions because when I stop talking, or listening to her say she doesn't know; when I have anything more than a moment of silence to fill, my head takes me to other places.

Horrific places.

What has happened to this dead person who might be my daughter? What condition is this body in? Is it covered in wounds? Is it hanging from a tree? Has it been broken as the result of one of those stupid, tragic, couldn't-have-been-foreseen accidents? Has it been violated – in life by a brute of a man or in death by animals feasting on the decaying flesh?

An image of a grey-green corpse, insects crawling over it, through it, comes into my mind and I run to retch violently into the sink.

I feel a hand on my back, rubbing softly. Just as I would have done with Nell when she was young and sick and needed the comfort of her mother. I don't know if it is Stephen or Heather. I don't care. I just want it to be Nell.

'I know I'm asking the impossible of you,' Heather says, 'but let's wait to see what DI Bradley has to say.'

'They're not sending the big guns round if they have any doubt the person they've found is our daughter,' Stephen says, his voice hollow, raspy. As if he can't get enough air into his lungs to breathe easily. I'm angry with him for letting go of whatever sliver of hope we had left. I'm angry with him for making a point that makes such perfect sense that I can't help but feel that same sliver of hope slide away from me.

Heather doesn't correct him. She simply replies that this DI Bradley, this big gun we've not met before, will know more. It's not her place to guess what information he will have.

'But I'm right, aren't I?' Stephen says, his voice angry, but alarmingly quiet. He is giving up. 'Why would such a senior officer come here to tell us what you've just told us? He can't have a doubt in his mind.'

Heather looks uncomfortable. I don't blame her. I almost, almost feel sorry for her and then I remember what is happening. It hits me again, like a wave crashing to shore. The realisation will ebb and flow and crash over me a million times until it has worn me away to nothing.

'DI Bradley is a good policeman. One of our best, and he likes to be very hands on with his cases. I believe he had planned to come and see you today anyway, but obviously this has expedited matters.'

'This has expedited matters' is a very posh way of saying 'this search might be all over before it's really begun'.

I'm shivering now even though it's not cold. Heather looks around, glances at the sofa in the sunroom just off the kitchen and sees the dark red throw rug that is hanging over it. Quick as a flash she lifts it and wraps it around my shoulders, crouching down to my height and rubbing at my arms. I want to scream; I'm not cold, but I can't stop shaking. My whole body is in spasms so violent that my jaw hurts as my teeth chatter together.

'Marian,' Stephen's voice, concerned more than I've heard him in years. 'Are you okay?'

'It's shock,' Heather says. 'Hot, sweet tea might help.'

'But the milk . . .' Stephen says. 'I'll go and get some.'

'Mr Sweeney, I don't think you're in any condition to drive. I can arrange for some to be brought here.'

But Stephen of course does what Stephen always does in a crisis. He grabs his coat and keys and leaves anyway and I'm too lost in my shuddering to call to him to stay. My breathing is funny now, tight, shaky. Small breaths that I try to force down into my lungs. My lips are tingling, my head dizzy.

I'm aware of Heather trying to get me to tune in to her voice. To breathe slowly and deeply. A memory slides into my mind. Nell, crouched beside me just as Heather is now, her warm hands over mine. 'Just breathe, Mummy,' she's saying. 'Look at me, breathe with me.' She has always been able to calm my panic. Always able to read me to know the signs of when I might spiral. Oh, God, I've put so much responsibility on her from such a young age.

I allow myself to believe that Heather is my daughter. That it's Nell I hear now, just as I did then. I allow her to bring my breath back to me, so that the dizzy, dark edges of my consciousness slip away and I'm back in the moment.

I hear my daughter's voice. 'That's it, Mummy. You're doing great. You're okay. It's all going to be okay.'

Much too quickly it changes back to: 'That's it, Mrs Sweeney. In and out. Count with me.' Nell is gone, again.

'I don't think I can do this,' I tell her. 'How am I supposed to do this? To listen to someone tell me my child is dead and then to try and get my head around the fact she's gone? It's wrong. It's not right.'

Perhaps out of things to say, I simply feel Heather rub at my hand. Soothing me with her touch. It must be an awful, shitty job. To sit with someone as their world falls apart. To be shouted at, or cried on, or even just to witness the devastation that comes with loss.

I look up, her eyes are that strange shade of neither hazel nor green but somewhere in-between with flecks of gold. Nell has blue eyes. A cool blue. Almost grey. She went through a phase in her teens of being annoyed about that. Blue was 'boring' she told me. She wanted her eyes to be green, like emeralds.

'I'm sorry,' I tell Heather. I don't say any more. I assume she'll know what I mean. That I'm sorry for having a panic attack. That I'm sorry for Stephen being so rude and storming out. That I'm sorry for everything.

'There's nothing to be sorry for,' she says.

But she doesn't know everything. She doesn't know how I told my daughter to move out. Told her to live her life. Not to come home to be suffocated by the tension between her

81

father and I. I thought it was the right thing to do at the time. I couldn't have known it would lead to this, but I don't think I'll ever be able to forgive myself for that.

Chapter Fourteen

Him

Two months earlier

He's delighted but not surprised when the video racks up hundreds of views in the first few hours. It's made all the sweeter by one of his naysayers from the night before putting his hands up and apologising.

'You're the real deal, man,' his faceless nemesis had written. That was enough for him. He knows it won't always be enough – he knows that quite quickly. This high, from posting the video to reading the comments cheering him on, to getting his apology is great but it won't feed him forever.

He'd like to go further next time. Do it better. Make sure not to get called out by drunk sluts stumbling out of the bar. Make sure to get a little closer to the woman he is hunting.

Hunting seems like an okay word for it. It fits.

He wonders if he could dare try reaching out and touching her? How could he make that work? Carrying something with him, a lipstick stolen from Jade's room, maybe. Reach out and touch his prey and watch her turn, scared, her eyes wide in shock and fear, her mouth a perfect 'o' – one that makes his cock twitch at the thought of how she would look, on her knees, in front of him.

Does that make him a pervert? A deviant? That he gets excited by it? No. Arousal is normal. It's a biological reaction. It isn't always controllable. He's not saying he'd force himself on anyone. He's not a rapist. He can indulge in fantasy.

All he wants to do is touch someone. Ask her if she dropped her lipstick? Wave Jade's sluttish red make-up in front of her face. Watch her shake her head and walk away from him. It's just the expression on her face he wants. A momentary glimpse of fear, up close, at touching distance. Close enough to see her lips part, her pupils dilate.

He already knows any to-ing and fro-ing he is doing in his head about this is redundant. He will do it. And he'll post the video and the other posters in the chatroom will think he is even more of a legend. It's just a matter of how soon.

He looks back at the post, sees the numbers of likes grow. There's one dissenter in the mix. Someone hiding behind an avatar of Austin Powers and the screen name BigMan.

'I don't know, bro. This has major creepy vibes about it. You don't know who you're following or what they might be dealing with. Why would you traumatise someone just for likes?'

It stops him for a moment. He wonders if BigMan (what a pathetic username) has a point. Is it just for likes? Is it a trauma?

He watches as the other posters come to his defence, rounding on BigMan. This is not a forum for 'snowflakes'. Everyone coming here knows what they are signing up for – they know they are going to the darker reaches of the dark web. A place where men like him should be free to say and do whatever they want. God knows there's worse than his fantasies on there.

He reads the replies.

HymenBreaker: *You're such a pussy. Trauma? He's only walking close to them. Men are allowed to walk close to women! They haven't* *taken that from us yet. Grow some balls, or leave us real men to get on with it.*

UppaReds: *Women want it all. To be taken as equals but no, don't walk too close to them or they'll be traumatised? Jog on, BigMan.*

Truth4Life: *The fightback has to start somewhere. Who's crying about all the trauma we've experienced as men being robbed of all our rights?*

They are all making valid points, he thinks. There does have to be a fightback. When he thinks of those slappers tumbling out of the pub and daring to call him names, he realises that. He wasn't the one dressed provocatively. He wasn't the one who had got so drunk anyone could've taken advantage of him. He wasn't the one who swore loudly in the street and called strangers names. He hadn't been creepy. He'd just been standing outside of a pub.

He types a reply. *'I agree. The fightback has to start. #IHaveThePower'*

And the likes flood in. One of the admins of the forum posts that he has banned 'BigMan' for 'not honouring the space' and that 'you're either with us, or you're against us'.

He goes to the kitchen and gets a beer from the fridge. He's earned it. He is buzzing. So buzzing in fact that when Cormac and Jade stagger in from the pub, laughing and talking just that little bit too loud, he doesn't disappear to his room. He joins them for a drink. Laughs a bit. Chats a bit. Feels almost as if he fits in. He feels his confidence start to grow. This is a new him, he realises. No, not a new him, but the him he was always meant to be.

Three bottles of beer down and he excuses himself, finally chilled enough to be able to sleep. He's smiling as he carries his empty beer bottles to the kitchen to put them in the re-cycling bin. He switches on the dishwasher, wipes down the worktops and switches off the light. As he passes the living room he hears the voices inside, still just that little bit too loud.

'I thought he was going to sit here all night,' Jade says.

Cormac laughs.

Even though he knows he should walk away and not keep listening – even though he knows that nothing good will come from listening, he stands and listens anyway.

'You have to feel sorry for him,' Cormac says. 'He's not exactly swamped with friends, is he? Goes to work and comes home and does little else. He never goes out. He never brings anyone home. A girlfriend or a boyfriend . . .'

'I think he's just shy,' Jade says, a hint of softness in her voice that acts as a salve against the wounds Cormac has just inflicted on him.

'Oh come on,' Cormac says. 'He's lived here for a year and not brought a single friend home. That's not right. There's something wrong with him. Don't you think?'

'I'm just trying to give him the benefit of the doubt,' Jade says.

'You're too soft. Why can't you just admit he's a creep. And a selfish creep at that. The incident the other night with the music while we were both trying to work is just typical of him.'

'I know, I know,' Jade says. 'But he isn't all bad. He cleans up after himself, and he did leave that takeaway for us as a sort of apology.'

'You're too soft,' Cormac says. 'The man's a weirdo and he's only getting worse.'

There's a pause before Jade speaks again. 'You're right,' she says, 'but maybe we need to keep on the right side of him all the same. We don't want to wake up to a horse's head in our beds or find all the doors and windows locked.'

She laughs and Cormac laughs along.

The noise cuts through him. It strikes every nerve as it does. He thinks again of what Truth4Life posted. 'The fightback has to start somewhere'. Maybe it needs to start right here and right now. He takes a deep breath and steadies himself. He wants to get this just right. He wants maximum impact.

Pushing open the door to the living room, watching as their faces change from creasing with laughter to colouring with embarrassment.

'Don't mind me,' he says, walking across the room. 'I forgot my book.' He looks across the room to the bookcase with a few scattered tomes. None of which he is reading. But they don't know that. He plays it casually.

'What's so funny anyway?' he says, keeping his tone light but their laughing has stopped. 'Did I hear something about a horse's head?' His face is a picture of innocence as he asks them. He looks from Jade to Cormac and back again. Jade can't keep eye contact with him, dropping her gaze to the floor.

'We were just talking shite,' Cormac says. 'Nonsense talk.'

'Wine in and wit out,' Jade mumbles.

'Yeah, but you must remember? I mean you've only just said it. I could hear you chatting away there while I was in the kitchen and walking up the hall. Was there something about someone being creepy?'

He knows, of course, he is being creepy right at that very moment. What's more he's enjoying it. He's loving watching them squirm. It's a huge comfort when all he really wants to do is tell them both to get stuffed. No, that's not entirely true. What he'd actually love to do is to knock their smug smiles to the other side of their faces – by whatever means necessary.

He's not a violent man, but there are always exceptions.

'I was telling Cormac about one of the researchers at the university. Real slimy character. Totally creepy,' Jade says, but she still can't look him in the eye. He's not stupid, he knows the tells for liars. He also knows what he heard.

Sitting down on the sofa, he thinks it will be fun to pile on the pressure a little more.

'Really? Tell me about him. You'll need to keep an eye on someone like that.'

Jade shakes her head. 'There's not much to tell. He's just a little handsy, you know?'

'Are you keeping a written record of every time he does something? It's important to document it.' He knows he can play the sympathetic listener very well. Damn it, he *is* a good listener. He's also a decent person. Not a creep. He wasn't the person who lied. He's just taking advantage of their dishonesty.

'I'm not sure it's that serious,' Jade says.

It's time to put the pressure on Cormac. 'Tell her, Cormac, that she should be keeping a record. I'm sure either Cormac or I would be happy to show up and have a word with him. Actually it might be better coming from me, don't you think, Cormac?'

Finally Cormac looks at him. 'If Jade thinks it's not that serious, then it's not that serious.'

'Sexual harassment is really serious,' he tells them. 'I really think you should escalate this, Jade.'

He's enjoying their discomfort.

'Maybe,' she says.

He wonders if he should turn the screw a bit more. 'There shouldn't be a maybe about it. What if he tries it on with the wrong person? What was it you said? Someone could wake up with a horse's head in their bed, or with all the doors and windows locked?'

Neither Cormac nor Jade speak.

He starts to laugh. 'That's it, I remember now. You said he was a creep, and a selfish creep at that. It's so strange though because by the way you were both talking it was almost as if he lived here and wasn't just some random researcher at the university.'

He watches as his housemates look at each other. He's the only one laughing now and it's a sharp, bitter laugh.

'Look,' Jade says, 'we were just sounding off. We didn't mean it. We've been drinking and you know I'm under so much pressure at the moment, what with the viva coming up and Cormac is feeling it in work. We've had a few drinks and . . .'

'Don't worry about it,' he says. 'No harm done.' His words don't match his tone, which drips latent anger. This isn't over. They should worry. And plenty of harm *has* been done.

Chapter Fifteen

Marian

Tuesday, November 2

Missing five days

DI David Bradley is a solemn-faced man. I search everything about his body language, his expression, his tone for a clue of what is to come. Even though the awful truth might just be a few moments away, it's as if I have to prepare myself for it.

He's dressed in a smart suit, his salt and pepper hair cut neatly. His face has the weather-worn look of someone who loves to be outside. I notice a small, sticky mark on the lapel of his coat. Like a child's handprint. Is the tiredness drawn all over his face due to the hours he's putting in on this case, or the presence of a child at home?

My mind flashes to an image of Nell. Four years old, running down the garden path, her arms spread wide in anticipation of a hug as she ran. Her then-blonde curls bouncing with each step. As she grew closer I could see smears of butter and a dusting of flour all over her dress. 'We cooked a cake!' she declared. I can still hear her voice now, as it was then. The soft lisp. The softness of her breath on my cheek.

'Mrs Sweeney.' I notice DI Bradley has stretched his hand out towards mine. I do what I should do and reach out to shake his hand. The warmth and firmness of the gesture pins me back to the here and now.

'I'm very sorry to be meeting under these circumstances,' DI Bradley says. I want to scream 'what circumstances?' I want to scream 'cut to the chase', but I also want to stay in this moment forever. In the before. I know everything will soon become defined in that way – before and after.

'Mr Sweeney has gone to get milk,' Heather says, sounding for all intents and purposes embarrassed that she was unable to keep him in the house.

'The shop is only at the bottom of the street. He won't be long,' I mumble. 'But please, you don't have to wait for him. Tell me what you've found. Is it her? Have you found Nell?'

'We have found the body of what we believe to be a young woman. From what we know of Nell, her height, build and age, we know that these remains match those details. But, due to the condition of the body, it would be impossible to make a conclusive identification at this stage.'

The knot tightens in my stomach. 'Well I'll come with you. I'll come with you and I'll know if it's her. We can go now.'

I feel a hand on mine. Heather and her pale pink polish. 'Mrs Sweeney,' she says.

'Please, it's Marian. Call me Marian,' I say. 'I know you think I might not be strong enough to see her, but I need to. I need to see with my own eyes and I need to know if it's her.'

'Marian,' DI Bradley says. 'I'm afraid that won't be possible.'

Blinking, I look at him. 'Why? Why isn't it possible? Don't you need an official identification? You don't know her. I know her. She's my baby.' My voice cracks on the word *baby*. I realise

I am shaking, my leg trembling so violently that my foot is tapping against the floor, a dull thud over and over again.

'I'm sorry to say that the remains we have uncovered are not fit for identification. It appears as if someone tried to dispose of this body. By burning it. I'm afraid there is nothing recognisable about it.'

A merciful numbness settles into my bones. I can't think. I can't feel. I need to shut out all of this horror. I feel the walls go up around me and around my heart. I push down the pain of what I've just heard. I push down the bile that is burning at my throat. I push it down because to allow myself to feel it at all will end me entirely. I know that I will die with the pain of it. I'm aware DI Bradley is talking. I can see his lips move, but I can't hear what he is saying. I'm aware of shadows moving around me. People moving. Coming and going. A phone rings, maybe. The doorbell. I don't know. Everything is blurred and I can't move.

It's only when Stephen is standing in front of me, his face contorted in pain – gruesome with grief – that I tune back in. I've wondered, you know, sometimes when watching the news or a TV drama and seeing someone fall to the ground when they get bad news, or scream, or lash out, how I would react. I don't think I ever thought I would simply freeze.

Noise swamps back in as I stare at Stephen, when I realise the roar I have heard is not the wind, nor a lorry passing by, nor a clap of thunder, but my husband.

'It might not be her,' I say, my voice so soft that none of them hear me. 'If the body can't be identified, it might not be her.'

'Marian?' Heather is looking at me. 'Did you say something?'

'You said not to panic until we knew for definite. We don't know for definite that it's our Nell. We don't panic. Not yet. You said.'

Her head tilts. I wonder if she thinks I'm just deluding myself. Maybe I am. But I need to. For another wee while yet. 'Marian, I think you need to prepare yourself for the worst,' she says.

'When will you know?' I ask, and I'm aware of DI Bradley sitting opposite me at the table. I hadn't been aware of him sitting down.

'We hope we can use dental records,' he says. 'If you can let us know Nell's dentist's details.'

I nod, aware of Stephen sobbing in the background, his cries like a weight on my chest. I tell him who has looked after Nell's teeth.

'That's very helpful,' DI Bradley says.

'I'm right though,' I say, looking at him. 'That it might not be her? I mean . . .'

'Marian,' he says softly. 'There is always a chance but I have to make you aware there have been no other women of Nell's age and description reported missing recently.'

I nod and take in what he is saying and the walls protecting me grow higher. Without speaking I get up and go upstairs to the room that used to belong to Nell. It's not a shrine to her. It's not just as she left it, with posters on the walls, and discarded make-up on the dressing table. We redecorated two years ago – made it into a guest bedroom, with a double bed, Laura Ashley wallpaper and curtains. Stupid things that Nell hated. It was too 'old-fashioned', too 'fuddy-duddy'.

'Ach, Mummy, would you not go for something a bit modern?' she'd said, but she'd helped me all the same. Helped me hang the curtains and make the bed. I want to get a feel for her, so I lie on the top of the bed even though I can already feel there is nothing of her here.

She is, was, only twenty-two. So many young women of her age would still be living at home. I had many friends who bemoaned their offspring's seeming uninterest in cutting the apron strings and going out on their own. He or she will still be looking for their socks washed and bed made when they turn thirty, they would say. Secretly I thought they enjoyed it. Enjoyed having their children at hand. Knowing where they were. Caring for them and cosseting them. Keeping them safe. But Nell had taken my advice and left as soon as she could. She'd forged her own life and I'd been – no, I am – proud of her for that. Doing everything for your children doesn't give them the resilience they need to do well in life.

But if she had been here, maybe she wouldn't have got into the trouble Clodagh told me about, maybe I could've stopped her going down the wrong road. Maybe she would be safe. Maybe I wouldn't be praying with every fibre of my being that the charred remains of some poor unfortunate were not those of my daughter.

I try to feel it. The way they tell you that you can feel these things. If your child or your loved one is dead. They say people know. They sense it. The loss of their energy, or soul or something. A shift in the universe as if one person means that much in the grand scheme of things.

I'm here. In the room she grew up in. I'm trying so hard to find her energy, not sure if I ever felt it in the first place. I find myself inwardly begging for some sign – from the universe, or God, or whatever of Nell remains on this earth to let me know she's okay.

I'm sitting on the bed when Stephen comes in. I can hear that his breath is still ragged. I don't need to look at him to know he is shaking. The bed dips as he sits down beside me. He reaches out for my hand but I can't bear to feel his touch. I don't want to feel anyone touch me. I don't want anything to break the numbness that I'm trying to build all around me.

'We have to prepare ourselves,' he says. As if he's talking about getting ready to go on holiday. Get ready to go on a picnic. Get organised for Christmas. I know how to do all those things. What I don't know is how I'm supposed to prepare myself for the death of my child. How can anyone prepare for that? Even those who know it's coming. It's impossible.

I don't speak.

'We need to be strong,' he says, his voice wavering. 'If it's her. We need to be strong to find out what happened and to make sure it doesn't happen to anyone else.'

I look at him. Is he really throwing out these clichéd lines at me? These tropes? 'To make sure it doesn't happen to anyone else'.

'I don't give a flying fuck what happens to anyone else,' I snap at him, and he looks as if I've just slapped him across the face. I've sworn, you see. He's not used to my swearing. He doesn't like it.

'Stephen, no matter what we say or do, bad things will happen to other people. I can't worry about them now. I can only worry about my child.'

'Our child,' he says, his voice soft.

'We let her down,' I say. 'We got it so wrong. All of it.'

'We did the best we could,' Stephen says and I glare at him, wondering does he really believe that? Can he really think we did the best we could?

I shake my head and I feel his hand on mine. I immediately shrug it off.

'No,' I tell him. 'We didn't. We might as well have walked her towards this.'

'Don't be absurd,' he says. 'We did the best we could for her.' His tone is conciliatory and I want to scream. In fact I have to use every ounce of my willpower not to scream. We didn't do our best for her. Stephen has never done his best for her, or for me. And I let him get away with it all. I taught my daughter it was okay to let him get away with it all.

It was our fault. But more than that, it was my fault.

Chapter Sixteen

Him

Five weeks earlier

He decides he's going to move out. He's talked to his online friends about everything and they've encouraged him to strike out on his own. They've told him that Jade is a controlling slut and she probably has Cormac by the balls.

'Leave them in the shit. Just pack your bags and go. Get a better place. A shag pad! You don't need the spare room in some shitty house-share. You're better than both of them,' Truth4Life has written.

'Don't get mad, get even!' UppaReds has typed. *'The best revenge is a life well lived. Bin them off, mate. Move on. You don't need their shit anyway. Let us know when the housewarming is. We'll show up with birds and booze.'*

There are other replies, all with the same basic message. All encouraging him to move on, and he realises that's exactly what he wants. He had shared before because he thought the company would be good. He thought he would be able to hang on to the halcyon memories of his student days where everyone gathered at the dinner table over vats of spag bol and cheap wine to talk about their days. He'd had visions of weekend parties. Intellectual conversations. A building of unbreakable bonds. But obviously it hadn't worked out like that.

The whole arrangement had only made him feel bad about himself – bad and emasculated. Jade liked to behave as if she owned the place. Griping over his cleanliness standards and rejecting the idea of his spag bol dinner. She was on a permanent diet. Or she'd eat out. Or she and Cormac would eat together, citing his shift patterns as reasons why they excluded him.

'I need to eat earlier in the evening,' she said. 'I can't wait for you to come in, and you're late so much. Always staying on to finish up your work.'

He'd mentioned she could at least consider plating something up for him and leaving it in the microwave, but she'd laughed it off. 'Nice try,' she said, her perfect white teeth on display in the brightest of smiles. 'But I'm not your slave, or your mum. So you can make your own!'

He'd looked to Cormac for some backup, only to see Cormac was laughing too. 'I'll give you this much,' his housemate had said. 'You have balls of steel!'

'Don't worry,' Jade had said with a laugh, 'I'll make sure to leave the tin opener out for you to make your beans on toast. And I'll pin any takeaway menus onto the fridge.'

He'd hated her after that. He hated her even more now. His online friends were right – he was better off without the pair of them. They could shag each other to death for all he cared. He wasn't going to be around to see it any more. And the rent was due the following week – they could whistle if they thought they were getting any from him.

They were both at work the following day when he packed up his belongings, took the tin opener out of spite, and left. He's decided to move into a hotel until he gets sorted with his own place. He has savings. Actually, he has quite a lot of savings. He works hard, but rarely goes out. He'll be able to find a place that makes his previous home look even more like the shit-hole it is.

He'll do exactly what his online friends have suggested and make it his own shag pad. Now is the time to get out there again. Onto the scene. God only knows there are enough slags like Jade around – willing to open their legs in exchange for a cheap dinner and the taxi fare home. He doesn't want to date them. Doesn't care if they are using him. He'll be using them back. Twice as much.

Maybe he'll be able to hook up one of his cameras in his bedroom? If he gets some slutty girl back for a quick shag he can film it, upload it. Prove to 'HymenBreaker', who clearly considers himself to be some sort of alpha male with that gratuitously offensive username, that he isn't a 'pussy'.

He feels better when he has checked into his hotel room, some of his belongings unpacked and a cold beer and a burger delivered by room service. It's quite blissful not to hear Jade's annoying laugh or be forced to listen to Cormac cheer over some sports event. It's just him and a king-sized, super-soft bed and hotel Wi-Fi.

He sits on the bed and scrolls through his phone to the chat forums where he sees a tonne of notifications waiting for him. Much more than usual. Much more than he could ever expect. With a mix of excitement and trepidation he clicks on them. His eyes widen.

Something is happening, something he hadn't anticipated. There are several threads, each with multiple replies. Each beginning with an excited poster sharing that they couldn't help it, they'd had to try his technique for themselves to see if it was the high he'd told them it was. And it seemed, for the vast majority of posters, that it was.

'*You should've seen her face,*' one poster writes, with a laughing emoji afterwards.

'*For me it was about control. I knew that I was going to walk away, but she didn't. It was a rush. There was power to it,*' another wrote.

'*I'm definitely going to do it again. I'm going to record it too so I can watch it back. That's a high I want to keep a track of,*' a third wrote.

His cheesy hashtag, the one he'd created without much thought, is trending on the site. #IHaveThePower is, one poster said, a 'battle cry for all men who have had enough'.

A battle cry? He likes the sound of that. He likes feeling as if he was behind a movement and women are getting scared. Not too much though. There's no harm in it, he tells himself. He can't be held responsible for the years of oppression of women, of crimes against women, which caused them to be frightened of lone men walking home on the same streets they are.

He opens a new thread, wanting to share his perspective. He wanted to let people know why there is nothing wrong with what they were doing and, in fact, if men don't start taking a stand they might as well cut off their balls themselves and make them into earrings.

He thinks of Jade's smug smile. Her sense of self-importance. She thinks she is better than him and it eats him up inside.

It's okay for women to take a stand. Women say they won't modify their behaviour because of men. They will walk where they want. Wear what they want. Behave how they want. Men need to learn that doesn't mean a woman is ever 'asking for it'. But what about us? Are we asking to be seen as predators just because we walk down the same streets alone? Should we be ashamed of our size? Our power? Our strength? These are things that are biologically part of who we are – we can't change them. We shouldn't have to walk around in pairs any more than

100

women should. I've had enough of being pushed into second position. I've had enough of being made to feel like some sort of deviant just because I'm a man.

He presses 'send' and posts the message online and while he starts to read the replies that flood in, he sees the first video uploaded after his own. A dark street appears on the screen, the soundtrack distant traffic and heavy breathing. Footsteps. In the distance he sees a lone figure – walking away. The camera grows closer before he can see for certain that the figure is a woman. She's wearing a red bobble hat, a black duffel coat, with a tartan skirt popping out from under it. Black tights, high heels. She has her hands stuffed into her pockets. He watches as the camera grows closer still, the breathing of the mystery man behind it growing heavier. She glances, all too quickly behind her, and speeds up, before crossing the road.

There is the quietest, almost imperceptible laugh from the mystery camera man before he crosses behind her. He speeds up until he is close enough to hear just how laboured her breathing has become. The fear rises in clouds from her mouth into the night air.

Her steps speed up further, until she is running as fast as her high heels can carry her. The cameraman speeding up for a while until he hears the softest of sobs from the woman in front. Then he stops, lets her continue on her journey and he turns – his camera catching the street he has just walked up. 'Brilliant,' he breathes, in a Geordie accent. 'Bloody brilliant.' And he laughs before the screen goes dark.

In his hotel room in Derry, he who started it all raises his cold beer to his lips and realises he has not felt this relaxed – and this powerful and respected – in years.

And he feels the urge rise up in him to get out and do it again for himself.

Chapter Seventeen

Marian

Tuesday, November 2

Missing five days

Stephen and I were married for five years, and Nell was three, the first time I found out he had been playing away from home – which is a polite way of saying he had smashed the heart of our marriage to pieces.

I'd been tidying in the kitchen, sorting out the pile of paperwork that had built up on top of the microwave. Nell had been in the living room, singing along with the Tweenies. Dancing – her dummy still in her mouth. My heart had been full.

And then my world had been pulled out from under me. A receipt – such a cliché – for a hotel. A hotel close to home for a night he hadn't been away. That made it worse, I think, that it was an afternoon frisson. That the people working in the hotel would know exactly what it was for. That when he had checked out just a few hours later, they would have had it confirmed for them.

I had asked him for an explanation, of course, when he came

home. I desperately wanted there to be some perfectly innocent explanation that I just hadn't been able to think of, even if I knew in my heart what it all meant. At first he didn't admit it and for a moment or two I allowed myself to believe him when he said he couldn't remember what it was all about. As if checking into hotels in the middle of the day was such a normal and regular occurrence it would be easy to forget the minutiae of it all.

When I probed further he explained it away with an excuse about a client from work staying over after a business meeting, and Stephen being a good and caring business associate had covered the bills.

But when I asked for more details – the who and the why and the how – his story started to crack apart until we were both crying and talking about the strain of being parents and how we had lost each other along the way.

It was funny how quickly it had turned to that. How it had been down to parenting. How it had been down to my being 'obsessed' with Nell to the detriment of our marriage. He had needs too, he'd said. He needed to be loved too.

I don't think whatever happened in that hotel room that afternoon had anything to do with love.

I became mired in grief and guilt. Devastated at the betrayal but convinced he was right. It was my fault.

I'd pushed down my anger at the betrayal in case I pushed him away further. I'd decided to show him that I could love both him and Nell. That came with its own mess of feelings. Was I betraying my feminist beliefs by morphing into a Stepford wife?

Dinner was on the table each night when he came home – no matter how busy my own day had been, or how clingy Nell was. I stopped changing into joggers and sweatshirts, or pyjamas as soon as I got in from work. Instead I freshened up.

Slipped on something trendy, figure-hugging, a little bit sexy even. I wore red lipstick. I was every cliché and more. I laughed at his jokes and listened to his long and terminally boring conversations about work.

But there was only so much a lay person can take in about engineering before their knowledge is exhausted and their interest gone.

He made an effort too, of course. That time. He sent flowers. Bought perfume and jewellery. We agreed on a 'date night' once a week and Nell would go and stay with my parents even though it pained me to have her out of the house. But he took me to nice restaurants or cooked for me. He told me he was so very sorry. That he had been weak and feeling neglected but he realised, completely, that he was an arsehole. He cried more than once until I became the one who comforted him and reassured him that it would be okay. All I really wanted was for someone to comfort *me*. To tell *me* everything would be okay.

'We'll look back on this one day and see it as a bump in the road,' he'd said. But he never did tell me her name. The mystery woman who had slept with my husband in a hotel. Sometimes when we went out I'd see him look across the bar at someone, or catch the eye of a passing woman as she walked across the room. I wondered each time if it was her. Or worse, was it someone I knew? I looked at our friends with increased suspicion. Until he told me I was being unreasonable and I needed to 'let it go'.

'It's over and done with and we need to move on. I can't live under the shadow of this for the rest of our lives,' he said, his face pained. 'I can't keep saying I'm sorry,' he said one day but what he didn't realise was that I *needed* him to say he was sorry. Over and over. I had trusted him with every part of me and he had let me down. This person who was supposed to be my partner in life had veered horrendously off course without so much as a second thought.

But apart from that first day, I didn't cry in front of him. It was different when he was gone though. I would cry and howl and find myself staring into space for an hour or more at a time, Nell playing around my feet until she would climb up on my knee and hug me. 'Don't cry, Mummy,' she'd say, giving me her teddy to hold.

She, even at three years old, felt a need to fix me and I, being weak and selfish, let her.

I've come back downstairs and DI Bradley is talking. He is updating me as much as he can. They've tracked down the taxi driver who picked up Nell. He had one of those dash cam thingies in his car, so they were able to verify his story that he'd dropped her off in town, close to the Foyleside Shopping Centre and had gone on to his next job. It wasn't a lead they would be pursuing further.

Police have spoken to some of the people Clodagh had told us about. They've not been terribly forthcoming with information.

'Probably scared to get into trouble themselves,' DS King said. 'If what Clodagh has said is right about their casual drug use and other antics. But we'll get more out of them. We've a couple more of that gang to speak to.'

'And this Rob character?' I ask. 'Wasn't someone going to speak to him?'

DS King shifts a little in her chair. 'Well, someone did go to speak to him, but it seems he isn't at work today. Off sick. So an officer was despatched to his home address to speak to him there.'

'And what did he say?' I ask, feeling for a moment as if I'm pulling teeth.

'Well, he wasn't there either, but we did speak to Jenny, the nurse at the hospital who saw him on Saturday and she confirmed that they spent the night together.'

'But that was Saturday. Nell went missing on Thursday. Tell me you're still looking for him?'

'We will be speaking to him, yes. We have left messages at his work, at his home and on his phone – which he seems to have switched off,' DS King says.

I nod, but inside I want to scream at them. Leaving messages isn't enough. It isn't going to find him, or her. I have to believe they haven't found her yet. I have to think the body they have is someone else. The alternative is unthinkable. I close my eyes to try to blank out the unbidden image of Nell, lying charred on a table, but of course the image is embedded in my head. It wasn't ever going away.

'Where did they find her?' I ask, not quite believing that I didn't ask this already.

'There are some outbuildings near the border at Culmore. A farmer walking in the fields was checking disused properties on the outskirts of his land when he found the remains. We don't believe the victim was killed on site, or that the body was burned there,' DS King says. 'We're combing the surrounding land now.'

I nod while my stomach turns.

The language of it is all so jarring. DS King didn't refer to 'her' when she talked about the farmer. She talked about 'the body', or 'the remains'. Whoever it is, even if it's not Nell, is so much more than just a body or just remains.

We fall into an uneasy, heavy silence. Waiting for the worst news possible. They've asked us if we want to call anyone over to sit with us. I can't think of anything worse. It's bad enough with six of us sitting looking at each other, occasionally asking questions we don't really want to know the answers to. I don't need my friends, or Stephen's family, or anyone else to worry about. In some ways I don't want them to know – which is ridiculous because I want everyone to be looking for her. But if my family know, my colleagues, my friends, it makes it real. I don't want it to be real.

A phone rings and DI Bradley takes his mobile from his pocket and looks down at it. I see how he glances at DS King and as he stands up to leave the room, I feel Stephen's hand reach for mine. Instinctively I pull away. I can't countenance the thought of someone touching me. Every nerve ending is fizzing. It's too much.

I refuse to look at DS King for any facial tells. I want to put my hands over my ears in case I hear what DI Bradley is saying. This kind of news can wait. It can wait forever.

I feel a dip in the sofa as Heather sits beside me. She's not terribly subtle, God love her. She might as well be carrying a box of tissues and leaflets for undertakers.

The thought is enough to make me laugh. One of those highly inappropriate bursts of laughter that is borderline hysterical. I've pushed down so much worry, terror and anger that my emotions have to come out in some way. Any way. The look of abject disgust on Stephen's face makes me laugh harder, until my sides are aching and tears are streaming down my face. Tears that very quickly turn to hysterical sobbing. Burying my head in my hands I think that I want to die. Right here. Right now. In this moment because the pain is too much.

'Marian,' DI Bradley's voice cuts through. I feel his hand reach for mine. I glance up and see that this senior police officer is crouched in front of me, his dark eyes looking directly at me.

'It's not her,' he says. 'It's not Nell.'

Chapter Eighteen

Him

Four weeks earlier

He has never considered himself someone people would look up to. He hasn't given it much thought, not until now anyway. Not until he started a trend that is taking on a life of its own. Now he comes home from work to see he has been tagged in different posts – some of which read like manifestos for the rights of men. Some of which are barely intelligible rants – huge swathes of text with no punctuation and very little in the way of correct spelling.

Others have recorded videos of their own, posted clips of scared women in dark, unfamiliar streets. He gets a buzz from them, of course he does. Just not quite the same buzz that he gets from doing it himself. But he knows he has to be careful now. Derry isn't a big city. The population not much over 100,000 – and most of those people seem to know all the others. There's no Six Degrees of Separation in Derry. Two degrees, three at most maybe, and the average Derry person can find out all they need to know about their neighbours with minimal effort.

News spreads like wildfire — it always has. Even before the days of social media. The jungle drums wouldn't be long in sharing any gossip, women chatting over the garden fence or at the school gates, men chatting in the queue at the dole office. Derry was a place where so much was hidden, but only just under the surface. The slightest cut and it can all spill out.

So he knows there has been a little talk already of a fellah behaving oddly in the city centre. Of course, no one can put their finger on it. It isn't as if he was doing anything illegal. He is, after all, just walking the same streets those women are. He is just making his way home.

He never makes any direct threats — or indirect threats for that matter. That these women are scared isn't specifically his fault. But still, he doesn't want to get in trouble. He has no doubt he would be scapegoated as an example of everything that is bad and awful about men in this world. He'd lose his job. God only knows what people would say about him. What they would be willing to make up to feed their own narrative.

Besides, if he is being really honest with himself, he needs something more now. It's been four weeks since he started this crusade. He has made ten videos. In the last three, he went so far as to reach out and touch the women he was walking behind. Just a tap on their shoulders. A quick 'Excuse me, did you drop this?' and they would shake their heads and scurry off like rats.

It has been a high, but it's not giving him the same hit as it was before. He wants to shake things up. Now that he's settled in his own place, he wonders sometimes what it would be like to bring one of those women home. Play the gentleman and gain their trust. Romance them a little with flowers and choc-olates and all the clichéd shit that women like to be bought with. Wait until they get comfortable, and then take control. Just enough to leave an indelible mark in their memories. A feeling of a cloudy, fuzzy place between comfort and unease. Between consent and coercion.

Is it wrong, he wonders, that he gets turned on thinking about that? That he gets hard. It's fantasy, after all, and fantasy harms no one. But making those fantasies become a reality is something he is craving more and more.

He craved it today, at work. When his boss was on his back all day. When she stood by his desk and he noticed her shirt was unbuttoned just that little bit too low. When she had laughed at him in their morning meeting. Told him he needed to do better. That he should know better by now because he's been in this job a while. And then, in the staff kitchen a little later, she had leaned back against the worktop, cradling her coffee cup, her dark eyes looking up at him from under her wispy blonde fringe. If he hadn't known better, he'd have sworn she was teasing him. Giving him a come on. Giving him a slutty look just to unnerve him. Fucking prick tease.

There had been no one else around then. If he wanted her he could've stood up, waited until she turned to put her cup in the sink and pushed up against her, hard, from behind. He knew how to hold her. How to restrain a person. One hand would cover her mouth, while he'd pin her tighter, groping her, pulling her shirt open, exposing her breasts as he ground against her. It would be so easy to overpower her. She was only small. It wouldn't really be a fair fight – but maybe she'd learn her lesson. Maybe she would learn not to laugh at him again.

At home in his new place, later that day, he thinks about that fantasy. Feels a mixture of excitement and then shame. He's not a misogynist. He knows right from wrong but it would be so much easier to stop the lines from blurring if he was treated with the same respect he was expected to hold his female colleagues in.

Fantasy hurts no one, he thinks again. It doesn't mean

he actually wants to do it, does it? Even though the thought of actually doing it invigorates and excites him.

He's starting to enjoy these little adrenaline bursts. Enjoying living just on the edge. But it does make him restless. Fantasy, he realises, may hurt no one but it's not always enough.

He changes into his dark trousers and jacket. Pulls his beanie hat on and grabs his GoPro. He slips his black gloves onto his hands and tells himself he's going out for a walk. Just a walk to burn off the nervous energy that has fizzed through his body since that interaction in the staff kitchen, and which has only been empowered in his chatrooms. He wants to dampen down the shame he feels nipping at the corners of his mind and the only way to do that is to drown out the noise with something louder.

The night is wet, rain is bouncing off the pavement and running in rivulets down gutters. There is a smell of chimney smoke in the air and he imagines most right-minded people are locked away in their homes and their perfect lives, curled on the sofa watching TV, or sitting around a dinner table with their loved ones. It's the kind of night that people only go out in if they really have to, the squalls of rain becoming heavier and more persistent.

The more he walks, the more he thinks it might not be a successful night for him. Even the roads are quiet, barely a car driving past. A man, older, in a long woollen coat is walking ahead of him. He glances around and walks on.

Determined not to give up, he crosses the road, walks along the river – hopeful he'll find a stray dog-walker or two along the popular walkway. Dogs don't care about the rain, they just need their exercise. He walks away from the city centre, water now running down his face and dropping off the end of his nose. He is soaked through, his skin clammy and cool. Until he sees her, her red puffy jacket illuminated under lamplight.

She has her head bowed, one hand tight in her pocket, the other holding a lead while a small dog in a stupid yellow raincoat scampers at her feet.

He has his prey in his sights and he sets off. GoPro switched on, gathering speed, the roar of the rain now drowned out by the roar of the blood pulsing through his veins. This was exactly the right thing to do. He can't stop smiling.

Chapter Nineteen

Marian

November, Tuesday 2

Missing five days

The relief that the body lying in the morgue is not my daughter's is short-lived.

She is still missing. There is still no trace of her. No activity on her cards or phone. No sightings. No productive line of inquiry. 'Rob' is still MIA.

And, of course, there is now a more serious case to draw the attention of the police. The discovery of charred remains of an unknown woman trumps a missing woman any day of the week. I know that.

'I can assure you,' DS King says, 'that finding Nell is still at the top of our agenda. Please don't think we'll reduce our efforts now.'

'Do you think what happened to this poor woman is related to Nell going missing?' Stephen asks. 'Could the same person behind it have her?'

I glance around, trying to read the expressions on the faces of the police officers in the room. They give nothing away.

'At the moment there's nothing to suggest that is the case, but we'll be looking at all lines of inquiry. It's still our hope to get Nell back to you alive and well,' DI Bradley says with more confidence than I feel, or at least he does a good job of bluffing it if he doesn't.

I nod, mutely because there is nothing that can be said. We're in the middle of a nightmare and I don't know how to feel. I want to find Nell and hug her, and shake her hard for putting us through this. I want to ask her what the hell she has been at. I want to tell her how sick to my very stomach I have felt thinking she was dead, her body destroyed. Most of all I want to blot it all out. All of it. I can't continue to feel this level of extreme fear, extreme anger, extreme grief and extreme love all at the same time. It will kill me.

I wonder if Stephen is feeling as guilt-ridden as I am. Guilty that she moved out and that we didn't keep her at home to look after her. It's sad that part of me wonders if it's even crossed his mind.

He's standing there now, across the room, and I wish things were different between us and I could reach out to him and find a proper, comforting connection and not just this sense of going through the motions. Of it not quite being enough. Not genuine. It used to make me so incredibly sad. But now, instead I just feel a bubbling anger towards him.

Anger at his concerned face. At his running out to get milk. At his huge display of love and concern for her – too little, too late, I think.

God, it really might be too late.

'You can be straight with me,' I say to DI Bradley, hoping that he absolutely won't be straight with me. 'What do you think? What's the chance that we're going to find her safe and sound? I don't want the soft soap. I know you all know things. How the first forty-eight hours are critical et cetera. I've watched enough crime dramas.'

'For goodness' sake, Marian,' Stephen interrupts. 'Those aren't real life. This isn't an episode of *CSI*.'

I tense. I'm not stupid. I want to shout at him that I'm not stupid, that there has to be some truth in what these shows portray.

'The first *seventy-two hours* are important,' DS King says. 'But we don't know for certain when Nell went missing. It's possible she was at home at some stage and Clodagh just didn't know about it. We have to work on what we know for sure, and that's that she didn't show up for work yesterday, and there has been no activity on her accounts since Thursday. So our next move is to escalate this to the Missing Persons Bureau. But please remember, we've no proof that anything bad has happened to Nell or that she's come to any harm. It's possible she's gone somewhere of her own accord – and by all accounts she has been mixing with new people recently.'

'I don't think speculation is useful or wise,' DI Bradley says, and he glares at DS King who seems to shrink under his gaze. 'Try to focus on the facts and hopefully they will lead us to her.'

'Of course. I'm sorry,' DS King says. 'DI Bradley is absolutely right.' Her face is flushed and I feel momentarily sorry for her. After all, I was the one who asked the stupid question knowing full well they wouldn't be able to give me a straight answer.

I nod because I have run out of things to say. I'm tired now. The sleepless night catching up with me. The urge to blank it all out with a long sleep washes over me again, but would it be a complete betrayal of my daughter to fall into a restful sleep while she is God knows where? What kind of a mother would that make me?

'Marian?' Heather's voice cuts through my fugue and I blink

in her direction. 'I know this must be awful, but we're doing all we can. You look done in. Why don't you get a rest? I'll be here and I'll wake you if there are any developments at all.'

I shake my head. 'No. I want to be awake.'

Heather is crouched in front of me, talking to me as if I'm a child and taking my hand in hers. 'We could be at the start of a long road,' she says. 'You're not doing Nell any favours by burning out now. You need to be well rested so you can be in the best place to help us find her.'

I nod but my limbs are too heavy to move. The weight of it all is pushing down on me now and I know if I let it, it could crush me completely. And we're only, as Heather says, at the start of a long road. I don't know if I can bear it. I want to scream at the top of my lungs. I want to call her name and I need to hear her voice tell me she is okay. I need it as much as I need to breathe.

I've heard people say they felt as though they were crumbling before, but I didn't get it. Not until now. Now I feel as if I am disintegrating, bit by bit. I can't exist without her.

I don't want to exist without her.

'Marian,' Heather says. 'Let's get you upstairs. You'll feel a little stronger after you've slept.'

I do as I'm told, not because I want to, but because I don't have the strength to argue.

Chapter Twenty

Him

Four Weeks Earlier

He has a bit of swagger about him. His walks at night, coupled with his growing status online have given him an extra air of confidence. He feels it every day. When he gets up in the morning and looks in the bathroom mirror, he no longer hates what he sees.

He no longer feels like an observer in his own life. He no longer feels uncomfortable in his own skin. He feels as if he has been reborn. He feels like a leader. He knows, actually, that he is a leader – that there are people online hanging on to see what he does next. There are people – men – online who are telling him that they have followed his lead and they are reaping the rewards.

Videos are popping up on the site now, several times a day – men from all over sharing that they have completed the 'challenge'.

Someone has started a league table, keeping score. Ten points if the woman shouts, twenty if they manage to reach out and touch her. There's no guilt. After all, none of them are doing anything wrong. They aren't actually causing any hurt to the women they follow and if a woman wants to be stupid enough to go out walking in a quiet area on her own, in the dark, then she must be aware she's taking a risk.

'*Maybe she likes risky behaviour?*' a user called NotAChad asked with a winky face emoji.

That question has been on his mind ever since he read it. He has seen a lot of reckless or stupid behaviour in his line of work – from both men and women. He's not a psychologist, but it does seem that some people really seem to get some sort of a kick out of taking chances. They know things could end badly but they do it anyway. That says a lot about people. Maybe we're all just conditioned to take risks. We need it to keep us fresh. He certainly feels refreshed, no – reborn, just now.

Other people are noticing the change in him too. If he's not mistaken, he's been getting some unexpected attention in work. From one of the new girls – only in the job six months. She has definitely started spending more time at his desk. She says she wants to learn the job from him, but he knows it's more than that.

Just as he could see the disdain in Jade's eyes, he can see the sparkle in Natalia's eyes. Natalia – it's such a lovely name – young, vibrant. He'd even go so far as to describe her as beautiful. And she's smart. She wouldn't take a risk by walking in a dark place, alone at night. She has more cop-on than to do that.

She listens when he talks and he was sure she had sat a little too close to him on purpose earlier as he tried to show her something on his computer. She could easily have seen the screen from further away, but she had pulled her chair closer – so close in fact that he could feel the heat radiating from her body, warming his own skin. He'd turned his head to talk to her, finding his face just inches from hers. He hadn't imagined the frisson of attraction between them. He was sure of that. He might just ask her out — although if he starts seeing someone he isn't sure how he will feel about his evening walks. What would Natalia think?

He'll have to think about it. Weigh up the appeal of asking Natalia out — with her deep brown eyes and olive-coloured skin — and possibly building a relationship with her, versus continuing with his hero status online. He doesn't have a good history with relationships. In fact, his history with relationships is pretty shockingly bad. A couple of not really official couplings. Casual arrangements — or at least they had been casual to the other person. He had always gone all in, and history had shown him when he let someone else see the real him they didn't usually stay around too long.

Natalia feels different, in his gut. Maybe because of his growing confidence, or maybe it's the case that she is that mythical 'one' that people talk about. She laughs at his jokes, even the nerdy ones. Actually, especially the nerdy ones. She seems impressed with his work, asks him countless questions and even in the kitchen he's noticed that she'll sit opposite him whenever she can. She is keen. She treats him with respect — as if he is important.

But it is still a risk, and women are notoriously fickle. A growing number of his online friends have decided to give up on women all together. Or at least to give up on the notion of forming a lasting relationship. They believe the world is unfairly weighted against men, and against any man who isn't rich, good-looking and overly confident.

Some of them, those online friends of his, identify as incels — shorthand for being involuntarily celibate. He can see the appeal in it. Who wants to put their heart out there time and time again for women to trample on — women who only ever see men like him as place-holders until the real deal comes along. Women who have grown too big for their boots.

119

He looks at Natalia. She is sitting across the office at her computer, her brow furrowed in concentration. She is beautiful. Too beautiful for him, he thinks. She catches him looking – looks up and smiles at him. A broad, genuine smile that makes him feel warm inside.

He'll definitely have to think this through. Will meeting the right woman be enough to ease his anger? Will he be able to trust her not to be like all the other women who spout their feminist agenda while not thinking about the damage they are doing to a generation of men?

Will the high of being with the right woman match the high – the adrenaline rush – of feeling as if he has power over someone? Does he want to be with her, or control her?

He drops his gaze from hers and tries to focus on the work in front of him. He'll think more about it later when it feels less messy in his head.

This wasn't in the plan.

Logging on that night he sees a number of private messages waiting for him and he clicks into the folder, running his eye down the list of first lines to see if there's anything that looks worth reading.

He's received at least a hundred private messages recently. People congratulating him, sharing their videos with him, asking him if he ever considers actually hurting a woman. Some say they fantasise about that. About going further than he ever has. Some are pretty sick, even for him. He's all for teaching people a lesson but he's not a psychopath. He doesn't actually want to hurt anyone. Apart from his boss, and maybe Jade. And even then he really doesn't think he'd have the balls to hurt them. Not in the way some of these guys describe anyway. And they do like to go into detail – forensic, intimate, terrifying detail. Assault, rape, murder, defiling the bodies of their victims.

Heinous acts. Treating women as lumps of meat. Using vile slurs – whores, sluts, cum-dumps. Dehumanising women. Advocating rape as something normal and acceptable. Sex is a human right. A male right. Men need to have sex and if a woman has a sexual history then she should be forced to spread her legs to allow that need to be fulfilled. There are vivid descriptions of torture. Or disfigurement. There is one message that calls for cheating women to be publicly executed – advocates for a new form of Sharia law that controls women to a whole new level.

It makes him feel uneasy. It's much more than just getting a kick from scaring a woman. It's a million miles from indulging in some seedy fantasies alone in his room. Choosing not to engage with the most violent of posts, he's about to click out of his private message folder when a username grabs his attention. Doire92. *Doire* being the Irish spelling of Derry. Perhaps it's coincidental, but the first line of the message intrigues him.

'*Can I ask you a question?*'

He clicks to open it and reads on.

I've been watching your videos. Well done, lad. First-class stuff. I'd be right in saying you're in Derry, wouldn't I? I recognise some of those places in your videos. Gotta say, you've got some balls, man. I admire the fuck out of that. About time someone put all those snobby bitches of this town in their place. All fake as fuck with their hair extensions, and fake tans and three tonnes of make-up. Crying about wanting a decent man while spreading their legs for any dickhead with a better fake tan than them and some funds in the bank. The state of them, dressing like sluts and then crying about respect. It gets right on my tits. You've inspired me, lad. I want to chase that high. I'm going to go for it. Maybe we could buddy up? You could give me a few hints and tips. Or we can go on the hunt together. Can you imagine that – send 'em running in one direction only to have one of us waiting for them there. It would be pure class. Drop us a wee line, mucker. Let's do this.

Clicking onto Doire92's profile he sees that this poster is someone new. He only registered a week ago and has yet to post anywhere else. His avatar is a cropped image of Liverpool football club manager Jürgen Klopp. His bio gives nothing away.

Breaking out in a cold sweat, he wonders if this is some kind of set-up. Could this be someone he knows on his trail? Could this be part of some sort of ruse to out him? Maybe those rumours of a dodgy character annoying women are escalating a bit.

And there was that one post that circulated on Facebook – from the woman walking in the rain with the dog – which turned into a rant about how women should be able to walk the streets alone whenever they want.

It had garnered a response – a mix of women berating creepy men, men who clearly thought it made them look eminently fuckable to voice their solidarity with the sisterhood, and brave souls willing to tell the poster she shouldn't be taking risks. Boys will be boys. Men will be men.

One poster had replied recalling a similar experience the week before. It was more than likely one of his own expeditions. There was something familiar about the face in the profile picture, but not enough for him to be sure. He'd clicked into her profile but she had it locked down tight.

But regardless, neither post had launched a manhunt or inspired a gang of vigilantes to try to track him down. Unless Doire92 is a lone vigilante of course. He can't rule that out.

In his gut he feels that his would-be partner in crime is for real and he doesn't know how to feel about that. He certainly doesn't want to team up with anyone. This has always been his own little secret. His lone adventure. Inviting someone else in would escalate things to a level he isn't comfortable with. Plus, there's something about this Doire92 person that gives him a really bad feeling. Even if it isn't a set-up to lure him out of hiding, it's not good. No good will come of it.

He clicks back into the message and reads it again before deleting it. His finger hovers over the 'block' button. He doesn't need this person in his life. Instinctively he knows the less he has to do with this person, the better.

He clicks the button and shuts down his computer, but he's on edge. Really on edge. So he decides to go out on a run. No GoPro, no phone recording this, just him releasing the tension in his body as he pounds the pavements, step by step and mile by mile.

Chapter Twenty-One

Nell

Monday, November 1

Missing four days

I think it has been four days. Maybe five. It's hard to keep track but this is the first day I've been on my own in this place.

Elzbieta was here until yesterday. Not that I saw her, but I heard her. I heard her the first day I was here. When I woke up in this . . . this . . . cell. I'd started screaming, clawing at the walls, trying to haul myself free. That's when I heard the voice from somewhere else in the building.

'No one can hear you,' she said, her accent thick and her voice familiar. 'I've been shouting for days,' she said. There was something resigned about the way she spoke. 'He is the only person who comes and he comes when he wants to.'

As she spoke I realised where I knew her from. She had been working on the same ward as me for months and now we had both ended up here. That first day – before he came, we talked. She told me how he had taken her – there was no pretence of a dinner invite with her. He had simply forced her into his car. Brute force and threat. She told me that he'd said he was disappointed in himself. That he hadn't got it right. That he had to get the game just right. That's all he talks about, she told me. His game and his rules. How his game will make him famous. How he told her he would make us famous too. That our sacrifice would be for the greater good.

My blood had run cold.

But Elzbieta was strong. Even though I knew she had to be scared, she was a fucking badass. She was so determined that she was getting out of here alive. That we would both get out of here alive. We just have to play the game, she told me. If we played the game and didn't break the rules, we'd buy time enough to find our way out of here.

But that first day, when we'd spoken, we hadn't realised we were already breaking them. We didn't get any food that night. That was our punishment. That was the consequence of our actions, he said to me first, and then I heard him repeat the same script, almost word for word to Elzbieta, the timbre of his voice stern, authoritative and laced with disgust. It would be worse the next time, he said. Someone would get hurt.

We didn't dare speak to each other again. Although sometimes we would sing the line of a song or speak loudly to ourselves knowing the other one would hear – little messages of hope. Little drops of compassion. I had clung to them.

Without them, without her, it's worse. The silence is so much scarier now that I am alone. Truly alone.

All I have to keep me going is the hope that she is okay. I know that's probably very naïve of me. Or maybe not naïve – it's a survival technique. I need to believe she is okay because nothing else makes sense.

He took her from here last night. I heard his deep voice rumbling as he spoke to her in the next room. I heard her crying – but they seemed to be happy tears. If she's free, I know she will be trying to get help for me right now. Help could arrive at any time. I just have to be patient. I just have to behave myself and try not to get into trouble with him.

He won't tell me what his rules are. I've asked him. I've told him I should at least know. He just winked, tapped the side of his head with his finger to let me know it's all in his head. That's all that matters. He doesn't feel the need to share. It would be no fun if I knew the rules, he says.

If I'd known the rules, I would never have taken my phone to the bathroom when I was having dinner at his house. According to him, if I'd just left my phone in my bag I would be going about my normal life now. We might, he says, even be planning a second date. I might not be aware of what he is really like.

I'd only taken my phone to the bathroom because I realised no one knew where I was. Clodagh would probably think I was with Rob – I hadn't had the chance to tell her yet that that had ended up as a non-starter. That he wasn't looking for anything serious. Instead, I'd gone with my stupid, reckless, obviously broken gut instinct.

I've always considered myself to be a sensible girl. Probably too sensible. Or so Mum tells me. 'Don't make the mistakes I did,' she'd told me once, when she'd had two glasses of wine over dinner. 'Don't rush to settle down. And live your life. Do things!'

She looked so sad. I wanted to scream at her to live her own life. I was doing just fine. But her words had niggled at me, as had the sadness in her eyes. My mother lives a quiet, unassuming life. Subservient to my father – theirs is very much an unequal marriage. She wants more for me.

She *wanted* more for me. Fear swoops in again. I might not ever see her again. She will be so worried that I'm missing. If she even knows I'm missing. Please God Clodagh doesn't assume I'm off misbehaving somewhere.

This madness of the last few months has ripped holes in our friendship. I just wanted to live a little. I wanted to rebel. I suppose I wanted it to be a two fingers up to my dad, who has never let my mother shine.

I love him, but I hate him too. My dad. The longing for him right now is visceral. I want him to storm in here and give out to me about worrying them both to death and march me to the back of his car and we can drive home in blissful silence. I want to be grounded in my room, even though I'm twenty-two. I want to live a small life with my mother and father. I want to apologise to Clodagh. I want to turn back the clock and change it all.

But I can't. Just like I can't get out of this room. That will be his call. I am at his mercy. I'm so, so angry with myself that I can hardly breathe. My chest is tight, my throat sore, my heart heavy.

I thought I knew how to keep myself safe. I thought I'd learned my lesson. I had decided to take fewer risks after that weirdo chased me, waving his camera in my face when I turned to challenge him. The look in his eyes had scared me. I'd realised I'd been taking stupid chances and for what? Friends who only cared about going on 'the sesh'? Rob and his flashy lifestyle of fine wine, great sex and hard drugs that made me feel detached from myself.

There was something about the whole episode that had completely freaked me out and I'd promised myself I'd be extra careful from there on in.

I'd only wanted to call Clodagh. That was the only reason I'd taken my phone with me to the bathroom that night. Things have been tense between us and I wanted her to know I was okay, and I was going to make more time for us in the future.

The appeal of spending all my money on nights out and then falling short on the rent had worn off.

Eddie had already made it clear he hated it when people were out together and spent their evenings staring at their phones instead of having proper conversations. There was something in the way he had said it that had made me feel uneasy. There was a lot about Eddie that made me feel uneasy. It never had before – when we were at work together. But here, in his house, he was giving out seriously creepy vibes. I didn't want to cause a fuss so I vowed to just eat my dinner, be polite and get out of there as quickly as I could.

As it happened I didn't even get to speak to Clodagh or send a message or leave a voicemail.

The mobile signal was rubbish from his house and as I moved about trying to get an extra bar of service, he had pounded on the bathroom door and asked if I was okay.

There had been something in his voice and in the heaviness of his knock on the door that made my blood run cold. But by that stage, of course, it was already much too late.

That first day was the hardest. He must've put something in my drink because I know I hadn't had enough to be anywhere near drunk, and yet I couldn't keep my eyes open. For hours and hours, I didn't know what was real and what was a dream. I don't know how many times I woke and tried to pull myself into consciousness before losing the battle and slipping back under.

It was like I was trying to crawl out of a deep, dark hole and every time my hand reached up into fresh air, I'd lose my grip on reality and fall back to the bottom. All those hours of half-sleep and strange dreams, I knew deep down that something was very wrong – but I couldn't make sense of what it was. Clarity eluded me.

It was as if I was having one of my recurring dreams – the

one where I'm desperately trying to make a phone call but can't. Where every time I try to punch the numbers on the screen I misdial, or the numbers move about, or morph into something else. My panic was growing with each failed attempt, but when I eventually woke there was none of the sense of relief that usually follows such a frustrating and stressful dream. Because things were not okay in my waking world.

Things were very, very not okay.

All I have are hazy memories of eating dinner, and something feeling off. Something smashing. It might've been my glass. Lying down on a sofa, my neck sore. I remember that, that it was bent at a strange angle and my head had pounded. Someone over me. No, someone on top of me. Him. Eddie.

I've pleaded with him so many times. Each time the door has opened and a tray of food has been slid in. When he has come in and stood over me, asking me if I'm ready to play nicely yet. I have begged. I have shouted, and cajoled and cried. I have tried to find a hint of humanity – something of the shy man who I would chat to in work. The man I thought was harmless.

So harmless that I'd agreed to go for a last minute dinner to his house on Thursday. I don't even know why I agreed to it. Eddie is not my type. Not now, not then, not ever.

I suppose I was angry with Rob, and Clodagh and I hadn't been getting along, and work had been tough, but still it was a bad idea. Rational me knows it was a bad idea, but he said it was just as friends. Just colleagues sharing a glass of wine and a home-cooked meal and sure what else would I be doing anyway?

'Sure, it's not like you don't know me,' he'd said. 'I'm hardly an axe murderer.'

Stupidly, I'd laughed along with him and believed him. I thought I did know him. Eddie who seemed so harmless. Who was helpful when I needed a patient's file pulled, or a clinic follow up arranged. Reliable Eddie who worked in administration and frequently called to the ward. Who always took the time to stop and chat.

I've been so stupid. If only I'd been more careful. If only I'd said no. If only I'd made up an excuse about wanting to get home to sort things out with Clodagh.

God, I miss her. I miss my best friend. I miss her ability to say and do the right thing. I miss her sensible head. I wish, God I wish, I was at home and she was handing me a big mug of hot chocolate and telling me everything is going to be fine. Telling me I'm safe.

I'm not safe. The thought takes my breath for a moment. I know I'm in so much danger. Even if I hope that Elzbieta has got away, I know that's just me trying to comfort myself, because I can't bring myself to think about the alternative. I can't allow myself to think that this entire sick game is weighted against me and, ultimately, it doesn't matter what I do or don't know. It will end the same way. He won't let me walk away from this. Not when I know him – his face, his name, where he works.

I draw my knees to my chest, hugging them close to try and find some comfort. It is bitter cold, and so damp. I can feel the moisture in the air sitting thick in my chest, seeping its way into my clothes, settling with the dirt and dust under my fingernails and on my skin. I feel it – the cold and the damp and the dust – burying me, minute layer by layer.

The walls are bare breeze block – rough. My hands are scraped and bloodied, my fingernails broken, torn from their nail beds by futile attempts to dig at the mortar around them, try to find a weakness in the creases of this tomb.

I assume I'm in a half-built house, a bungalow maybe? I don't hear any feet stomping on stairs when he arrives. There are two doorways in this room. The one he uses to come in and out of is complete with a heavy padlock that sticks some-times. I've heard him swear as he fumbles with his key, fighting with it to do what it should.

I don't know what I wish for more – that he can't open the door, or that he can. I don't want to see him. To have him touch me, but the thought of being abandoned here with no way to escape is a thing of nightmares. I don't like the dark, especially now that I'm completely alone.

The second doorway leads to a tiny room, an en suite, which mercifully has a working toilet plumbed in. A dim, bare bulb hangs from wooden rafters in that small room. It provides a cursory amount of light – not enough to light the darkness of the bigger room. I'd guess at most it's a forty-watt bulb, but I'm grateful for it.

There is space for a window in the wall closest to me, but the aperture has been boarded up. I've tried to break through it. My shoulder is swollen from where I've run at it, hefting all my weight into an attempt to splinter the wood. It hasn't budged or cracked or given way. It's as stuck as I am.

The only natural light I have – the only way I can tell the difference between day and night – is through the small crack at the bottom of the main door, the one he walks through. I have to lie down, my head sideways on the floor to see it – to believe there is still a world outside of these walls. If I get my head at just the right angle, I can feel a slight breeze.

I never know if or when Eddie will arrive. It might be first thing – his voice dragging me from whatever fitful sleep I've managed. On that first day, when I was trying to figure out what was happening, he didn't come until night-time. Or maybe he had come earlier too, and I was just too out of it to notice.

So out of it that he had been able to shift me from the warmth of his sofa to this place. To this sagging divan bed, with its damp pillows and scratchy blanket.

He has told me one of his rules is that I should greet him warmly no matter what time he arrives. Morning, afternoon or middle of the night. That I should respect him. If I don't, he can change everything. What I eat. What I drink. If the lightbulb stays in the bathroom. If I get a blanket to try to keep me warm.

He has brought me a two-litre bottle of water each day. That's what I get to drink, and to use to clean myself. I have one towel, which is now mouldering on a nail that has been crudely knocked into the wall. It never dries. It just stagnates. Nothing is ever really dry here.

The sole source of heat is a rusty Super Ser, which he switches on only when he is here. It pumps out heat and a sickly smell of gas that can't be safe. Despite the bitter cold, I'm glad when he turns it off. My head can stop swimming and I can feel clarity return. My senses sharpen. That's a blessing and a curse. I've always been a 'coul rife', as my mum would say. Cold at all times. Hugging the radiator whenever I can. But I don't think I ever truly felt cold until now. This is next level.

And in the middle of the night, when my teeth are chattering so hard my head hurts, and I can feel the cold wrap itself around me, the heater sits there, taunting me, just out of reach.

Because that's the thing, you see. I'm chained up like an animal here. A heavy, cold chain is linked around my ankle, the other end attached to the floor with a thick iron bolt, cemented into the ground. Yes, I've tried to scrape at that cement too and been as successful as I have been with the mortar on the walls.

None of my personal possessions are here. Not my shoes, my bag. Not even my own clothes. I'm in a tracksuit – cheap and flimsy. Dirty and smelling of my own sweat, and damp.

He only ever brings flimsy plastic cutlery, paper cups and plates when he brings food – takes them away with him when he leaves. He's not stupid. I'll give him that much. He is making sure I have nothing that could possibly be used as a tool or a weapon.

I hope and pray Clodagh has alerted someone to the fact I'm missing. That she isn't so cross with me for being the worst friend in the world recently that she is just enjoying the peace and quiet. That she doesn't think I'm off somewhere with friends who aren't really friends.

I hope someone is looking for me because the thought that this may all be happening without anyone on my side is unbearable. I can't deal with this much longer. I don't want to. I just want to go home. I just want my mum.

I curl up on the bed, wrap the blanket tighter as if that will make a difference, and try to remember if it has been four days or five.

Chapter Twenty-Two

Marian

Wednesday, November 3

Missing six days

I have slept. Thanks to fifty milligrams of Diazepam. I probably slept too well, but thankfully it was dreamless. Lying in my bed, I hear Stephen's slow, deep, rhythmic breathing. He's still asleep. I wonder if he took some Diazepam too. Probably not. Pills aren't his thing. He sees them as a crutch – an admission of weakness. Probably even now.

Julie-Anne, one of my oldest friends had arrived at my door sombre-faced with a strip of the magic pills 'borrowed' from her own stash. It had been too late to get a prescription from my doctor. Stephen had given me a lecture about how it was illegal to share prescription drugs and did we not have enough to worry about without getting off our heads on someone else's pills while there was a policewoman in the house.

I'd told him to go to hell. But in less polite language. I considered hiding them in case he took the notion to take one before bed – but I'm not heartless.

Julie-Anne had pulled me into the tightest of hugs and I had sobbed on her shoulder as if I would never stop.

'My mammy has the holy candle lit,' she whispered. 'She said to tell you she's praying for you. For Nell.'

I gave a half, watery smile. God love Julie-Anne's mammy and her holy candles. They are a thing of legend among our group. Known to work wonders in almost every situation. I don't think they've ever been tested this hard before.

I'd invited her in for a cup of tea but she'd given her head a shake. 'You're exhausted. You can barely stand up. Get one of those down you and go to sleep. You're no good to Nell if you can't function yourself. You can't fill from an empty cup. But I am here for whatever you need, whenever you need it.'

I love Julie-Anne. With every part of me. There is nothing she can do. Not really. But I like that she tries and that in the face of feeling useless she is doing what she can – getting the candles lit and doing surreptitious drug drops.

I must call the doctor. Ask for a prescription myself and then I can give Julie-Anne hers back. It's easier to focus on the small tasks, lying here in bed, than to try to work out the big ones. Besides, my head is still foggy. I can feel the horror of my missing child nagging at me, but it's like that horror is behind a veil, somewhere my brain can recognise but not quite feel.

The horror will come. I know that. The realisation is creeping in that not only have I slept well, but no one has come in the night to wake me. No one has come to tell me they've found her. I've not been ushered to a police station, or hospital to hug her and tell her I love her.

I drag a reluctant breath into my lungs, counting in and out. Slowly. Slowly. If no one has woken me to tell me she has been found, it also means no one has woken me to tell me she is dead. She could still be out there.

I lift my phone and blink until my eyes come into focus and I can see the time. It's not long after seven. There are notifications on my phone screen – but none of them with the information I need. None of them are from Nell. I type a quick message into the WhatsApp group I share with my friends. I thank them for their concern but ask that they don't message me. I can't bear jumping with every notification – a mixture of hope and fear with each ping, then followed by the mixture of disappointment and relief. I tell them I'll update them whenever there is news. Then I hit 'send' before copying the text and sending it in every other WhatsApp group on my phone. I log out of Facebook. Out of my work email. Out of everything I don't need so that my phone is free for the call that matters.

Pulling back the duvet, I feel the cold morning wrap itself around me. The heating hasn't come on and the bedroom is like an icebox. I wonder if Nell is cold before shaking my head, as if the physical act will dislodge the painful questions.

In the kitchen, I fight with the thermostat until it whirs and clicks into life. I boil the kettle. Notice the wash I did two days earlier is still mouldering in the machine. I throw another scoop of powder in and set it to wash again. The house is coming alive with white noise.

I switch on the radio, just in time for the half-seven bulletin. They're leading with the body, of course, and even though I know that's exactly how it should be, I bristle. What good will leading with the body do now? It won't bring the poor unfortunate soul back to life. All eyes should be on finding Nell.

Nell, who is four stories down the bulletin in a 'And meanwhile . . .' clip that lasts no longer than ten seconds.

'Police are appealing to the public to help them locate missing nurse Nell Sweeney. The twenty-two-year-old has not been seen since Thursday evening.'

That's it. That's all she gets. I switch the radio off. Today I will go to the hospital myself, if I need to. Speak to some of these new pals of hers. Let them tell me – a terrified but determined mother – that they know nothing. Let them tell me they're sorry but they can't help. See if they have the brass necks to watch my pain up close and not blink. Someone must know something. They simply must. They might know where this 'Rob' has run off to.

I wonder if the police would tell me the name of the taxi driver if I asked them. Or what firm he drives for. I could go and talk to him too, maybe? Have they checked his record? Are they sure he isn't telling them lies? I'm not sure I would have dismissed his involvement as quickly as the police did. I'll ask Heather for his details when she arrives, assuming she will be arriving. Assuming she's not sitting with the family of that poor, murdered woman right now, holding their hands and trying to ease their pain.

Switching off the radio again, I look around for something to do. I need to be busy. I can't sit, zombie-like, with nothing to do but think. I wonder if I should go to work. It might be a great distraction, but I realise it's likely to cause more stress. Co-workers asking how I am. Looking at me with pity in their eyes. Jumping each time the phone rings. Dealing with clients coming in and asking if that 'wee Nell Sweeney' is anyone belonging to me. I shudder at the thought.

Is there a protocol for this, I wonder? What if she never comes back and we never find her? Is there a statute of limitations on how long a parent can grieve a child who may or may not be dead? Will I be expected, at some stage in the future, just to live my life as if nothing has changed?

Right now, I know I need to release some energy, so I decide I'll get dressed, put on my walking boots and go out. Go to the Bay Road nature reserve and walk the loop along the river.

It'll be quiet, if I'm quick. I'll get there before the traffic really starts moving over the Foyle Bridge as the journeys to school and work begin. Being by the river will ground me, I hope. I need something to anchor me because I feel dangerously close to losing it.

I pull a jumper and jeans from the basket of clean laundry on top of the dryer and dress in the utility room, slipping on a pair of Stephen's socks because there are none of mine there and I don't want to wake him. I don't want to talk to him, to explain or field questions. I don't want him to ask me if there is any news and have to shake my head and say 'no'.

Grabbing my phone and my keys, I set off walking at a pace that I'm probably going to regret in five minutes. When my phone starts to ring, I freeze, right there on the pavement, knowing that now the only calls I can expect are important calls. I take a deep breath before I look down at the screen, only to see Julie-Anne's name flash up. I want to scream, except I know Julie-Anne would only call if she really had to. My heart leaps – maybe, just maybe, Nell has showed up at her door and . . .

I try to hit the answer button, my gloves rendering my fingers absolutely bloody useless when it comes to using a touch screen. Swearing, I haul one off and tap the button hoping that the call still connects.

'Is she there?' I blurt down the phone. 'Did she come to your house?'

There's a pause – a pause in which a hundred different scenarios flash through my head and very few of them good. If she was there, there would be no pause. *Yes* would trip off her tongue and I would run – actually run despite my disgustingly awful fitness level – to her house and pull my child into my arms . . .

I'm not sure which is worse, the crashing realisation that no, of course she's not bloody there or the guilt that washes over me for putting Julie-Anne, the softest of soft creatures, in a position where she has to tell me as much.

'I'm sorry,' she says, and I can hear the pain in her voice. 'And I'm sorry for calling, but, look I found something. Well, I didn't find something. Mia did, on Facebook. It's a video, of Nell. She's being chased or something.'

'What?' I stutter. 'What do you mean being chased? What video?'

'I think you need to see this and I think you might need to get the police to look at it too. It's . . . it's not pleasant.'

I can feel adrenaline course through my veins in waves, building with every beat of my heart as it pumps raw fear into my system. I want to ask her what she means, what exactly she has seen and why the fuck it's on Facebook. I can't speak though. I can't actually form any words.

'Marian, I'm sorry,' Julie-Anne says, breaking the silence. 'Mia said there are a few videos like it, of different girls, not Nell, doing the rounds. Some stupid internet challenge or something – scaring people for likes. I went mad at her when she told me it was all harmless. Sure it's not harmless if your daughter is missing?'

'Can you send me the link?' I ask.

'I can get Mia to,' Julie-Anne says. 'Or how about I bring her round? She can show you?'

I hate myself for wanting to scream at the very suggestion. I've no desire to see Mia, my goddaughter, just a few years younger than Nell. The last thing I could cope with right now is her sitting opposite me, in my house, at my table. Where Nell should be. I don't want anything to do with anyone who is not my child. I just need to see this video. I don't want to see it, but I have to. And the police need to.

'No,' I say, biting down my irrational response. 'No. There's no need for that. Just send the link. I'll pass it to the police.'

'Is Stephen there?' Julie-Anne asks. 'Or that policewoman you told me about. Heather, was that her name? Are you in the garden? You sound like you're outside. I don't want you alone when you see this. It's not violent or anything. But it's sinister.'

'Stephen's here,' I lie. 'And yes, I just stepped out to get some fresh air. I'll be fine. Honest. I have support. Just get her to send it now if you could.'

'I will. I absolutely will,' she says and even as I go to end the call I hear her speak to Mia and tell her to do just that.

I am rooted to the spot. A runner passes me, his breath coming out in white clouds into the cold morning air. He huffs and he puffs, his calf muscles tight. I imagine this is part of his routine. His normal day.

The word normal taunts me. I don't know if I will ever feel normal again.

Forcing one foot in front of the other I walk to a nearby bench where I sit down and stare at my phone until it lights up with a notification. Mia has sent the link, added a quick 'I'm sorry' message before it. As if it is her fault.

It's a strange form of torture, watching the screen come to life. This video was made at night; rain is falling. The camera is aimed at a person in the distance although whoever is holding the camera doesn't take too long to catch up with her. Her – my daughter. Just as I know her face, I know her shape. Her walk. The curve of her shoulders in her green coat, a colourful scarf I'd bought for her in Monsoon wrapped around her neck. I notice the dark trousers of her uniform. The black backpack she is carrying. There is a momentary glimpse of her face as she turns her head to see who is behind her and I want to reach out and touch her. I want to feel her skin, the softness of her cheeks, but she quickly turns away again and she speeds up. The traffic noise, the slap of the rain on the pavement, is joined by the heavy breathing of whoever is holding this camera. There is more to it than exertion, I think. There is excitement.

I want to scream at her to shout for help. To take her phone from her pocket, turn and video this person and catch him red-handed. I want to see her turn, her face set in defiance, and threaten to knee him in the balls if he takes one step closer. I want to scream at her to stay safe.

But that moment has already passed. I can see that. This isn't a live feed. There is no way to know when it was recorded, except I know I only bought her that scarf on her birthday in September so it has to be relatively recent. Could it be from last Thursday night? Could this be the last sighting of my beautiful girl?

I sit frozen as he gains more ground on her, watching as her head turns slowly towards the camera, her eyes wide, her skin white. Her beautiful face, scared. 'Leave me alone!' she shouts confidently. I'm proud of her in that briefest of moments. There is some nondescript mumbling from the bastard holding the phone. I want to hurt him. I don't think I've ever wanted to hurt anyone else more.

Then I watch as she speeds up and walks away, glancing back one last time and I just want to scream at her to come back. Warn her. Just tell her I love her.

The coffee I drank earlier rises in my throat and without warning I'm bent double, my stomach emptying, not sure if the tears that are running down my face are coming from the force of the vomiting or my grief for my daughter. Whatever, I allow them to fall before I pull myself back to sitting straight. That same runner passes me again, still focused on his training. If he has noticed my distress, he's absolutely not showing it.

Looking at the screen again I read the comments below the post. Look with horror at the laughing emojis. The congratulations from people. The caps-locked 'LEGENDs'. The assertions that this is 'great craic'. The stern words. 'This isn't funny, lads. How would you like it if it was your girl, or your sister, your ma?'

A short, well-meaning post from Mia. 'This is my mum's best friend's daughter. She's missing, now. The police are looking for her. This isn't funny.'

The little shocked face emoji has been hit 283 times under Mia's post. The sad face, 400 times. Fifty-four people have clicked the laugh emoji. I click on their names and look at the sad excuses of bastards that they are. A sad mix of men in football tops with beer cans in their hands, and heavily filtered and made-up women. Sneering banter dripping from their posts.

'That'll learn her,' one has replied – I want to correct his language. I want to tell him he's a bastard. I want to track him down and ask him just what is so funny about my missing child.

I'll get Heather onto this. These amoebic arseholes who want to laugh and joke about it. How will they feel with police attention right at their door?

I look to see if I can figure out who was first to post the video and find myself chasing down a rabbit hole of links and badly written comments. Until that is, I find a montage of clips. Different girls, different expressions all on a theme of fear. Clip after clip. Some I recognise from Derry. Others in unfamiliar streets. In the top right-hand corner there is that hashtag #IHaveThePower.

What the fuck is wrong with this world?

Chapter Twenty-Three

Him

Three Weeks Earlier

The next message arrives five days later. From a different username. Doire92 has morphed into Doire69 it seems.

He wasn't expecting to hear from him again after his unceremonious blocking of the account but like a bad penny, there he is back in his inbox.

Lad,

Not sure what happened there but I couldn't send you another message. Weird, isn't it?

A glitch in the matrix or something. This message should get through though. Wondered had you thought about my proposal any more? It would be class to buddy up. I've been out myself. I did it. Do you want to see the video? It's a cracker! Such a buzz. I can see why you do it. Gets the blood pumping, doesn't it? You shoulda seen the face on the girl last night, I got so close without her hearing. She was wearing them earbud things — absolutely perfect.

I was able to tug on her ponytail. She nearly shit herself, turned around and had her hand raised as if she was going to lamp me one. This wee tiny thing. Like she'd have had a chance, LOLZ. I faked innocence and when she walked away it was like she hadn't a notion what had just happened.

The link is at the bottom of this message. I'm putting it up on the forum soon.

Watch it and hit me up if you want to get in on the action. Seriously, mate, we could send this shit viral. People will be talking about this for years. #IHaveThePower

With a sense of foreboding he clicks the link Doire has posted. He feels a little shaky. Uncomfortable. Before now, it had been a good day. He had sat with Natalia in the staff kitchen at tea break and they had chatted. He hadn't felt self-conscious or freaked out. The conversation had been relatively easy. They chatted about work stuff. And then they'd chatted a bit more about TV. Their latest binge-watches on Netflix. She likes true crime too, and the American version of *The Office*. He'd recommended an old series to her – one she hadn't watched and she'd told him she was going to give it a go. There had been just something in her expression that made him think she wouldn't mind, not one bit, if he watched it with her.

She's beautiful, Natalia. And feminine too. But not slutty. She doesn't flirt with everyone. She doesn't dress like she's going out clubbing instead of to work. She's demure. That's the word. Demure. And respectful. She makes him think there is a chance that finding love isn't as impossible a task as he might have thought. Not all women are playing a game. Natalia would not play games.

He hasn't gone out hunting in days. He doesn't feel the same need to chase that particular high. He still looks at the forums and reads the messages. He still revels a bit in the praise, but just maybe not quite as much as before. More people are doing it. More people, like Doire69 are pushing it further. Pushing it too far, he thinks. Into the realms of those sick fantasies he once had. Natalia would hate him if she could see inside his mind. He never wants her to know that part of him exists.

He has a feeling something special is happening with her and he doesn't want to risk it. He has been given a second chance. He knows he is lucky. Most people who have watched his videos don't have a clue who he is or where he is, and until now he has felt in control of how things are going. He has always been clear in his own mind on where the ultimate line would be drawn. He expected he would be able to decide when to take a break from it all – when to end it.

But it's bigger than him now and he can feel that control slip away, and if he can't control it, he can't contain it.

He gets up and pours himself a drink before sitting back down and pressing the play button.

A dark street. It looks like Magazine Street – which runs parallel to the historic City Walls, within the city centre boundary. Even in the dim lamplight he recognises the cobbled streets, the slope downwards towards the Tower Museum.

The figure, small, slim, shoulders hunched over in a grey woollen coat is maybe twenty feet ahead of the camera. She's wearing a cream beret, a scarf, a short skirt and thick black tights. The camera gets closer and closer to her but she doesn't speed up, or change direction. This isn't how the game is played. The game is to get into their heads – to induce fear of attack. Not to actually attack them. It feels wrong.

On the screen he sees a hand reaching out towards a glossy dark ponytail and he feels his stomach tighten knowing that this poor girl has no idea what is coming. This isn't the game of cat and mouse he started. It could never be described as 'innocent fun'. He doesn't feel anticipation, he feels dread, as a gloved hand wraps its way around the hair. What Doire described

145

as 'tugging' is much more. He hauls the girl backwards and she stumbles, falling to the ground and landing with a sickening thud. And still he has her hair in his hand – pulled taut. He is pulling it, winding the hair around his hand, forcing her neck to bend backwards so he is towering over her – looking directly down at her. He can see, even in the dark of the video, her eyes are wide with terror, her hands scrabbling for purchase on the slippy cobbles to a soundtrack of heavy breathing, and her crying and pleading.

Then it's over as soon as it started – mercifully. Her head is released, pushed forward with such force that there is a sharp smack as the bone of her skull collides with her knees, which she has pulled up to try and find her footing. The camera swerves around, Doire walking away, then running up the street and his heavy breathing turns to laughter. Laughter that is so cold, so manic that he can feel his blood run cold.

This man is dangerous. Dangerous in a way that he could never be himself. And now this feels really messy. He knows he has fucked up and he has absolutely no idea how he is going to extricate himself from it all – or more importantly how to make sure Doire doesn't do any more harm.

He downs his drink, JD and Coke, and hopes he'll feel the alcohol hit him quickly. When he closes his eyes the image of that girl, her face a mask of terror, is there. It hits him, hard, that he never acknowledged how wrong it was when he did it. Not that he ever went that far. Not that he ever physically hurt someone. It was always, always, only about the game. He's not as bad as Doire. He's not in the same league as him. Doire isn't making a stand for men; he's a predator. But seeing that video – he knows how what he did *was* wrong.

Just then his inbox pings with a new message. Doire is back.

Well, did you like it? Brilliant wasn't it? I could've had more fun with her if no one else was around but I heard voices, probably up on the Walls, and I'm not taking any chances. I've been banged up before. I'm not going back inside. We really should meet up – I can tell you about my idea for a whole new game. Tell me this – have you ever thought about keeping one of them girls? Can ye imagine?

Naw, I'm joking, like.

But we should talk.

With a deep, sinking feeling, he downloads the video. He might need it. He knows he should take it to the police, but that would mean admitting his own offences. There'd be no coming back from that. None.

He wishes, with all his might, that he'd never started any of this. 'I have the power'? As far as he can see he has no power any more. Doire with his 'joke' that probably isn't a joke has stolen all the power from him in that one small message.

Chapter Twenty-Four

Marian

Wednesday, November 3

Missing six days

'You have to look into this. And now. You have to call DS King or that Bradley person and tell them to find out who posted this,' I tell Heather, who is scanning the video clip on my phone.

'I will, of course. I'll call them now.' She can't hide the shock from her face as she clicks from the clip of Nell to the montage.

'I wonder . . .' she begins, but stops herself. 'I'll call them. Okay.'

'You wonder what?' I ask.

'Oh, nothing. Look, I'll make this call outside.' With that she hands back my phone and reaches for her own. She doesn't make eye contact. I'd go so far as to say she is actively avoiding eye contact at this stage.

'I spoke to my goddaughter after I watched it,' I tell her as she retreats from the room. 'She says these videos – this hashtag

– has been appearing over the last week or so. On TikTok and Facebook, but she hadn't really paid attention to it until she saw that one looked as if it was filmed in Derry.'

'We can tell all this to DS King and DI Bradley,' she says. 'They may well want to speak to your goddaughter themselves.'

'This one was only posted last night though – look. And on the same day we released Nell's name to the press. It can't be a coincidence. It really can't. You need to find who posted it. What if this was made by the man who has her? What if this can lead us directly to her? Maybe it's this Rob character behind the camera? There'd be a way to find out, wouldn't there? Search his phone?'

I am ranting now. Sure as sure can be that if they find whoever posted this – whoever is behind that camera – they will also find Nell. They'll find her before she ends up like the poor, unidentified creature lying in the morgue.

Heather crosses the room back to where I'm standing. 'Please, Marian, try and stay calm. Yes, this is a big lead and my colleagues will look into it. Have enough faith in us to allow us to do our job, which includes letting me phone DS King.' She nods, offers a small, sympathetic smile. I wonder if that is part of her training – appropriate facial expressions. But I know, all the same, that while she is smiling, I'm annoying her now. My ranting. My demands. Well, I don't give a ha'penny damn if I'm annoying her. I'm fighting for my child.

'We'll do everything we can to trace the video and who's been sharing it but I want you to be realistic too. There have been more than 5000 shares of this in the last twelve hours alone,' Heather says, biting her lip. 'It might be like searching for a needle in a haystack, and that number is rising all the time . . . Exponentially, tens of thousands of people will have seen it by now. And that's if it's only sharing on Facebook.'

She points to the screen as I watch the number of shares

update in real time, the number of views now soaring to 32,000 escalates in seconds to 33,000.

'And what? You only need to find the first person to share it. You just need to go down that road. Christ, I'm no detective but that seems obvious. And then how about those people laughing at it – posting those despicable comments?' I poke at my phone trying to bring them up but my hands are shaking and I feel a sheen of sweat break out on the back of my neck. On the third attempt I find the comment I was looking for. Mr 'That'll learn her'. 'See! That says he lives in Derry. He works in that garage in the Waterside. He can't be that hard to find.'

'We don't normally police people's ill-thought-out Facebook posts,' she says.

'Not even when they feature a missing person who could be in danger? You haven't ruled out that poor creature who was found yesterday being connected to this in some way. You might have a serial killer on your hands. You haven't even found this Rob character yet – he's not around. He might be with her right now. This could lead us to them both right now! Or God, what if we're running out of time? He could be hurting her!' There is more than a hint of hysteria in my voice now and I don't care. I'm not even going to try to hide it.

As calmly as she can, but very, very firmly, Heather tells me she is going to phone the detectives leading the case. She tells me that she needs to do that now. She reminds me that she is on my side. On Nell's side.

'Thank you,' I say, the wind gone from my sails. 'I appreciate that.' She nods and leaves the room, out through the utility room into the back garden, just as Stephen pads into the kitchen in his stocking feet looking half-asleep.

'I heard raised voices,' he says, hesitantly. 'Is everything okay?'

I can't even speak. I just burst into tears. I hate that I will have to tell him about this video. I will have to show it to him. I will have to put the weight of this horror and pain on his shoulders too.

'Marian! You're scaring me, what is it?' He reaches for me, taking me by the arms and trying to make eye contact with me but I do not want to see the look in his eyes when I tell him someone was chasing our daughter. That our daughter, scared and vulnerable, is being watched by countless people online. That people are laughing at her fear.

'There's a video,' I splutter, the words feeling as if they don't belong in my mouth. I bring my gaze to his, see the fear I'm feeling reflected in his expression. 'Julie-Anne called and Mia had seen it on Facebook.'

'Mia? What? What kind of video?'

'Some online trend thing but it's awful, Stephen. Someone is chasing her until she's terrified.'

'The person who took her?'

'I . . . I don't know. It could be. Heather's calling DS King now to let her know. It's some new thing – men are doing it all over. Scaring women and posting their reactions.'

Stephen loosens his grip on my arms. 'So this might not be a lead at all?' he says and I don't know whether that makes him angry or relieved.

'It would be a bit of a coincidence to have it posted online just when she goes missing, just when we reveal her name to the press? Don't you think?'

He turns and stomps away from me, turning back, dragging his hand through his hair. 'So the police can track it? Who posted it?'

'I don't know . . . you know I'm not technologically minded.'

'Jesus, Marian. You just follow the link. Show me!' I lift my phone and hand it to him and he taps at the screen like a pro.

151

I didn't realise my husband was so proficient in social media use. He furrows his brow and looks at the screen again.

'The person who posted this originally,' he says, looking up at me, 'is a troll account.' He waves the lit screen in front of my face but doesn't give me time to focus on the words and images in front of me. No personal pictures. New account. No friends. No privacy settings to see – just no information at all. He scrolls up and down the screen until he clicks on the video, which he has avoided watching until now. I see his expression change as he watches the screen. His eyes darken, and his face contorts. He reaches to the screen as if touching the pixelated image of our child could somehow feel like actually touching her face.

I listen to the soundtrack, the steps, the breathing, the rain hitting the ground. The gasp as Nell turns to look at the camera. I don't need to see it to know what is happening – it is now completely ingrained in my consciousness. It won't ever leave.

Stephen takes a few steps to the table and sits down on one of the kitchen chairs. His head in his hands, he says nothing. He barely makes a sound and I am frozen, unsure of whether or not I should comfort him or steer clear.

'Who would do this?' he says, eventually. Looking up at me.

I shrug, brush away a tear that is running down my cheek just in time for another one to fall. 'Will they be able to find who posted this?' I ask him. 'Even if it's a . . . what did you call it . . . a troll account?'

It's a defeated voice that answers me. 'I don't know. Depends on a few things. They can trace the IP address, I suppose. But there are ways around that. VPNs and the like.'

'What's a VPN?' I ask, thinking Stephen might as well be talking a foreign language.

'A virtual private network,' he says, but that clarifies nothing to me. It's just word soup. Seeing the confusion on my face

Stephen simply says, 'There are ways to hide yourself online. Or at least to make it more difficult for you to be tracked down. You have to be a bit computer-savvy to do it well, but it's certainly not impossible. The internet is a dark place.'

He drops his head in his hands again, scratches at his stubble. His skin less supple now, wrinkling and sliding under his touch. When he looks up I see he has aged ten years in the past couple of days. I don't push him further on how he knows all these little internet secrets. He works in tech – in sales. Maybe the ability to hide your tracks is a selling point these days. God knows, Stephen is adept at it with or without the use of a computer.

Silently I make him a cup of coffee, mostly because I need to be doing something. I need to be moving my body even if it's just to lift a kettle because I know if I stand still I will crumble to the ground and I might not be able to get back up.

'Do you really think this might be the person who has her?' he asks. 'If he's some sicko who posts videos of it?'

I sit his coffee cup down in front of him but I don't speak. I can't. My brain is playing out a myriad of horrific scenarios, which all start the moment that short video ends. We are in our silent horror, a metre apart, unable to look at each other or God forbid, comfort each other, when Heather comes back into the room. Like startled meerkats, we look at her in unison – our wide eyes begging for some new information.

'Did you talk to DS King?' Stephen asks. 'What did she say?'

'I didn't speak directly to her,' she says. 'But I believe she's at the hospital taking witness statements from the rest of Nell's new friends. I do have some news though. This Rob character made a statement this morning at Strand Road Police Station. He's been in Belfast visiting his parents the last few days – something his parents, and staff at a restaurant they visited, have verified. So he's now in the clear.'

I feel a strange disappointment wash over me. We're further from finding her than we ever were. Even knowing he had been out with one of the other nurses at the weekend hadn't stopped me doing all sorts of mental arithmetic to try to convince myself they might be together. He might be 'normal'. She might be safe, despite the growing collection of evidence to the contrary.

'Well, I think DS King should be focusing her attention on this video that's doing the rounds instead of talking to some eejits up at the hospital,' Stephen says, sitting back in his chair. His tone is sharp and I resist the urge to tell him again that Heather is not our enemy – even though only a few moments ago I was giving her a hard time myself.

'I'm pretty sure it'll top her list when she sees it,' Heather says. 'She's having a very busy morning but I'm told she'll be shown it as soon as possible.'

There is a strange something in how Heather is talking, as if there is something happening we're not aware of. Maybe it's that her words sound too scripted or her tone is off. But I sense it all the same.

'There's something you're not telling us,' I say and it's a statement not a question. She looks at me, her face expression-less as if she doesn't quite know how to react. 'Has something happened? Have they found something out?' I don't dare allow my brain to fall down the rabbit hole of wondering if they have found our daughter. Maybe they already know that she isn't safe. Maybe DS King isn't even at the hospital. Maybe she is with Nell right now. Or what is left of Nell.

'I'm not in a position to say,' Heather says.

'But that's your job,' Stephen snaps. 'You're our family liaison officer. It is your job to fill us in on any developments.'

'Mr Sweeney,' she says and I notice that while she has switched to using my first name, she still gives my husband his title. 'As

154

we have explained to you before not all information will be passed on to you immediately for procedural reasons. We have to verify everything. There are other people involved. I know it must be very frustrating, but we do have good reasons.' Her voice is gentle, soothing even, but I don't feel soothed.

'So there is something then,' I say. 'If there wasn't, you would just say "no". You wouldn't have to be in any position to say no.'

Heather blinks at me. I can see the cogs whirring in her head as she tries to think of the best answer. 'DS King will be here as soon as she can. I know this is frustrating, but she has the information necessary to update you. The worst thing I could do at this time would be to give you false information.'

'Just tell me – have they found her?' Stephen asks, his voice barely a whisper. 'Is this development that they've found her?'

Heather shakes her head. 'I'm sorry, but no. Nell is still missing.'

Relief washes over me for the briefest of seconds. If she is still missing it means there have been no more bodies.

Glancing at Stephen, I see that he is wound tight. The muscles in his jaw are taut and I know he is doing everything in his power not to lose control of his emotions. I've seen that expression a million times before and I know exactly what happens when he loses that particular battle.

'Okay,' I say, trying to exude a calmness into the room. 'That has to be a good thing, doesn't it? No news is good news, isn't it?'

Heather doesn't react. She doesn't agree with me that the absence of a body is a positive to cling on to. She has no comforting statistics to mollify me with. We all know that this is serious. We all know that someone being missing for six days, with no activity on their bank cards, phone or social media

155

doesn't usually end well. But none of us are ready to say that out loud yet, so we stay quiet. We don't risk speaking. Heather walks to the window and looks out, swearing under her breath.

'I can't believe this,' she mutters, before turning to look at us both. I hear a car door close outside.

'Who is it?' I ask, trying to look over her shoulder to see out the window. Surely DS King can't be here already? And if it were King I very much doubt that Heather would be swearing. She'd probably be delighted to hand us over into someone else's care for a bit.

I spot a woman, slim, blonde, mid-thirties maybe, walking up our driveway. There's something vaguely familiar about her but I can't quite place her.

'Ingrid Devlin.' Heather says her name as if the words conjure a foul taste in her mouth. 'The journalist.'

It clicks with me where I've seen her before. I've seen her on *The Late Late Show* talking to Ryan Tubridy about her latest book. She came across as a smooth operator. I thought that's what she was concentrating on now – her books. I'm about to ask Heather why Ingrid would be arriving at our house when she tells me to stay where I am and that she will handle it. With that she's gone, closing the door behind her.

It isn't long before there are raised voices – very professional-sounding raised voices, but raised all the same.

'Look,' Ingrid says, 'I think this is really important and I think that the Sweeneys have a right to know. I'm happy to go ahead and publish without a comment from them, but I'm the person who got this information. The source came to me.'

'With respect, Ingrid, this is a very stressful time for the family. We're waiting for DS King to arrive to update them and I think it's appropriate that it's she, not a journalist, who imparts that information. I'm sure if you speak to our press office there will . . .'

There is a laugh, a dismissive tinkle. 'C'mon, Heather, you know full well the press office are of no use to me. The Sweeneys are going to want to get as many people as possible looking out for Nell, especially now.'

'This has to be dealt with through the proper channels,' Heather says.

'It seems to me the proper channels aren't getting very far. If the girl's been missing since Thursday . . .'

'Ms Devlin, I'm not going to debate this with you. The Sweeney family are not speaking to the press,' Heather says and I sense some movement behind me as Stephen brushes past, pulling open the door.

'I think that should be down to the Sweeneys, shouldn't it?' he says. 'Do you know something, Ms Devlin? Can you tell us anything?'

Clearly that is enough for Ingrid to feel she can walk into our house and she does so without so much as looking at Heather.

'Mr Sweeney, I'm very sorry to be troubling you both at this time. It must be incredibly stressful for you. Contrary to what the PSNI might want you to believe, the media actually want to help you get to Nell.'

'You said you had new information,' Stephen says. 'What do you know?'

'It's probably better if I come in and we talk about it,' Ingrid says, taking a step forward, but Heather steps forward too, making sure Ingrid cannot cross over our threshold.

'Ms Devlin, please,' Heather says and there is a genuine pleading to her voice.

'Have you seen the videos doing the rounds on social media?' Ingrid asks. 'Nell is in one. Have you seen it?'

'If this is all you've come here to tell us then you're wasting your time. Yes, we've seen the video of Nell. We saw it this morning.' I sag. This isn't exactly anything new.

'Are you familiar with the name Elzbieta Kowalski?' Ingrid asks.

'Ms Devlin, you really should leave this to the PSNI. This is a sensitive stage of the investigation.' There is more than a hint of panic to her voice.

'No,' I say, glancing to Stephen who shakes his head. 'Who is she?'

'I've a source who informs me that the remains discovered yesterday are thought to be those of Elzbieta Kowalski.'

'Ms Devlin!' Heather's voice is loud now; she is determined to be heard. 'DS King will be here presently and I really think this will be more appropriate coming from the senior investigating officer.'

'We've never heard of a . . . what did you say . . . Elizabeth Kowalski?'

'Elzbieta, but I believe some friends called her Eliza,' Ingrid says as she teeters on her tiptoes to see over Heather's shoulder. She is about to say something else when the sound of a car pulling into the street distracts us – and I immediately recognise it as the car DS King travels in, with DC Black. They both get out, followed by a uniformed officer from the back seat.

'Ingrid Devlin,' DS King says. 'I should've known you wouldn't be long getting here. There's nothing gets past you, is there?'

'Not much,' Ingrid says. 'I wish I could say the same for the PSNI.' She smiles as she says it. There is clearly a long-established to and fro between the pair but I want to tell them both to shut up and leave their sniping for somewhere else. This is not the time or the place. I need to know who Elzbieta Kowalski is and what else Ingrid Devlin knows. Or DS King knows. To be honest, I don't give a damn who tells me as long as someone does, and soon.

'Indeed,' DS King replies, her face expressionless. 'Mr and

Mrs Sweeney, if we can just all come inside, away from our local roving reporter here, we do have some news for you.'

I look from her to Ingrid, whose eyes are directly on Stephen. I step back without really thinking and allow the police to come into my house but I don't immediately turn and follow them. I watch as Ingrid blinks and breaks her gaze with my husband, and I watch on until I feel a hand touch mine. Heather is pulling me gently towards the living room.

'Elzbieta Kowalski worked in the hospital. In the same ward as Nell,' Ingrid calls as DC Black closes the door on her. 'I'll be right here if you want to talk.'

Chapter Twenty-Five

Him

One Week Earlier

He is relieved, at first, when Doire goes quiet. He thinks perhaps his nemesis has become distracted with something in real life. Something that takes him away from his growing obsession with incel forums. It's entirely possible, after all. Hasn't he experienced it himself, with Natalia?

She hasn't made everything in the world better, but she has made him feel better about his place in it. Feel as if he matters. As if he is important. Most of all, she makes him feel as though he is visible. He's noticed how she smiles when he looks at her. He's even noticed that, one time, she waited for him in the staff kitchen just to say hello before rinsing her mug out and putting it on the drainer. She'd handed him a mug of freshly made tea, just how he liked it, having already sussed that just a splash of milk and two sugars were just to his taste. It's the little things that matter.

Maybe, just maybe, Doire has found someone like Natalia. He scans the forum every night looking for more videos – checking to see if Doire has uploaded anything and hoping he hasn't. He breathes a sigh of relief each time he sees there is nothing new online.

There is silence for five days, but then a message arrives in his inbox – the subject field reads: 'Ready to play the game?'

He knows without opening it that this will not be good. There is something dark in this, he can feel it, and it is about to be unleashed into this forum of angry men. More than that, it is about to be unleashed on the unsuspecting women of the world. But first, given Doire's location, he knows it will be released on Derry women first. Women like Natalia – who aren't cold and hateful. Who don't think they are God's gift to the universe, like Jade does. Women who are caring and considerate.

He doesn't want anything to do with it, he realises. He wonders if he should just block Doire again – just shut down his account – then maybe he can pretend this whole sorry episode in his life has never happened. That this has all been a blip. A breakdown of sorts, maybe. Behaviour that can only be described as 'out of character'.

But he knows he can't do that. He might have done some stupid things but he is not stupid. He knows it's better to know your enemy – and there is no doubt in his mind now that Doire is his enemy. They are not the same. They could never be the same. Doire's soul is darker.

He clicks on the message, sees that it is long and no doubt rambling. With a heavy heart, he starts to read.

You'll be ragin' at yourself for not getting in at the start here, lad. This is going to be epic. I mean people will talk about this. Probably write about it. Make a TV show or a movie about it. This is my fifteen minutes of fame but it's going to be longer than fifteen minutes. I've the stamina to keep it going.

Not like you. Running away and hiding when shit gets real.

Did you really want to make a change or are you just full of shit? Ha ha! Don't answer that. We both know the answer.

Maybe you think you're better than me? Is that it? Are you the kind of person to look down your nose at others? Think you're fucking special because you have people sharing your wee hashtag? Or maybe, just maybe, you're jealous because you know I've a bigger set of balls than you are ever likely to possess. I can take this where it needs to go.

I'll take it to a place where people will pay attention. Properly pay attention. Realise that we're not messing. That this isn't a joke. Men have been fucked around with for too long and castrated by feminists who think they have a right to make all the decisions while we should just feel guilty for being born with dicks.

See all them people who laugh at us and judge us, they're going to learn and soon. They're going to learn it's not our fault. They're going to learn that they need to take the blame too. Consequences have actions, my friend, and you reap what you sow.

You could've been a part of it. You could have gone down in history. Maybe you'll want to play the game too – when you see where it goes. When you see what I do. But it'll be too late then. You'll be too late. You missed the boat, fellah!

Or maybe, thinking about it, I'll take pity on you. After all I owe you. In a way, you started it. You built the fire and left the rest of us to light it. But if you ask nicely. Or you beg. Yes, that's it – I'd like to see you beg to be a part of this revolution. See who has the power now, eh?

It won't be you, when you're on your knees begging for a second chance. Ha! I'm only joking – but maybe I'm not. Maybe I've given you a wee clue there. You'll know when it's me. Everyone will know when it's me.

Do you remember those choose your own adventure books? Where every decision took you to a different ending? I loved them when I was a kid. Always went back and changed the ending if I didn't like how things were going. Well that's all I'm doing now. Changing the ending. And the girls – they'll be choosing how things end too. They just won't know it.

They won't even know they are part of a game. That's the best bit, don't you see? They think they've been winning all these years but they have just been playing directly into my hands. Into our hands.

He reads the message over and over again, thinking about this man and who he might be. Wondering if he is serious, or if, as Derry people would say he was 'all mouth and no trousers'. There are plenty like that – people who talk like big men but do nothing of merit to anyone.

He knows he is kidding himself with the thoughts this man will do nothing, though. He knows Doire has already acted on his impulses, imagined he has been given a green light to do whatever he wants. He'd already sent that video and posted it on the forum, of the poor girl he hauled to the ground by her hair.

No longer able to stomach the beer he had been drinking he sits the bottle on the floor and scans the forums. Searches for clues as to what Doire's next move will be. If only there was a way he could track him down without drawing any attention towards himself. He can't think of one, not now anyway while his mind is racing.

He clicks through Doire's posts to see what he is posting publicly now. There may well be clues there. He may well be able to stop the next phase of this game – whatever it is. What he sees, added to the message he has just read, convinces him that Doire is a sociopath. Then again, he thinks, desperately wanting to convince himself there is nothing to be worried about, most of the men posting in this dark corner of the internet seems to have some kind of sociopathic tendencies. It doesn't mean they act on them – they just vent their frustration. Isn't that what he, himself, did? He didn't actually hurt anyone. He didn't actually break any laws.

His stomach tightens as he reads through the threads on the forum again. It's as if he's seeing them from a new perspective, from a place where his anger has dissipated. These threads, he realises, go beyond frustration. They are filled with hate. There's no other word for it. Brutal, honest, raw hate. And there, amid the rabble – describing some of the darkest of his fantasies and being praised for his creativity – is Doire. He's there, teasing forum users that something big is coming.

Feeling trapped in a prison of his own making, he isn't sure what to do. He decides not to reply straight away. He must think very carefully about what to say. The last thing he can risk is making things worse.

But he can no longer be naïve about it all. He has to prepare in case the very worst does happen and Doire makes good on his promises.

Making a dedicated folder on his computer, he copies and pastes the most horrible of the posts to a Word document. He takes screenshots. He made notes of the IP addresses attached to Doire's posts – not that it is ever the same address twice. He tries to find clues in what Doire has said, the videos he has posted. He hopes he can pick out details that might just identify him.

He rereads all the old posts not only from Doire but from himself as well, and feels the beer in his stomach start to curdle. He can see clearly how close he had himself come to madness. The urge to delete all the files, folders and links from his devices is strong. He's even tempted to destroy his hard drive and spring for a new laptop. It's not possible, he knows, to wipe all his internet activity but he can make himself harder to trace. He thinks of the videos, those where his voice is heard. Would it be possible for him to be recognised by that alone? And what if the videos were tied up with CCTV images? Could he be found? Angry with himself he realises he has been so very stupid. So foolish. He has risked everything.

Now, he knows he has to fix it all because if he doesn't he risks losing everything: Natalia and all he hoped for from their time together, his job, his career. It would all be utterly unsalvageable if this got out and he's not sure how to tackle it without landing himself squarely in the frame too.

Maybe, he thinks, he can urge a bit of caution. There was respect there at one stage. This Doire character claimed to think he was a legend so surely he should be able to appeal to that side of him – the side that admired him.

Realising he doesn't have much to lose, he starts to type his reply:

I've been watching your work. Great job. You're really teaching those girls some lessons they won't forget in a hurry. Maybe they'll think twice before they start their slutty carry-on, thinking they're better than us. Nothing wrong with knocking them down a peg or two. Or three.

But look, if you want my advice – and I'm only saying this to try and help you – be careful. I know you want your fifteen minutes of fame but if you take your time, take a more measured approach, you can make a real difference. Don't be a flash in the pan – make sure we're taking you seriously and not just as some psycho on the internet.

Play the long game. The slow burn. This requires patience. Planning. The last thing you want is to get into trouble – to have this ended before it's even begun.

I'm talking as a friend.

He hits send and sits back. He doesn't know if it will work but all he needs to do is get Doire to slow down just long enough for him to find a way out of it. Maybe Doire will come to his senses, he thinks. Everyone has moments of madness. Everyone has a breaking point. But people can come back from the brink. If he can figure out how to either give Doire a scare, or a wake-up call – or if he can appeal to his better side (assuming he has one) – it could make all the difference.

It scares him how close he had come to the point of no return. Sometimes, when he wakes in the middle of the night, images of women, in the dark and rain, their faces white with fear, the tremble in their voices, he wonders if he did in fact already cross that point. Then he remembers Natalia, and her sweet smile and how they flirt together. How she listens to him. She's pure. So pure and decent. She could be the person to save him. She makes him want to be a better person.

He has hauled himself back from the abyss and he has to believe that Doire can too.

Restless, he tries to watch TV. Tries to read. Tries to lose himself in work or in more research around those stupid forums and how they're allowed to operate in the first place – although it's accepted not all corners of the world wide web are concerned with following rules.

He can't sleep. His beer tastes sickly in his mouth and his appetite is all but gone. When Natalia texts him to ask him the name of the boxset he recommended to her, he replies as succinctly as possible. She might save him, but what if he is so broken inside that he destroys her in the process. In another world, a world where she hadn't smiled at him as he walked into the office, Doire could be him.

He startles when a new message pings onto his computer screen. Doire has replied Hoping that his strategy has worked, he opens the message – almost immediately wishing he hadn't.

You don't get to tell me what to do. You don't control me. You can't stand this because it's now bigger than your stupid little videos. People like ME now. People are listening to ME and you are old news. I don't need any 'slow burn'. I want to light this place up. Go big or go home, isn't that what they say? Well how about I go big, and you go home?

He's not entirely surprised when Doire blocks him almost as soon as he has read the message. He'd love to walk away from this forum now, but he knows he can't. Something big is going to happen. Doire is power-hungry.

He sets up a new account, one that will be able to see what Doire posts and it isn't long before it appears. A manifesto of sorts. A call to arms. A 'watch this space'.

With his head in his hands he wonders just what the hell he has started. It was never meant to go this far.

I've had enough of women telling us we're not good enough. We're not important. We're not relevant. I've had enough of women tarring us all with the same brush. Enough of #MeToo and women rolling their eyes when we point out it's not all men. We're not all creeps. We're not all oppressors. This is the world we were brought into. It's not our fault. Stop blaming men for every little thing in your life that is shit. Stop making us the butt of your jokes. Stop writing us off before you've even got to know us. Stop with the double standards. All the fucking double standards. They want equality but when push comes to shove, they still want to be treated like pampered princesses.

Women have to realise they are responsible for their own actions. They are responsible for their own flaws. For their own fuck-ups. And we have to show them that. We have to make them see before all that is left of us is a bunch of pussy-whipped eunuchs.

I'm going to show them how their actions have consequences.

167

I'm going to show them they've pushed us too far. It's up to them if they walk away or not. They have the power. We just have more of it. As it was meant to be.

Those viral videos? They were a good starting place but they are little more than child's play. It's time for the big boys to get their turn. This is a whole new game – and we're setting the rules.

Are you with me?

The affirmative replies flood in thick and fast. There is no stopping this now.

Chapter Twenty-Six

Marian

Wednesday, November 3

Missing six days

The police are increasing their efforts at the hospital. Running checks on staff members. Those Nell had become friendly with, those she worked with or may have come into contact with. Seeing if anything pings on the system. They are looking for any hint of violent behaviour – although they've told us, once again, not to get our hopes up. All hospital staff will have had Access NI checks before their appointment, any criminal records will have been flagged up already. And with so many agency staff, and visitors, there's nothing to say they are looking for a staff member. Thousands of people come through those doors every day. Any one of them could be the person we're looking for.

It's about all they've got to go on for now though, so I have to pin my hopes on them finding something – and fast. It's too much of a coincidence that Elzbieta also worked at the hospital, and that means the likelihood that whatever monster defiled that poor girl also has Nell. My stomach tightens.

I want to go and look for her. Physically go and look for her. Knock on doors and check outhouses, and poke overgrown areas with a big stick and scream her name on every street corner until I hear her reply, 'I'm coming, Mum!'

I want her to walk through my front door, face pink with embarrassment. I want her to tell me that she didn't want to worry anyone. She just wanted to get away for a bit and there was a last-minute holiday and she had forgotten her phone and wallet and sure it was okay because her new friend had paid for everything . . .

I want to scold her. Really scold her. Tell her she's selfish and immature and that she had us worried half to death and the police have been looking for her. I want to shout and scream and rant and then pull her close to me, into my arms and sob that I'd thought I'd lost her and it was the most unbearable pain of my entire life.

I want to get the chance to be a helicopter parent. To drop my laissez-faire attitude to parenting an adult and hover over every aspect of her life. I want to see the strain gone from Stephen's face. I want us all to sit down as a family and talk about what really matters. The cracks in our foundations. The mistakes we have made. The blame we all carry a little of. I want the three of us to move on. I want to forgive Stephen, but to let him go and live the life he deserves.

I want to free him of any duty to be there for me as our older years approach – a duty multiplied by the tragedy of our lost daughter. How can we pull apart now, in this time of absolute horror? What if it makes him angrier and he turns that anger on me, as he has done in the past? 'You're such an easy target, Marian,' he'd said at his cruellest. 'You don't even have the respect to fight for yourself.' It had cut deep because it was true. Or he had made me believe it was true – gaslighted me into believing all I deserved was to be eternally punished for not being his idea of perfect.

He doesn't love me – and I don't love him. Not any more. Not enough anyway. Not in the right way. But just as I haven't had the courage to fight for myself, he hasn't had the courage to walk away. If all that fight and courage has to be directed at simply existing in a world without our daughter, how can we ever make the break from each other that we need to?

I want to tell him it's over. That we both deserve more. The hurt that was there has faded – drowned out by the knowledge that what we are facing now is worse than anything we could have done to each other. Drowned out by the fear that somehow, this was our fault for not acknowledging the chasm that opened up in our marriage a long time ago.

What would it have been like if we hadn't lived in this powder keg of hurt and recrimination? Maybe she wouldn't have moved out so early. She'd still be under our roof and I could have kept her safe. Maybe we wouldn't be in this position now. Sitting in this awful space – a conference room in a city centre hotel. Uniform in its blandness. Looking at the surreal site of a long trestle table, four seats behind it. Pop-up banners emblazoned with the logos and contact details of the Police Service of Northern Ireland provide the sombre backdrop.

There is a picture of our daughter, blown up, on another pop-up stand. A phone number beneath her name for people to call with information. I stare at it. I try to take in every detail of her face – the crinkle around her eyes. The smattering of freckles across her nose. The tiny scar on her left cheek – a reminder of a childhood bout of chicken pox. I look at her eyes, blue. But flecked with grey, with traces of green. I can see them so clearly now that she is magnified in front of my face. I stare at the slight turn of one of her front teeth – not enough to warrant braces but enough to mark her out as herself. I push down thoughts of Elzbieta Kowalski and how her identity was confirmed through dental records.

Looking at Nell, frozen in a moment of time, I think of all the versions of this beautiful person I have known. A tiny baby. An inquisitive and dramatic toddler. A shy schoolgirl. My girl. A young woman getting giddy over a glass of wine with Clodagh when they found out they had got into their nursing course. A young woman telling me it was okay to leave him. A young woman who had so much to offer the world. I wonder what Stephen sees when he looks at her.

DS King had been very gentle with us, after Ingrid Devlin had been unceremoniously exited from our house. She'd told us Elzbieta was a foreign national – a student from Poland – who was a member of the cleaning staff at Altnagelvin Hospital. Elzbieta was twenty-four, and she was beautiful. Flawless. Conscientious.

No one had reported her missing because she didn't socialise much and she had been on a week's leave from work. When she didn't show up for her shift on Monday, her supervisor had tried to contact her by phone and left a message. They'd assumed that Elzbieta may have decided she'd had enough of mopping hospital floors, or that she had gone back to Poland. She had been quite homesick, DS King told us and that made my heart ache. She'd never see her home again.

When the police had launched a detailed appeal to help identify the woman whose body had been found yesterday, one of her co-workers had approached a police officer who was part of the team speaking to hospital staff about Nell and mentioned she too hadn't shown up for work.

That one of the wards she cleaned was also the surgical ward on which Nell worked seemed to be too much of a coincidence, DS King told them, so they went to Elzbieta's house-share and discovered she hadn't been seen in days by anyone there either.

Having quickly learned from a housemate that Elzbieta had a filling done just a month ago, police had been able to confirm her identity using dental records. I try not to think about the call they had to make to her family in Poland – how awful that must have been.

Instead I do everything I can to keep looking at the picture of my daughter and not at the large photo on the other side of the table of Elzbieta, her pale face framed by chestnut brown hair. Her smile shy, but warm. Her eyes a stark green. She had been a very beautiful young woman before . . . I can't stand to think of it. Bile rises to my throat. My stomach is empty and still I feel as if I could be sick at any moment, as if I have to expel grief from me so that it doesn't drown me from within.

A squeeze of my hand, Stephen's in mine, pulls me back to the moment. Back to looking at my daughter's familiar face hoping that we are not too late and we will see her again. Oh God, I need to see her again.

'Are you feeling okay?' Heather asks and I shake my head. It's a ridiculous question in the first place. How on earth could I be feeling okay? But I realise Heather knows that. She knows that I'm broken and all she needs to know in this moment is if I'm okay enough to do what is needed of us.

'I'll be okay,' I croak, reaching for the glass of tepid water in front of me and then taking a sip. My mouth is dry, my throat sore.

I think of all the times I've watched police press conferences. Watched appeals from tearful parents and partners just pleading with their missing loved ones to come home. The pretence always there that the missing person is, of course, free to just leave wherever it is they are, get on the bus and come home. That all it takes to change the mind of a kidnapper is a tearful parent.

'Stick to talking about Nell,' DI Bradley says, and I blink at him as I try to make sense of just how utterly insane and terrifying all this is. 'The statement Stephen prepared is perfect. It tells her how much she is loved. How she is a great nurse. Whatever you do, don't go rogue and show anger towards whoever took her – it's entirely possible the person you're appealing to is unstable. I know you might want to kill him right now but it's better to get him onside. If he's the same person who took Elzbieta, then we know he is capable of murder. This is a very delicate process,' DI Bradley says as the word 'murder' crawls under my skin and strips my nerve endings raw.

He has clearly done this before. These words don't affect him. His voice is deep, calm and reassuring. I wonder does he use the same script every time.

I feel Stephen squeeze my hand again. His hand is warm, sweaty. His grasp a little too tight. If she doesn't come back, I think as my stomach turns, he will be all I have. He will be the only other person who will know just how I feel. It's not a bond I want to share with anyone.

'Ms Devlin will ask the first question,' DI Bradley says, with some disgust. I overheard DS King tell him about Ingrid's impromptu visit to our home, adding it was best to try to keep her onside. She seems perfectly polite to me, but what do I know? I'm not used to being at the centre of a media storm.

'She has been well warned as to what she can and cannot ask,' he continues. 'The press questions will be directed at myself and DS King. You do not have to answer anything. Keep to your short statement. We'll try and get this wrapped up as quickly as possible. We want to get this on the evening news – and all those journalists will be wanting to hit their deadlines. That works in our favour.'

I try to care about Ingrid Devlin and all the other journalists. I try to care about making sure this press conference goes well. I try not to think about how many people will watch our grief-stricken faces and wonder if we are hiding something. I try not to think about the person who took her – because I know in my heart someone has taken her. I wonder will he watch this. Will he get some perverse pleasure from our pain? Will he taunt her with it?

'Marian . . .' I am jolted back into the room once again by Stephen's voice. Turning to look at him I see that he is rubbing the hand that had been holding mine as if he is in pain. Had I squeezed back too hard? I don't know. I mutter that I'm sorry because I am so very, very sorry. For everything.

'It's time to do this,' he says, not acknowledging my apology. I nod and we stand up to walk to the front of the room. He doesn't take my hand this time. The world is fuzzy around the edges as cameras click and a silence descends in the room. I want to escape from this place. I cannot do this.

Chapter Twenty-Seven

Him

Tuesday, November 2

One day earlier

Work has been brutal. If he could pack it in and never go back he would. He's seriously contemplating just throwing the bare essentials into his rucksack and clearing off. He could start again somewhere else and leave this whole sorry mess behind him.

He hasn't slept more than an hour at a time since yesterday. He knows it is time to put an end to all of this, and that he has the power to stop it going further. He can end it before anyone else gets hurt. He saw so much hurt today and he can't shake the heavy black cloud that is hanging over his head.

'Are you okay?' Natalia had asked him shortly before he'd gone home.

He'd looked at her – didn't know how to answer her honestly but didn't want to lie to her either. He'd shaken his head. 'It's been a tough day, and I've a headache. I think if I can just get a good sleep, I'll feel better,' he'd said. All of it true. But he knew the chances of him sleeping at all were gone.

Doire had made good on his word. He had started his game and he was making sure that people would pay attention.

He'd hoped that he'd been wrong. But when he heard about that woman's remains being found – her body burned beyond recognition – he had wanted to throw up. He knew, instinctively, that Doire was behind it.

It was happening.

With a sense of dread like a lead weight in the pit of his stomach, he logs onto the forum again. He's pretty sure that if Doire has, as he suspects, been behind the grisly discovery, he will be unable to keep quiet about it. People like him thrive on attention and sure hasn't he said his goal is to get noticed? He wants to be famous, or infamous, and remembered.

If only he'd taken him more seriously, taken proper action instead of just storing his folder full of IP addresses and screen-shotting diatribes. He could have made a difference to that poor girl. Maybe, he thinks, he can still make a difference in the future. There's another young woman missing, after all. Is it possible that Doire has her too? The forum should tell him. He searches through the posts – the users are in a frenzy. Word is clearly getting out and there in the middle of it all. Holding court is his nemesis – revelling in his new-found notoriety.

That's one in the bag. The game is in play, lads! I've taught one of them a lesson that none of them will forget in a hurry.

I gave her so many chances and she just kept making bad decisions. If she had only played by the rules it could all have been so different. Some people just don't want to learn though, do they?

I'm sorry I didn't post about her over the last few days. You see I wanted to iron out all the wrinkles. I wasn't sure how it was going to go. She might have surprised me.

177

She was a smart girl, you know. Sexy too. And her accent? It drove me wild.

Her first mistake was turning me down when I asked her out for a drink. You see if she'd made a different choice, or even been nice about it, it would've gone differently. But she sneered at me — like she thought she was better than me. Why do so many women think they are better than us? Where has the respect gone?

It's time we got that respect back — by all means necessary. That was one rule broken, so I had no choice but to take her. She brought it on herself. The rules are the rules. They are not negotiable. Not in this game.

Then, you see, she fought me. She was feistier than I thought she'd be. I'll give her that much. If she had only been polite and compliant, it could've been different for her. But the filthy tramp spat in my face! She just wouldn't listen. The rules being the rules, that meant I was forced to restrain her. It was the biggest fucking turn-on of my life, lads — not that she appreciated it, if you know what I mean . . .

It's all written down — actions have consequences. I told her that and she laughed at me. That was another mistake.

You see it wasn't my fault, but it has been my doing. And I've enjoyed it. Enjoyed my little plaything. I'd have loved to have shared her with you. I think you'd have enjoyed her too. Maybe you'd all like to play? I might just invite you all in — if you play by the rules too.

He sits back and stares at the computer screen, the dread in his stomach now replaced with nausea. The man is mad. He has as good as admitted that he is responsible for the dead woman currently lying in the morgue at Altnagelvin Hospital waiting transport to Belfast for a post-mortem. That's surely what he's talking about. Swearing, he decides to respond to the message

178

thread knowing his reply may well get lost in the sea of responses filling up his screen. There hasn't been this much activity in this forum in a long time — maybe ever.

People asking for more details. For pictures. Is there a video? What does he mean when he says 'in the bag'? Doire is, according to posters 'a legend', 'a hero', 'a God'. But none of them know the full grisly reality of what he has done. He's been clever not to post identifiable details. The forum is well moderated — hidden deep in the dark web away from the prying eyes of people overly worried about keeping things strictly legal.

'Is this about the remains found today in Northern Ireland?' he types. He tries to keep it general. He doesn't want Doire guessing who he is, but he wants to make sure. He wants to lure him into boasting more. Perhaps giving away some details.

There is no response. He watches his screen as it updates periodically and there are no further posts from Doire at all. Surely he has to run with the information he has and take it to the police right now. Before anyone else gets hurt. That Sweeney girl is still missing after all.

His phone is resting beside him on the sofa. With just one call he knows he could start a process that would bring whatever this stupid game is to an end. Staring at the screen he wills himself to find the courage to do just that.

He grabs his phone, unlocks it with his fingerprint and takes a deep breath and scrolls through his list of saved numbers, while trying to think of what exactly he will say.

'Well, there's this guy on the internet and no, I don't know his real name. Oh, and it's the dark web too. How do I know about it? Ah, well . . . I just . . . Look. There's a guy online and he hates women. Really hates women and . . . yes, well I know that could be describing just about every man on Twitter, but this isn't Twitter and this guy is local. He's here. He's boasting about doing something big. He wants to teach women a lesson. I have these videos . . .'

He can see it. His boss's face. That way she raises her eyebrow as if she is expecting little else than for him to be some sad case who hangs out on the dark web, chatting with incels about toxic masculinity and why feminism is a bad word.

And in that moment he is torn. This game isn't so easy to play after all and he doesn't know the right thing to do. No, that's not true. He does know the right thing to do. It's the only thing he *should* do.

He just can't bring himself to do it.

Maybe he is the weak creature he fears he is. Maybe it isn't all those women who have been sneering at him all along. Maybe it isn't a female voice that whispers in his ear late at night to mock him for his flaws, of which there are many. Maybe the loudest voice of all is his own.

In frustration he throws his phone, watches as it cracks against the wall and falls, splintered, to the ground. 'Fuck!' he shouts into the empty room. 'Fucking fuck.'

Chapter Twenty-Eight

Nell

Wednesday, November 3

Missing six days

I've been trying everything I can to stay warm. I've walked back and forth and back and forth the length of the room – this cell – until the chain has rubbed my ankle raw and blood carves a pattern through the dust on my foot before leaving prints on the floor as I walk.

I've tried waving my hands around – anything to keep moving and keep my circulation going at full speed. At some stage last night, I found myself in a state of mild hysteria, dancing as I sang Kylie Minogue's 'Can't Get You Out of My Head' and tried to remember the dance routine Clodagh and I used to do to it.

I had started laughing but that had quickly descended into sobbing and screaming. I didn't care that I was breaking his stupid, fucking rules. I couldn't just sit here and wait for whatever would happen to me. I screamed until I couldn't any more. I can feel my throat now, jagged and swollen. I screamed into the void until I was sure I could feel the fibrous tissue in my throat split and tear.

No one had come. Not through all the hours of darkness. Not when that smallest sliver of light started to slide under the door and I lay, exhausted, as the draught washed over me.

No one has come all day. The gas heater taunts me. I'd even take its noxious smell and taste right now if it meant I could be warm. I've finished the bottle of water he left yesterday. I finished it this morning. I tried to eke it out for as long as I could but I was thirsty – and hungry. He doesn't leave much food. Yesterday morning he left a couple of prepacked sandwiches from Tesco, yellow stickered with the previous day's date on them. I'd eked them out too, half a sandwich at a time for each meal when I had been so ravenous I could easily have eaten the two full sandwiches in one go and still have looked for more.

I've had nothing to eat since lunchtime. That I can just about deal with, but the lack of water? With my throat so raw, a cool drink of water would be like heaven. It would be so soothing and it might just quiet the gnawing hunger pangs for a while.

I haven't done it yet, but if he doesn't come soon I will see if I can prise the lid off the cistern in the toilet and scoop some fresh water out of there. The thought makes me feel nauseous, but I remind myself it's a fresh water supply. And it's so cold outside that it's bound to be so cool it will numb the pain in my throat as I swallow.

Numb. I'd like to be numb. And not just from the cold. I'm scared. This is a terrible, terrible nightmare but I know from the way my bones ache, the way the cuts on my skin sting and how dust and grit scratch at my eyes, that it's not something I'm going to wake up from.

I'm awake. And waiting.

'The waiting's the worst part.' I say that to our patients and their families all the time. To the patients as they wait for the porters to come to bring them to theatre, to their family members as they wait for the porters to bring them back.

They always nod and agree with me. A lot of the time we share a small smile – a wee gesture of solidarity. But I don't think I really got it. Not until now. I mean, I've never had anything serious to wait for before.

Not life-and-death things. Not like those families who are waiting while their loved ones are carved up, poked at, bits of them removed, complications found, incisions made and stitched back up again. On an operating table, with their lives in someone else's hands.

Like my life now, in this space, not knowing when or if he will come. The sliver of light under the door has faded to black again.

As strange as it sounds, I'm terrified he won't come back. Ever. As much as he scares me, and as much as I hate him, I'm scared that I will just be left here to starve to death or freeze to death. The temperature has dipped more – or maybe I'm just not able to keep warm any more. I'm hungry, tired and my body is using up all my reserves. Still, I don't want to die this way. What if no one ever finds me? What if this is my grave?

I've tried to reach whatever humanity remains inside him. I am so sure there has to be some in there somewhere. He seemed so normal, nice even, at work. He'd always been quite polite, shy but harmless.

He had always been friendly with me, but not overly so. His face used to redden when we spoke, which I thought was sort of cute, but Lucy, one of the third-year students, said she thought there was something a bit creepy about him. She said it was in the way he looked at her. 'He gives me the dry bokes,' she'd said in her much too loud Belfast accent. So loud in fact that

I think he might have heard her. He had only just walked away from the nurses' station and I'm sure I saw him pause momentarily before walking on.

Thinking about it now, I'm sure Elzbieta had been there too. Yes, she had been. Definitely. She'd laughed at the turn of phrase and repeated it, not quite mastering the Northern Ireland accent. 'I love how you talk,' she'd said.

I'd glowered at Lucy, but she took no notice of me and went on to talk about her latest date. Lucy was flighty and flirty and everything that I wasn't. Confidence oozed from every pore and she seemed so assured.

I don't know why I felt the need to do so, but when I next saw him I apologised to him on her behalf. He'd blushed and told me not to worry about it. Then we'd shared an awkward conversation about a new cop drama that had been on TV the night before. It was stilted – harder work than it should be, and I felt even more sorry for him. His confidence had clearly been dented by Lucy and her cruel words.

I'm not the most confident person in the world, so I thought I understood him. I was trying to be kind to him, so much so that I was worried I'd crush his esteem altogether if I said no when he offered to make me dinner. I didn't tell Lucy, or anyone for that matter, where I was going or with who. It was 'only as friends' after all.

She, and my new 'friends' (I now realise how stupid I've been to consider them real friends) wouldn't have understood. They'd have mocked me mercilessly. And Clodagh? Well – I'd blown it with Clodagh by falling in with Lucy and co in the first place. It had felt nice to feel different for a while. To live on the edge a bit. To take risks.

I'm paying for that now though. God knows I'm paying for it.

I'd cry but my eyes are dry, my stomach tight. I ache so

much and I'm so cold that I can't stop my teeth from chattering. Curling up as tight as my chains will allow, pulling the damp, fusty blanket around me, I close my eyes as tight as I can and pray hard that someone will come and rescue me. Someone has to.

The clang of a key being rammed into the lock on the outside of the door makes me jump. My muscles constrict further – almost as if they are trying to make me as small as possible – small and hard and impenetrable. Every inch of me hurts.

If I could will myself to pass out at this very second, I would. I would very gladly lose consciousness if I could escape what he will do. I'm broken enough.

There's a blinding light, the torch on his phone I think, when he walks in. He has it pointed directly at me.

He takes a step towards me and I want to crawl inside myself to get away. I need to get away. I look behind him and he has left the door open. I blink past the light and can see that much. My heart races. If I can get free from this chain, if I can get past him . . but how? I don't know how.

The light gets closer and brighter with each thud of his heavy boots on the cold cement floor. 'You're famous,' he says, his voice low and booming, the light from his phone still blinding me. 'You've been all over the news tonight. Quite a celeb, in fact.'

He stares at me, daring me to talk but I know enough to know it breaks the rules if I speak without being given direct permission. It takes all of my willpower not to beg him for information. Are they looking for me? Surely this means they are looking for me. If I'm on the news, police must know I'm not where I should be. I feel a flicker of hope ignite somewhere deep inside.

'Poor Elzbieta, not even getting her fifteen minutes of fame without you stealing her limelight. What does a girl have to do to get an appeal all to herself?' He keeps his phone pointing at me and I can't see past its beam.

I don't speak. He pauses and crouches down, taking my chin in his hand and twisting my face towards him. 'Are you not happy to see me?' he asks.

'Of course, I am,' I choke out. 'I missed you.' The words stick in my throat but I can't risk angering him, not now when I know they are looking for me.

'I suppose you miss her too?' he asks.

I nod.

'Me too. Maybe I should've given her another chance but rules are rules. How many men get a second chance with you lot? You'd rather write us off quick as look at us. We have to live with the consequences of our actions and so does Elzbieta.' He stops for a moment and pulls back, the expression on his face grotesque and mocking. His camera is still on me and I want to reach up and block it, push him and it away as hard as I can. When he starts to laugh it is a low rumble at first, a laugh so fake it makes my blood run cold. Narrowing his eyes and shuffling closer to me again, he speaks. 'It's funny,' he says, 'having to live with the consequences. Because she doesn't. Live, that is.'

I feel the weight of his words like a kick to my solar plexus and I have no idea how I manage to keep quiet because inside I am screaming. She can't be dead. This is insane. I know he's mad, but to kill her? She can't be dead. She just can't be.

His eyes never leave my face, I can feel them bore into me – begging me for a response. His phone held aloft. He's recording every second of this, the bastard. My mind flicks back to that man, the creep with the phone who followed me and then laughed when I was frightened. Recording me then too and my sense of horror is replaced by a sense of anger.

An anger so strong I have to ball my hands into tight fists, what is left of my nails digging into my palms, to stop myself from lashing out.

Lashing out would give him just what he wants. I'd break the rules. I'd face the consequences. The same consequences that Elzbieta did.

Very calmly, very quietly, I keep his gaze and then I look directly into the light from his phone, into the camera lens. I have no idea who will see this. I don't know if it's something he keeps to himself but I'll play along. I'll do whatever it takes to get out of here and then make sure I get justice for Elzbieta. 'She was asking for it,' I say softly and I am rewarded with a pat on the head and a 'good girl'. I swallow the bile that has risen to my throat.

Chapter Twenty-Nine

Marian

Thursday, November 4

Missing seven days

Harry Styles curls his way around my legs. He clearly knows something is up and has been hiding upstairs under the bed in Nell's old room for most of the last few days. Today though, he seems to be finding his way under my feet with alarming regularity.

I should pick him up. I should pick him up and stroke him and then maybe feed him some chicken from the fridge as I would normally do. But I don't want to think about him. I don't want him near me, brushing against me, periodically letting out a pitiful miaow. I don't want that stupid cat, or anything or anyone else in my space. Except for Nell.

I'm not sure what I expected from the TV appeal. Perhaps a flurry of phone calls and a rescue operation. Derry is a small place, we're always being told. A city with a village feel where everyone knows everyone else's business. Where you can't do anything without the rest of the world knowing about it.

Except, it seems, kidnap two girls and murder at least one of them.

That's my darkest thought, right there. The 'at least' because if whoever has Nell could do it once, there is nothing to say he can't, or hasn't, done it a second time. We could be searching for yet more charred remains and not even know it.

My eyes are heavy with the need to sleep but I don't want to close them. There are no happy scenarios playing out in my head. My daydreams are not of tearful reunions but of the bottom of my world falling out. Of my daughter – the greatest love of my life – being taken away from me and there is nothing I can do about it. There is no door I can knock to beg for mercy. There is no figure I can plead with to let her go. I have done what I can. I have played the role of the dutiful wife and mother and cried my tears on TV for everyone to see. No one knows that those were fake tears. Tears squeezed out as a performance. It wasn't that I hadn't wanted to cry. Of course I'd wanted to cry, but if I let myself go and cried the tears that I really felt inside of me I would have roared and screamed like a wounded animal and no one would've heard a thing Stephen or any of the police had to say.

Not that they'd said an awful lot. The pictures did the talking – two smiling girls in the prime of their lives. It doesn't bear thinking about, except that I can't think about anything else.

My head is fuzzy through lack of sleep. I'm not sure if I'm hallucinating half the time. As predicted, there is a scrum of reporters outside of our house, while we are inside now. The curtains pulled as if there is a wake in progress. It gives the day even more of a surreal feel to it. Sitting in this half-light.

Stephen is talking to Heather. That tall, lanky police officer – DC Black – is here too. He's sitting opposite me, folded into an armchair that looks too small with his frame in it. He is made of right angles, I remember how I used to say that about

Nell when I was pregnant. She was constantly kicking and poking and wriggling in my tummy, tiny bones pushing so fiercely that I could feel them from the outside. I could watch as they moved from right to left as my stomach undulated with her determination to stretch out and claim her place in the world.

I place my hand on my stomach again now, as if I'll be able to conjure those sensations again if I think about them long enough.

'I'd best be heading off,' DC Black says and I blink, try to focus on him. 'Join the team at the hospital. We're really hopeful that the CCTV will pick something up that will give us a link to Miss Kowalski and Nell.'

'They worked together,' I say. 'That's the link. You don't need CCTV to find that out.'

He shifts uncomfortably, makes to get up. 'Well, of course,' he stammers, 'but we're trying to establish if maybe there was someone they both interacted with or would have come into contact with. If we can see either of them entering or leaving the hospital with someone, it might just give us a clue.'

I shake my head. It feels like a spectacularly small needle in a very large haystack. Literally thousands of people pass through the hospital every day – from staff to patients, to contractors, to delivery staff to taxi drivers to . . .

'We're running out of time,' I say. 'I can feel it. We're running out of time and meanwhile all we can do is go through CCTV footage and talk to her friends and colleagues. The same friends and colleagues presumably who had nothing of note to tell us yesterday, or the day before.'

My voice is hoarse. I know I'm stumbling over my words – speaking a little too loudly. I feel as if my grip on reality is slipping away from me and that bloody cat is rubbing against my leg still, and I fight the urge to kick him out of the way.

190

I fight the urge to break things and shout and scream and destroy everything. I think it's only sheer exhaustion that stops me from doing it. The cat will be relieved. I imagine from the look on DC Black's face that he is also relieved.

'Marian.' Heather's calming voice enters the room just before she does. 'I know this is very hard but you must believe we're doing everything we can to get your daughter back to you.'

I nod. 'I've no doubt you'll get her back to me,' I say, blinking slowly – my bloodshot eyes so dry I can feel my eyelids drag up and down. 'It's what state she will be in when that happens. What if she is like Elzbieta? What if I can't hold her hand, or kiss her forehead? What if nothing comes back but the dregs of her remains?'

'Marian!' Stephen's voice is loud, it makes me jump and, slowly, I turn my head to look at him. 'I don't want to hear you talking like that. Ever. Do you understand? I don't want you to give up on her, and I will be damned if you have her dead already when the rest of us are doing all we can to look for her.'

His words pierce the fog in my mind. 'The rest of us are doing all we can'. Does he think I'm doing nothing? Does he really feel that I'm capable of doing nothing when my child is out there, in danger? A bubble of anger rises from the very pit of my stomach. I can feel it build, grow and get ready to erupt from me. I think of how I have spent so much of my life doing everything I can for everyone else to make their lives easier. Not to cause a fuss. To make everyone's passage through life as comfortable as possible. Of all the anger and hurt I have buried. Of how I want to scream at him that it's his fault. This isn't my fault.

It dawns on me, that I've been blaming myself for so long. For not being enough for him, so he felt the need to look else-where time and time again. For not biting back my pain enough to keep completely quiet about it. For not being brave enough to walk away from it. For making life so uncomfortable that I couldn't bear to have our beautiful daughter learn to walk on eggshells around her father like I had done. That I had to set her free before I was ready.

I *had* tried so hard to make things comfortable in our home. I *had* tried to make it work. And it was Stephen who put up obstacle after obstacle and continued living his life without a care for how it was destroying me and how it was pushing our daughter away.

My voice is quiet at first. 'How dare you,' I say and it is almost a whisper.

I see his brow crinkle, his head tilt ever so slightly as if he can't quite believe what I'm saying, and that I'm saying it in front of two police officers at that. He opens his mouth to speak but I am not done and I feel the anger grow.

'How fucking dare you,' I say, and my voice is louder now. Firm. Assured.

I see the colour rise in his cheeks. He is embarrassed by my outburst, so he does what he always does in situations such as these: he tries to minimise my feelings. He tries to make out that I'm being a hysterical woman and little else.

'Marian, you're tired and emotional . . .' he says as he raises his hand to signal that I stop talking.

If he thinks I'm going to stop talking now, he can go to hell.

'I'm tired and emotional?' I say, and how I stop myself from screaming at him I don't know. 'Of course I'm fucking tired and emotional. Our daughter has most likely been abducted by a murderer. She may be dead. What emotional response did you expect from me, Stephen? Did you want me not to cause a fuss? Or not admit my deepest fears? Or not call you out on your arrogance and bullshit? How dare you stand there and say to me that everyone else is doing all they can and imply I'm not. How absolutely dare you. How dare you imply that I'm being hysterical or that I've given up. God only knows there are plenty of times over the last twenty-two years when I could've become hysterical and given up, and none of them relate to our daughter and they never would. She is my entire life – do you understand that? I doubt you do. The biggest love in your life is yourself, you selfish, smug absolute prick.'

Harry Styles darts under the sofa for cover at the harshness of my voice. DC Black looks stricken, and very much as if he would also like to dash under the sofa and hide with the cat.

Stephen will not like that I'm saying this, but I don't care. I am finally saying what I have needed to say for years. I am not brushing my emotions under a rug any more to save face for him. I can see the mixture of embarrassment and anger on his face. I can see how shocked he is that I have raised my voice, that I have sworn at him in front of Heather and DC Black. He blinks at me, his face a perfect portrait of indignation.

'Marian and Stephen,' Heather says, 'I know this is a hugely stressful time for you both but let's try and concentrate on getting Nell back.'

I almost tell her to go to hell, but I don't. It's not her fault my marriage has been stuck together with plasters for years.

'Of course,' I say, calmly as if I haven't just let out years of anger and frustration. 'What can I do? Since I'm not doing all I can yet . . .'

Stephen doesn't speak and I revel in his silence. I'll pay for it later, of course, but for now I know I've made my point.

'The best thing you can both do is try and rest. Look after yourselves, and each other. We're still hopeful the TV appeal will reap rewards.'

A mobile phone rings – a tinny theme tune I can't quite put my finger on – and DC Black nods and leaves the room,

193

lifting his phone as he goes. I imagine he is deeply, deeply relieved to leave.

'Stephen,' Heather says, and I notice she is no longer calling him Mr Sweeney, 'why don't you put the kettle on? Your neighbour dropped in some lovely home-baked wheaten scones before. Maybe we could have tea and scones?'

Still mute, my husband nods and does as he is asked. Heather looks at me as if she is seeing me for the first time.

'I've seen worse,' she says, calmly. 'Situations like these bring a lot to the surface.'

I don't apologise or try to minimise what I've said. I'm using all the energy I have just to keep breathing. 'That might be the only good thing to come out of all this,' I say, weakly just as DC Black comes back into the room.

'No big leads at the hospital yet,' he says. 'Miss Kowalski's parents are flying in this afternoon. I've been told they'd like to come and see you.'

I don't want to see them. It's not that I don't care. I do – but I don't want to see a preview of what may well be waiting for us.

'You can say no,' Heather says, but I don't feel I can.

'We'll see them.' I nod, feeling a little sick at the thought. 'Although I'm not sure what use we will be to them. We didn't know her. I don't think Nell ever mentioned her to me before.'

'That's very kind of you,' DC Black says and if I'm not mistaken he looks as if he's struggling to hold on to his emotions.

Chapter Thirty

Him

Thursday, November 4

He gets into his car, hands shaking, and turns the key. He wants to get away from here. From this house and this street and what he has to face this afternoon.

Jesus, he can barely breathe at the thought of it. He had barely kept it together when Natalia had called him. He had to maintain his professional demeanour. He couldn't let anything slip — except he knew now that the time had come when he had to make a huge choice.

He either sentences himself to a life of guilt by staying quiet — knowing he already has blood on his hands and is likely to have more before this is all over. Or he mans up and shares all the information he has; including the damning evidence against himself.

It had been bad enough when he had seen the video that was doing the rounds on Facebook — the one Marian Sweeney had demanded they look into. He thought he would pass out as he recognised his own handiwork. He could hardly believe that he hadn't connected the smiling picture of Nell that the

Sweeneys had handed over with the scared face he had captured on camera one night as he was on the prowl. Fear had transformed her face and he'd thought in that moment of realisation he might be sick but he'd managed, God knows how, to keep it together. He still, back then, had faith that he could find a way out of this before setting his entire world on fire.

He had thought that slipping a little information to Ingrid Devlin might have been enough. That she would've found some angle to it that kept his name out of the fray. But he had been stupid to think that.

Doire shows no signs of slowing down, in fact he seems to be absolutely revelling in his new-found celebrity status. He is an idol to the men of the incel boards, and he is someone to be feared by the women of Derry.

He has hardly slept since Elzbieta Kowalski's body was found and he saw Doire's boastful posting. He has been battling with himself. He has even been short with Natalia – swearing down the phone when she called to pass on a request from the higher-ups in work.

And this morning, as he watched Nell Sweeney's mother howl with grief he'd had to fight the urge to run from the room. Marian Sweeney, he imagines, is quite a formidable woman in her day-to-day life. He had seen her across the room from him, out of her mind with fear and exhaustion, crumbling in front of him. Fearing all she will get back of her daughter is charred remains. He thought he had seen what broken looked like before – God knows he has had enough experiences of horror in this job – but this was a new level of broken. To see a parent so despondent, so frustrated by their inability to help their child. So terrified they will never see her again.

He can't tell Marian Sweeney that's she's wrong to worry. He knows more than anyone how bad this is, and how bad it is likely to get. He knows that to Doire this is a game. One that is being followed online by countless others. Those others baying for blood like Romans at the Colosseum. He knows that Doire believes he is fighting the good fight. That he is making a political statement, issuing a violent manifesto against feminism and toxic masculinity. He knows Marian Sweeney's fears are justified.

Most worryingly of all, he knows the exact level of sociopathic madness this Doire character has. He won't stop. He won't get bored or wake up to his madness. He is thriving and the bigger a response he gets, the bolder he will become.

Sitting in his car, he feels sick to the very pit of his stomach because while he had wanted women to realise they too had to face the consequences of their actions – that they too could make bad decisions – he is facing the consequences of his own.

When his phone had rung, he'd been delighted to get away from the storm that was brewing in the Sweeney house but he didn't realise there was a bigger storm waiting on the other end of the line. He wasn't to go to the hospital to continue questioning staff and reviewing CCTV as he'd thought. He was to go to Belfast International Airport, meet the Kowalskis and escort them to meet the coroner where they would be shown what was left of a small emerald ring – all that remained viewable of their eldest child.

He'll have the best seat in the house to witness their raw grief and he doesn't know if he will able to look them in the eye.

DC Mark Black, who has inadvertently opened the doors to hell and let 'Doire' walk through knows he is done. He cannot sit with the Kowalskis knowing his role in their daughter's death, and he does not want to see the Sweeneys face the same horrors.

All his pleas to Doire's good side have gone unanswered, presumably because the man doesn't have a good side to begin with. Getting Ingrid Devlin – who he has been feeding police information to for a number of years – on board hasn't uncovered anything of any great help. He should've known it wouldn't. He didn't give her much to go on. He wonders if he could trust her with the full story – will she keep quiet about him if he leads her directly to the forum and to this psychopath?

No. She loves a good story too much. There is no way she would cover up the fact a PSNI officer has started a stalking craze – one that has spiralled into kidnap and murder.

He has no choice, he realises. He has been backed into a corner and the only way to stop this happening to anyone else is to fall on his proverbial sword. With shaking hands, he unlocks his phone and scrolls through his contacts to find DS King's number. She'll enjoy this, he thinks bitterly. Hasn't she always kept her distance from him as if she knew from the very start he was damaged goods?

Taking a deep breath, he listens as her phone rings three times and she answers – her tone brusque and business-like.

'Mark,' she says, his name sounding like a sigh of exasperation on her lips. 'I hear you're going to Belfast. I know this is going to sound really insensitive, but try not to let them drag it out too much, you know. We need you here. I don't know how we're supposed to get through this work with our current manpower levels. You'd think they'd give us more resources.'

'DS King,' he says, using her full title, 'can you assign someone else to the Belfast run?'

'Oh for fuck's sake, Mark,' she begins, 'you know we have no one. Constable Williams would be the obvious choice but you know Heather needs to be with the Sweeneys now. Especially given this Facebook video debacle.'

He cuts her off, wanting to say what he needs to before what little courage he has deserts him altogether.

'I have new information about the case. And about the

Facebook video,' he says, his voice cracking just a little and to his utter shame he thinks he might break down.

'What? What do you have?' his superior asks, her irritation clearer now.

'It might be better if we meet at the station to talk about it,' he says. 'And if DI Bradley can sit in.'

'Jesus, would you not just cut to the chase? I really need to be here if I can be, not driving back to the station to look at whatever little nugget you have.'

He winces at her words, and at the disdain in her voice. One thing he has been right about all along is that DS Eve King is a grade-A bitch. That's not misogyny talking, it's just a fact, he thinks.

'It's more than a little nugget,' he says, a part of him perversely pleased to have more information than she could ever give him credit for. 'If you want half a chance at getting Nell Sweeney back, you'll meet me at the station in twenty minutes.' With that, he hangs up. She will be enraged, he thinks. DS King is not a woman who likes to take orders, especially not from a lower-ranking officer. She'd be well within her rights to reprimand him officially for this, but he's not worried. He knows he is facing much, much worse than a reprimand.

His heart thumping loudly in his chest, he turns the key in the ignition, steadies himself and then sets off for Strand Road PSNI Station where he is about to throw a grenade into what goodness remains in his life.

Chapter Thirty-One

Marian

Thursday, November 4

Missing seven days

There is a shout from the scrum of journalists standing at the end of the garden. It's different from the others. This one is not a plea to come and issue a further statement, or a request for a childhood picture of Nell. It is not an attempt to get one up on other journalists – to pull at the heartstrings of readers who don't even live anywhere near Derry, who don't know Nell and who are unlikely to give a damn whether she is found alive or dead.

'Mr and Mrs Sweeney,' a male voice calls out, 'I have important information for you.' I don't have the strength to stand and look out the window, but Stephen does. He pulls back the curtains, that action alone seeming to set off dozens of camera flashes. He blinks, instinctively pulls back as if the brightness hurts him. It probably does. Everything seems to hurt at the moment. Thinking hurts. Breathing hurts. Being in this room with the weight of what I have said this morning to him hurts. He has been giving me the silent treatment since, but I'm too tired to care. I don't think there is anything we can say to each other.

I have taken a Diazepam. Even the promise of 'important information' isn't enough to cut through my mental and physical fog.

'Come away from the window,' Heather says softly and leads Stephen to the chair as if he is old and infirm and prone to wandering. 'There are officers outside who will talk to this person and see if he is genuine.'

'Why would he not be genuine?' Stephen asks. 'Why would anyone come and stand outside our house if they didn't have proper information?'

'Things like this can bring out the worst in people. And there are others who want to help so much they will do anything to get police attention, even if they have nothing concrete to share with us. Others just like to be at the centre of the action,' she says, having a quick peek out of the window before pulling the curtains closed again.

'This isn't a freak show!' Stephen says, and all I can think is that it is very much a freak show. Our dysfunctional marriage on display for everyone to see. Our daughter on the news because she is missing. The press en masse outside our front door and strangers shouting in the street that they have 'important information'.

'Of course not,' Heather says. 'But this is why we're here. To protect you and support you through this. You're not in this alone.'

I look at her and my husband. I think of Julie-Anne and Mia. I think of my work colleagues. My family and friends and all I can think is that I am alone. When push comes to shove, I am a mother without her child. There's no lonelier place.

When the doorbell rings, Heather gestures to us to stay where we are and leaves the room, closing the door behind her. Stephen and I look at each other but we don't speak. I don't think we have anything left to say. I hear voices – Heather, a man's voice, the clamour of the press. I hate this room. I hate being stuck here, waiting for other people to bring us news. Not actively doing anything that might help find her. Not being able to sleep to escape the horror for a while, because I'm scared not to think about her for a while. I'm more scared to sleep and to be woken with the worst news.

I haven't cried. Not really cried, but there is something in this moment – in this sitting in the darkened room, feeling so utterly disconnected from everything that was my family – that opens the floodgates. As I listen to other people talking like this is nothing more than a headline to them I start to cry. A tear slides down my cheek and I don't have the strength left to brush it away or to try to hold in the second tear that follows it. Before I know it, tears are flowing freely and my shoulders are shaking, my whole body tense. Every muscle is pulled so taut with grief and fear that it physically hurts and the only way I can think of to try to get rid of that pain is to sob. I don't care about staying stoic. I don't care that people might hear. I don't care about anything. I just sob, and I howl and I scream because this is not fair. It doesn't make any sense and it's not how things are meant to be.

If I had the strength I would be breaking things but I don't. I just want to slide from this chair, lie on the floor and scream. I want to bang my head off the walls to shake the pain and fear from my mind. I want to not be here. I can't do this. All I can think is that I can't do this.

As I wail and sob, I feel arms wrap around my body and pull me into a hug so tight that I can't lash out, even though I want to. I feel the warmth of another body against mine and I hear my husband try to soothe me. I hear that he too is sobbing and all I can do is cry with him.

We don't hear the door open again or notice that Heather has come back into the room. I'm not sure how long we stand there, but when we pull apart I feel completely spent. I feel like I might finally be able to sleep. Even for just an hour.

'Marian . . .' Heather says my name, softly as if she is afraid that I might break again in front of her.

'Stephen,' she adds. I steady myself and turn to look at her. Her face is pale and I know by her expression that something big has happened. Has the mystery man given the police a big lead? Has she been found? I feel Stephen's hand squeeze mine and no matter how we have shouted and fought, I sense comfort and strength from it.

'What is it?' I ask. 'What did that man say?'

'Oh, him . . .' She shakes her head. 'He was no one. Just a crank. Said he was psychic. No, it's not him. I've just had a call from DI Bradley and he's on his way over to talk to you both.'

'Don't start this again,' Stephen says. 'Tell us whatever the hell it is that you need to say.'

She blinks and I can see that behind her distress there is something more that in my fuzzy-headed state I can't quite put my finger on.

'I will, or as much as I know,' she says. 'First of all, she's still missing. I don't want to mislead you on that score. But there has been a break in the case.'

'What do you mean?' I ask, still trying to read her expression.

'Some new information has come to light and it might help us find who has Nell.'

'Well, that's great news,' Stephen says. 'Isn't it? New information is good. What is it? Can you tell us that?'

She shifts awkwardly, puts her hands in her trouser pockets and takes them out again. 'DI Bradley has all the details, but we've been directed to a website where it would appear someone has claimed both the kidnapping of Elzbieta Kowalski and Nell.'

My heart thuds. This has to be a help. It has to. They should be able to track down whoever it is using their IP address or whatever it's called. Surely, regardless of what Stephen says, the police have ways to track that down. Whoever it is, is unlikely to be that high-tech surely.

'What website?' Stephen asks as he lets go of my hand and lifts his iPad from the table.

'I don't have that information to hand, but I can tell you that while he has admitted to killing one woman, as things stand he is saying he still has one woman with him. That's as good a sign as we can hope for that your daughter is still alive.'

I feel hope surge inside and I turn to Stephen hoping to see that optimism mirrored on his face but he doesn't even glance towards me before he sits down and starts frantically typing and searching through the internet.

'Stephen, I don't think you'll find the site. I believe it's one in the darker recesses of the web. Not strictly legal.'

My stomach tightens again. Not strictly legal. I don't want to think about what that means.

'Where did you get this information from?' Stephen asks. 'Did someone call the inquiry line?'

'That's what DI Bradley wants to talk to you about,' she says and that awkward look is back on her face. There is more to this than she's letting on.

'Can't you tell us?' I ask.

Heather shakes her head slowly. 'No. I'm afraid I can't. But DI Bradley is already en route. Now I know that this probably goes without saying, but I have been asked to request that neither of you reveal what I've just told you, or post to social media at this time. The press office is taking care of all media related to this investigation and we'd prefer it that way.'

Stephen snorts. 'And there was me about to jump right onto

Facebook and post an update,' he says, his words dripping with sarcasm.

'Stephen, please . . .' I say my voice calm, my words more soothing to him than they have been in days, weeks even. 'Heather is doing her job.'

He looks at me and I half-expect him to vent his anger in my direction but he doesn't. He nods slowly, then turns his gaze to Heather. 'I'm sorry,' he says. 'I shouldn't have spoken that way.'

To my shock Heather looks as if she will cry. I know the signs. The widening of her eyes to try and keep hold of the glistening tears that are forming, the quick, shallow breaths, the fairly strangled 'It's okay' that emits from her throat and how she turns her back to us. 'I'll just wait out here with the other officers,' she says and the crack is unmistakable now. I don't think it's just Stephen's tone that has upset her. Something else is going on here and I don't like the feel of it one bit.

Chapter Thirty-Two

Him

Thursday, November 4

Missing seven days

DI David Bradley's voice is still ringing in his ears even though his superior officer has left, along with DS King, both of them with faces like thunder.

He knows he deserves everything that has been said to him and everything that will come. An immediate suspension from all duties pending an internal investigation, and possible criminal charges. He has impeded an investigation, DI Bradley has told him in no uncertain terms. A part of him wanted to argue that he didn't know for certain, not until the night before last, that Doire had anything to do with any of it. Technically, he still doesn't know Doire is behind it all. He could just be an opportunist claiming responsibility for a crime he didn't commit to make him look big and powerful in front of his internet followers. That's the best-case scenario.

Deep in his heart though, where there are no more straws to clutch, he knows that Doire is responsible. He knows, ultimately, that he himself has to claim a good portion of the responsibility too. He did not grab Elzbieta or Nell from the street but he did help create an atmosphere where women became pawns in a game. He dehumanised them so that they were simply people he could use to make himself feel powerful. To get likes on social media. To feel in control. His motivations don't matter. His own sense of frustration at how men are now treated like second-class citizens doesn't matter. What matters is that his stupid videos, and his stupid hashtag brought someone deeply disturbed out of the woodwork.

DI Bradley, a man known for keeping his cool in almost every situation, had lost it with him. He had roared and shouted and, at one stage, he had feared that he might actually hit him.

'Jesus Christ! What the hell have you been thinking?' he had bellowed, his voice so loud there was no doubt it would have travelled out of the door of his office and into the open-plan space where Natalia, among others, is working. Shame clawed at him. He didn't even see a point in trying to explain himself. There is nothing that can justify this to his colleagues. Life as he knows it is over.

He'd just sat and took the dressing-down, listened as DI Bradley told him at the very, very least he will have brought the PSNI into disrepute and 'it's not as if we don't have a fucking hard enough task getting the people of this city onside'. The ACC will lose the plot over this. He will be made an example of. He knows he is lucky not to have been marched to the custody suite, humiliated in front of his colleagues and thrown in a cell.

How he will walk out of DI Bradley's office and through the open-plan area where his colleagues – his fellow officers and civilian detectives are working – makes him feel sick. They know he has messed up, and each of them who has been burning the candle at both ends all week in a bid to find Nell Sweeney will be out for his blood.

That's not to mention the investigators who have been tasked with watching countless videos with his stupid #IHaveThePower hashtag. Or the poor bastard who is currently on his way to Belfast airport to pick up the Kowalskis – a job he'd had no stomach for himself. He doesn't even want to think about how DI Bradley is going to break this to the Sweeneys.

He thought of just how broken Marian Sweeney looked that morning. She'd gone beyond grief and fear and just looked hollow. As if there was no light or no hope in her world.

If he had just . . .

Dropping his head to his hands he tells himself there's no point in thinking about all the shoulds, woulds or coulds. What was done was done and he will have to carry this with him, whatever the outcome, through the rest of his life.

The look on DS King's face comes into his mind. His superior officer. The boss he has both in turn admired and hated over the last few years. He'd probably spent more on-duty time with her than anyone else. They had worked numerous cases together, caught a lot of bad guys. They have seen each other at their best and at their tired, stressed and frustrated worst. As much as he has come to hate her in recent weeks – at the way she has begun to sneer at him when he messed up, at the way she seems to lord her career progression over him – when push comes to shove, the fact that he has now completely lost her respect is the biggest humiliation of all.

While Bradley had been angry – incandescent with rage even – Eve King had remained silent. On another day he might have congratulated himself on rendering her mute with shock. On another day he might have enjoyed watching her face as she read his litany of complaints on how women needed to be taught a lesson. He might have enjoyed the slow dawning that he wasn't just this tall, awkward sidekick to her main act. He might have enjoyed her knowing that while she had been throwing her weight around, rolling her eyes at him and ordering him about as if he were a child, he had been creating something that would become a viral social media movement.

But he hadn't enjoyed it today. Because he now sees the problems with this viral trend – just like a virus it has spread and mutated and even though there has only been one death that he knows about, it has already claimed too many lives.

It wasn't anger that had flashed across Eve King's face. It wasn't even shock. It was huge disappointment. He'd seen in that moment any modicum of respect she'd had for him drain away. He had blown it all for the sake of what? It hardly takes courage to walk up behind a woman wearing headphones and make her think she is being followed. It hardly takes courage to rant on the internet to a collection of like-minded arseholes. Yes, it has taken courage for him to walk into this room and admit his grievous mistakes – but he'd only done that when he'd had no choice. When he realised he couldn't live with the death of another woman on his conscience. When he knew it was only a matter of time – be it days, or weeks or months until those videos now circulating on mainstream social media like Facebook and TikTok, led his colleagues back to him anyway.

And it was only a matter of time before they were able to ascertain that he had been behind the camera of the video in which a startled Nell Sweeney had looked so scared. He may have deleted that video from the forum, and from his phone, but once something is online it develops a life of its own. He'll probably never know if Doire recognised Nell in the video he had made. Had something in her expression made him want to take her for himself? Was it seeing a woman he knew – a woman he worked with – that tipped him over the edge?

He would like to think it was just a coincidence – but

nothing is ever just a coincidence. He's been in CID too long to really believe that could be the case.

He has been ordered to wait where he is until his superiors come back. He expects the door will open any moment and some of his colleagues will come in and start the grim task of reading through his posts, tracking IP addresses and the like. That there are things on this site that would make your blood curdle. He'll have to see the expression on their faces as they read his stupid manifesto. As they see him acting like a big man because people are praising his stupid videos, with his stupid childish hashtag. It's not going to matter that he has spoken up now. It's not going to matter that he is handing them 'Doire' as a breakthrough to their investigation because as he well knows, it is too little, too late.

They've not taken his phone from him – yet. It's only a matter of time. It will be evidence now. Everything in his life will be examined in forensic detail. His colleagues will learn every last sad little detail of his life. Unlocking his phone, he scrolls through the forum again as he sits, and he sees it for what it is. He sees its full pathetic nature.

And then, as it refreshes, and a new conversation thread is started by Doire, he feels the blood rush from his head and he swears if he wasn't already sitting down, he would fall down.

Game On: Livestream tonight. Going to teach this little bitch a lesson.

Even though no part of him wants to think about what it may contain, he clicks on the thread to read the full post.

Click back here at eight to see the live show – or click the link before for a preview.
It's not that hard to make a woman compliant and respectful.

If women won't do it the easy way, then we do it the hard way.
Remember: you have the power!

The thumbnail below is a close-up of a face – a scared expression that he recognises from his own video of Nell close to the hospital. She is somewhere dark, her face is dirty, tear-stained. Guilt washes over him again as he clicks play and sees a recording of Nell Sweeney in what looks like a prison cell, her feet bare and a chain around her ankle. He listens as the man behind the camera asks if she misses Elzbieta and Nell tries her best not to look as if she is absolutely terrified.

He is watching the video when the door to DI Bradley's office opens, but when he turns to see who it is – expecting one of the tech guys – he is shocked to see Natalia, her face a picture of disgust. He burns with shame and opens his mouth to try to apologise to her but what can he say? There is nothing that can make this better.

'I've been asked to tell you to go to interview room one. Someone will be with you shortly.'

There is a shake in her voice and all he can do is nod.

'I will. I just have to make a phone call first. This video . . . it's new.'

Natalia doesn't say anything else. She just nods and leaves the room, closing the door behind her.

DC Mark Black picks up his phone and calls DI Bradley to tell him that the clock is now ticking, louder and faster than ever.

Chapter Thirty-Three

Nell

Thursday, November 4

Missing seven days

When I woke this morning he was standing over me. Even in the dim light of this room I could see his face had taken on an extra manic quality.

He'd thrown a newspaper at me, *The Chronicle*, and my face, along with Elzbieta's had stared back at me. A third picture, an image of my parents, their faces creased with grief and worry took the breath from my lungs. My poor parents. My poor mother – she looked old and defeated. More defeated than I had ever seen her before. I couldn't stop the tears from forming in my eyes.

He hadn't liked that. Not at all.

'Why are you crying?' he'd bellowed. 'You're famous! Isn't that what all you young girls want now? To be famous? Isn't that why you pout and pose your way all over social media, and live your life behind filters? So vain and vapid. I'm giving you fame on a plate.'

I'd not known what to say. I'd nodded. Figured it was better to agree with him. To be honest, I didn't have the energy but to do anything but agree with him.

'I'm giving you everything,' he'd crowed. 'I'm going to make you more famous than you could have dreamed. Even more famous than poor Elzbieta. I always did like you more.'

I thanked him for his attention. I knew that was definitely one of his rules. Agree. Say thank you. Don't criticise. Don't fight back.

He'd left afterwards, happy with my responses. Hyped up and excited about whatever his big plan to make me famous entails. I don't want to think about it. I can't think about it.

I'm just so tired, and hungry and broken and all I want to do is go home to my mum. Despite my exhaustion, I've barely slept. Each time I close my eyes I see and hear Elzbieta. I replay our muted conversation that first night – before we knew the rules. When she had called out asking if anyone else was there and I had replied, initially relieved to hear another voice. In my hazy state, I was hopeful that she was free. That she could do what I couldn't and that she would come into this room and release me.

It didn't take long for her to let me know that wasn't the case. I think she was just as disappointed as I was that I hadn't come to save her.

No one ever came to save her.

Reading through the newspaper that Eddie left with me again, I try to take in what it says. That Elzbieta's charred remains have been found. That expression makes my stomach turn, and it makes me angry. 'Charred remains' sound so impersonal. 'Charred remains' don't say anything about the person Elzbieta was. She was shy, but funny. She was dedicated to her studies, and great at her job. She had only just been starting to find her feet in Derry; had only just started to make friends and now she was reduced to being referred to as 'tragic' and a 'gruesome discovery'.

Her parents are on their way to Derry, the journalist, Ingrid Devlin has written before going on to describe my parents as 'haunted'. I read on to what Ms Devlin has written.

Stephen and Marian Sweeney looked broken as the appeal was made for anyone with information about their daughter Nell's disappearance to come forward. An only child, Nell Sweeney was described as a 'loving and caring daughter' who is the 'heart of the Sweeney family'.

'Nell, if you are listening, please know that we are looking for you and we will not stop looking for you. If you are free to come home, then please, please get in touch. We won't ask any questions. We just need to see you again,' Mr Sweeney pleaded. 'If you are the person who has our daughter, we beg you to let her go. We don't know how to exist without her.'

My heart splits in two. My father is not a man to show emotion. Not openly. At times I have thought him to be cold and cruel. I have seen how he has treats my mother. How he does not appreciate all she does for him, and yet here he is publicly pouring his heart out. I wonder does he think I'm already dead. That I am just another gruesome discovery in waiting. Is he only able to be open with his emotions because he believes I'm gone and he wants to maintain the appearance of a doting father? Maybe I'm being just as cruel and cold. He does love me. He would want me to be safe. Just because he has chipped away at my love for him with how he has treated Mum, that doesn't mean he doesn't love me. That he doesn't want me safe. He's not a monster.

When I look at the picture of him and Mum again, I see the pain in his eyes. But it's nothing at all compared to the look on my mother's face. Not just her face – her entire demeanour. She is broken. I have seen this woman plaster on a smile through a lot. Through the repeated humiliations of my father's 'gallivanting' with other women. Through his passive-aggressive take-downs. Through the healing of the bruises she thinks I don't know about. She is the strongest person I know, and I see her broken. And it's all my fault.

A sob catches in my throat. For as much as I'm scared about what might happen to me, I am also terrified about what this will do to my mother. She has known a lot of hurt and here I am about to hurt her more than he ever has, or ever could.

Eddie has left me a clean towel and soap. And a dress he said he bought himself. By the look of it, I think he bought it in a charity shop, but it is clean and dry. Demure and mid-length, it might even provide me with a bit of the warmth I crave so much.

I'm to freshen up before he comes back. I told him that I had nothing to tell the time by and he'd told me it would be after dark. It doesn't matter that it's always dark here – I'll have to keep an eye on the sliver of light under the door and make sure that as soon as it disappears I am ready. I have to believe that if I play by his rules, he will be kind.

Well, maybe not kind, but less cruel. Less dangerous. If I can just fit into his ideal of what I should be, I might get away with it. I might stay here long enough for someone to find me. Now that I know they are looking for me.

I know, even as I think it, that's not how it is likely to end. There is no one near. No one has heard me scream. I can't help but feel time is running out.

Eddie is fixated on being famous. On making me 'more famous than I could ever imagine'. That won't end with me walking away from a madman. You become famous if your image becomes a faded, dated picture of someone who didn't make it. Of a victim. Of someone who has a foundation set up in their memory. If you become a warning story to others.

'You don't want to end up like poor Nell Sweeney,' they'll say. 'Look what happened to her.'

Chapter Thirty-Four

Marian

Thursday, November 4

Missing seven days

'We wouldn't recommend you try to hunt out the website,' DI David Bradley says as I try to focus on his face and his voice. 'I know that the temptation must be there to do so, but the dark web is a disturbing place. You may find a lot of distressing content, and at the moment we really must focus on the positives. Knowing where the original videos were posted is a big piece of the jigsaw puzzle, and we have our best tech people on it right now trying to trace the videos back to the original user. We are liaising with our colleagues in the Cyber Crime Unit at Scotland Yard to put traces on these users as quickly as we can. It's still a big task, but the haystack where our needle is hiding just got a lot smaller.'

'How did you find the site?' Stephen asks. 'The dark web isn't the kind of place to come up on a Google search.' I wonder how he can think so rationally as to ask a question that makes sense. I can barely think at all. My mind is screaming to see what has been written about my daughter on all those posts DI Bradley, ashen-faced and sombre, has just told me about.

'A forum user made us aware of it,' he says, not quite meeting our gaze. I've a feeling there's more to it — not only by his demeanour, but also by the grim expression on DS King's face.

'The investigation is moving at quite a pace at the moment and that's a good thing,' she says. 'This morning we had very little to go on and now we have news of this forum, where we know there have been discussions about both Elzbieta and Nell.'

There is a forced enthusiasm on her face, which only serves to make me think, even more than before, that they are keeping something from us. I'm about to ask her when DI Bradley starts to talk again.

'I think Heather has already impressed on you the need to keep this information under wraps for now,' he says. 'What we do know is that whoever has Nell is hungry for attention. He has posted about his desire to be famous; to be remembered for this. We can't rule out the possibility that he was responsible for spreading the original videos in which women were scared by men from his corner of the internet onto mainstream social media. He wants to create a huge discussion and if we starve him of the oxygen of attention, we have a better chance at drawing him out.'

'Or making him take drastic action,' Stephen says. He doesn't need to explain that further. I know exactly what he means.

'It's true we can't predict entirely how he's going to react, but we also want to try and contain any panic around this. We want to be able to focus our resources on getting Nell home safe, and finding this man before he kills again.'

'Why Nell though?' I ask. 'It doesn't make sense. Why did he target her? What on earth can he achieve by . . . taking her?' I can't bring myself to say 'hurting her' or 'killing her'. I can't allow those words any space in my head. 'She's never hurt anyone in her life,' I tell him. 'She's a nurse for the love of God. She even took on extra shifts as a student during the height of the Covid pandemic. She spends her entire life helping others.'

'We don't know why your daughter, or Miss Kowalski for that matter, were targeted,' DI Bradley says. 'But it's likely that the person we're looking for is attached to the hospital in some capacity. That's where we're concentrating our efforts now. We have officers speaking to staff, including contract and agency staff, as well as examining shift patterns to see if any likely suspects emerge; if anyone has displayed any suspicious behaviour or if they're anyone both women spent time with. From what we can see from the forum, Nell willingly went to meet this man. They must have had some existing relationship. All I can do is assure you both that we have all available eyes on this case and we're just as keen to get this person as you are.'

I doubt that they are just as keen as we are, I think, but I don't say it. Stephen gives a slight cough, in the way he does when he thinks something is utter nonsense. Normally I find it incredibly rude, but not now. Now I know it means he is thinking exactly the same thing as I am.

'These other forum users, have they just been cheering him on? Why haven't they reported him before now? What's wrong with them? I don't understand it. Did they know just what he did before today and kept quiet anyway?'

'It does seem as if he considers himself as part of a wider mission to make a political statement of sorts,' DI Bradley says.

'Political statement?' I ask, wondering what the hell kind of a political statement taking my child, and killing another young woman could possibly make.

'It's part of a movement for men's rights,' DS King says and I can hear the scorn in her voice.

'A movement for what?' I say, incredulous. 'Are you serious? These girls are being scared and taken and God knows what in an appeal for men's rights? I've heard it all now. Jesus Christ!'

'It's quite a big movement, and while it might sound ridiculous, they shouldn't be underestimated,' DI Bradley says. 'They call themselves incels – which means they consider themselves involuntarily celibate. They believe society has moved too far in favour of women, and that they're being denied their human rights and discriminated against, and rejected by women. There have been a number of fairly high-profile mass killings by followers – some of whom have developed martyr status. That's more than likely why no one from that forum reported any of this to us. They believe very strongly in what they're doing – that women are expendable, worthless. They have been cheering this man on. The other possibility is that they knew if they brought this information to us, they would be implicating themselves in something very dark and dangerous.'

'Jesus Christ,' I say, trying to wrap my head around this.

'You're telling me wee lads who can't get a girlfriend think they have some sort of duty or right to go about kidnapping women, and even killing them?' Stephen's voice is filled with anger and I don't blame him. Our child's life is at risk because some arsehole thinks he is being persecuted. I shake my head.

'It's not something we've had much experience of in this part of the world, but networks such as the dark web allow like-minded individuals a place to come to together and talk about their theories and form their own manifestos. Until fairly recently you could find some of these boards operating on mainstream social media sites, but there has been a crackdown, which has just served to drive the most militant of these individuals underground. I've no need to say that makes it harder for us to monitor them or see a threat before it's realised.'

Dragging my fingers through my hair, I feel a headache building right behind my eyes. This is so much to take in, let alone try to make sense of. What started as some sort of stupid video trend of men scaring women has turned into a living nightmare.

'I'm afraid movements such as these seem to bring all the crazies out of the woodwork. Clearly we're dealing with a very unstable individual,' DI Bradley adds.

And suddenly I want to know just how unstable this individual is. I don't care how distressing the forum posts are, I need to see them. I need to read him saying that she is alive. I need to feel even a little of what she is feeling. I need to try to understand what she is going through and just maybe if I read those posts I will see something that no one else does. A mother's intuition is a strong thing. A mother-child bond is stronger still. There's no force like it on earth. Maybe I'm clutching at straws to think there might be a clue of some sort – a secret message, a sign only I can read in the posts – but it has to be better than just sitting here doing nothing.

'I want to see the posts,' I say and DI Bradley starts to shake his head.

'As I said, I really don't think . . . at this stage of the investigation . . . well, it might cause you more distress than good,' he says.

'I can assure you that what is going through my mind at the moment is distressing enough. At least if I knew what was actually happening . . . If we read the posts,' I say looking at Stephen, who is staring back at me as if I've lost the run of myself, 'we wouldn't have to torture ourselves with thinking what they might contain. We might even see something in it that you've missed. She's our daughter after all. We have to do something. Can you not just open up this dark cesspit of the internet and show us? We've a right to see it.'

'I don't want to see any part of it,' Stephen says, his voice low and quiet. 'Not now. Not ever. I don't think any parent needs to read that and I've no idea why you think I'd want to read what those sick bastards are writing about or why you'd want to look at it yourself.'

His words, in this moment, feel like a betrayal. Like a judgement. Like he thinks there is something inherently wrong with me. Something twisted.

'I want to try and understand,' I say. 'And to do that I need to know what these people are saying about her. I want to do anything I can, no matter how uncomfortable or painful, to try and get her back to us.'

There's a look, a blink and you'd miss it, glance between Bradley and King and now I know for definite that there is something they aren't telling us. Maybe they're trying to protect us from something too horrible to contemplate. That thought lands with a sickening thump. Are they trying to hide the worst truth of all – that she is already dead? That she has already met the same fate as Elzbieta?

I look to my husband, hoping he sees the fear and the need to know in my eyes. Hoping he can move past his own terror and realise why I need to see what is written, no matter how horrific, no matter how grim. When we brought her into this world we made an unspoken promise to be with her through all of her life no matter how tough that life became. The true definition of for better or worse, in sickness and in health. A vow stronger than any promise we could've made each other – it was a promise that didn't need to be spoken. It is scored in my heart. No matter the horrors. We are her parents. I am her mother, for the love of God. It's my job to protect her.

'You're keeping something else from us,' I say, my voice cracking. 'You're not telling us everything and don't you dare give us that "you have to trust us to tell you what you need to know" crap again. What is it?'

'Marian,' Stephen says, 'you need to calm down.'

How dare he, I think. How dare he tell me to calm down. 'And you need to fuck off!' I bark before turning back to the police officers sitting across the room from me. 'So help me God, if you don't tell me what's going on I will not be responsible for my actions. I will get on the phone to that Ingrid Devlin woman and tell her about this forum, about these sick bastards, about this dark web.'

'We really wouldn't recommend you do that, Mrs Sweeney,' DI Bradley says, but I notice that he shifts in his seat and looks to DS King. She gives him a small nod.

I'm suddenly aware that Heather has appeared at my side, where Stephen should be. She takes my hand in a way that lets me know something bad is coming and instinctively I shake her off.

'I'm not listening to this,' Stephen says. 'You can sit there and torture yourself if you want to. Go ahead, but I won't be a part of it.' He storms out of the room, and up the stairs. Heather makes to follow him but I call her back.

'Let him go. If he can't handle it, that's up to him but I want to know. And I want to know now.'

'Mrs Sweeney . . .' DI Bradley says.

'You've been calling me Marian before now. You can keep calling me Marian,' I say, brushing off his attempts to keep me pacified. If he truly respects me, he will tell me the truth.

He nods. 'Marian, we need you to know there will be a full investigation into this matter. Both externally and internally. I want you to know all police officers are vetted and are expected to adhere to the very highest of standards. That said, it would seem that one of our officers may have been part of this movement, and responsible for some of the original videos.'

I hear what he is saying but I can hardly take it in. The look of utter disbelief must be written right across my face because DI Bradley keeps talking. 'It was one of our own officers who brought the website to our attention today, and who has been able to direct us to the poster we believe is responsible for taking both Miss Kowalski and your daughter.'

'One of your own officers? A policeman? And he's been part of this group of crazy women-hating madmen? Has he known about this case? If so, why has he only told you today? Why not on Monday? Why not on Thursday when Nell was taken or whenever it was when Elzbieta was taken?'

'We've not had time to examine all the posts yet or to fully question the officer, so I'm afraid I don't have that answer for you at present. I can only reiterate that we're redoubling our efforts to try and get Nell home safely. There will be time for a full investigation once we have her home with you, and we are hopeful we can still achieve that,' DI Bradley says. 'As I said, all eyes are on this case.'

'And should we not just share all this information now, get as many people as possible looking at it? Surely someone might recognise something about this man – his turn of phrase or something?'

'We did discuss that on the way over here,' DS King explains. 'But we would be concerned that shifting the focus directly onto him would have one of two possible outcomes. One is that it would embolden him to use Nell to make a bigger statement.' She doesn't need to tell me what she fears 'using Nell' would entail.

'The second is that it might drive him underground and any chance we have of tracking him with it. As it stands we have a username, which isn't much but it's a start. Our officer is speaking with senior investigators now and trust me, we'll get as much information from him as possible. He's co-operating fully with our investigation.'

'That's big of him,' I say, thinking that it all feels a bit too little, too late. 'Who is he? Have I met him?'

'I'm not sure I can release that information at this time,' DI Bradley says.

'But you're in charge of the case, aren't you? Surely if anyone could release that information it would be you?' I ask. I want to shake him. He has just told me that one of his own police officers may hold the key to finding my daughter. That the same police officer has sat on information about her abduction for valuable days.

'For operational reasons, and pending an investigation, we have to make these judgement calls. As I said, the important thing to remember is that he is co-operating now,' DI Bradley says, spilling out a word soup of buzz words and key phrases. I want to tell him I don't care about his PR disaster. I don't care about protecting whoever he is talking about. I just want Nell.

I'm about to tell him just that when a phone rings and DS King fishes her mobile out of her pocket. I watch her face, see her mouth the word 'Black' to Bradley and then get up to leave the room.

I am left sitting face to face with this senior officer. I imagine he doesn't get flustered very often, but he looks flustered now.

'Are you a parent?' I ask him.

'I am,' he says. 'A little girl. She's just a year old.' I see the hint of a smile, the love in his eyes, even as he mentions her.

'What's her name?' I ask, not sure why I need to know but I absolutely do need to know. I need to be able to connect with him on this level so he gets just how much I need him to find her.

'Lola,' he says. 'Her mother's choice.'

I nod, remembering how Stephen had told me Nell was an old woman's name – not one that should be given to a baby but how I'd known as soon as I set eyes on her that Nell was the only name that would've ever suited her.

'Marian, I can't imagine how this feels for you,' he says. 'You are living a parent's worst nightmare. We're aware of that and I'm pulling every resource at our disposal to get to the bottom of this.'

'Thank you,' I say, but it comes out choked and strained. I feel Heather's hand on mine again and I don't pull away this time. Tears I thought I had emptied myself of not two hours before smart at my eyes again.

When DS King comes back into the room there is an immediate change in the atmosphere. Her face can't hide that something else has happened. If I thought my stomach had plummeted as far as possible before, I was wrong. It dives again and I feel Heather squeeze my hand so tightly it is almost painful.

'What is it?' I ask.

'There's been a development and DI Bradley and I need to give it our full attention.'

'You also need to tell me what it is,' I say and I see her blinking, trying to frame her face into an expression that belies the underlying horror of what she's about to tell me.

'Eve?' DI Bradley says.

She glances at me and then to DI Bradley. 'A new video has been uploaded to the forum. It's of Nell – we believe it's very recent.'

'Well that means she's alive?' I say, hope flooding through me.

'It would appear so,' DS King says. 'But her captor has said he will do a livestream later. To teach her a lesson.'

My head spinning, adrenaline flooding my veins I am on my feet before I can even register the fact and I am throwing up into the sink, my body shaking so violently I'm not sure I won't just collapse under the weight of my fear.

Chapter Thirty-Five

Him

Thursday, November 4

Missing seven days

'What can we tell from this video?' DS King is leaning over the desk, as DI Bradley sits staring at the computer screen. They are both watching as the image of Nell Sweeney, who looks so very young and so very scared, comes into focus.

Mark Black has already watched it three times and each time he has felt worse than the time before. There is nothing powerful about seeing this young woman blinking against the bright light of a torch, being afraid to meet the gaze of her captor and coming to the realisation that her colleague – a woman she was held captive with – has met a horrific end.

He knows that Nell Sweeney must fear she will meet the same fate. God knows he has the sinking feeling that she will. As he well knows, Doire is not a man who possesses empathy or is likely to listen to any pleas to let her go. He has already told Mark Black that he, himself, is a no one now. Mark may have gathered the kindling, but it was Doire who lit the fire and he's content to keep adding fuel to the flames. The bigger the fire the bigger – and longer lasting – the impact. He is willing to sacrifice whoever he needs to in the name of his cause.

The promise of a livestream makes it all so much worse. The tech guys are trying to find a way to shut it down, but this is not Facebook or Twitter. There are no 'Contact Us' buttons. There is no simple path to getting the site taken offline.

This is some seedy corner of the internet in which there are no standards of morality or decency. He knows that. He has seen some things in these forums that should never have seen the light of day. Women being raped and shamed. Torture scenes. Women, clearly not willing participants, being forced to act out hard-core pornography scenarios. A snuff movie.

He told himself at the time he was only watching them for research. He'd been investigating a revenge porn case where exceptionally graphic footage of a local woman performing sex acts with her former partner had been shared on social media. As quickly as he could get the video taken down from one site, it would appear on another. He'd heard the links were being circulated through Snapchat and WhatsApp – that while openly on Facebook where the comment pages said that this was an awful disgrace, he had seen screenshots of men lapping it up. Describing the girl as 'up for it', as a 'slut'. Judging every curve and crevice of her body as if she were cattle at a meat market. Saying what they would do to that 'pretty little mouth'. He had even seen women post that if the girl in question didn't want her 'tits all over the internet' why had she let her boyfriend film them in the first place? He'd agreed with that. Agreed that there surely had to be some level of personal responsibility involved. He'd wondered if roles were reversed, if it was she who circulated videos of her ex, would he get as much sympathy as she seemed to think she was entitled to? Likely not. Sure it was different for women.

But still, it had opened something in him – a need to 'research' further. Some of the men were disgusting pigs, that much was obvious, but the more he read the more he started to agree with some of what they had to say. When you look at things through a different lens – when you think of how men have been vilified – you start to believe that women are not the real victims in any of this.

Until now, that is. Now, of course, he knows. He has seen it up close and for real. He has seen the devastation Doire's acts have caused. He has taken a teacup from the shaking hands of Marian Sweeney and seen first-hand how she too is in hell.

He has seen how Natalia now looks at him as if she never knew him at all. As if she is both disgusted by him and scared of him.

But maybe there's a chance he can still make this right? Maybe he can do something to crack this case before it's too late.

'It looks like a new build,' DS King says. 'Have we people out at development sites checking unfinished properties?'

There are so many new developments being built around the city, it could take hours to check each one. Most are still following Covid regulations, so there are protocols to follow, and that's only assuming it's a development in Derry. It could be in any of the villages or holes in the road between here and Strabane. It could be in the other direction too, he thinks. It could cross the border into County Donegal – God knows that there are still shells of ghost estates lying empty after the death of the Celtic Tiger.

'We should liaise with An Garda Síochána,' he says. 'In case he's just over the border.'

'Mark, if you know where he is then now is the exact time to admit it. Vague clues aren't going to be enough. Keeping quiet if you know something is only likely to make things worse for you,' DS King says. He notices that she doesn't seem able to meet his gaze. There is no way back from here.

'I don't know any more than I've told you. I've shown you all the conversations between us. I had no other way of contacting him. Nor him me,' Mark says. 'I'm just trying to think outside the box so that we don't miss anything.'

'Bit late for that now,' DS King replies. 'If we'd known a few days ago . . . even yesterday . . . The damage this is going to do . . .'

He is mired in shame, totally because he knows she is right. He will be as much to blame if Nell Sweeney dies as Doire will be. Maybe even more so.

'We'll get the chopper up,' DI Bradley says. 'Do a sweep of the area, look for any unusual activity.'

'There isn't much background noise in the video,' DS King says. 'I mean it could be down to the time of day, but surely if it were an ongoing build there would be noise or it would be risky to keep her there – surely it would be easy for her to make some noise.'

Mark shakes his head. 'Not if it's one of his rules,' he says, and for the first time DS King looks up at him. He is sure he sees something akin to shock on her face.

'His rules?' she asks.

'In the posts, he talks about the rules a number of times. It's how he expects women in his company to behave. He says women need training. They need to know there are consequences if they don't toe the line. He talks about not telling the women the rules – that it's a game to him. And look, here he talks about inviting the others to play . . .' Mark, scrolls through and shows the offending posts. 'I've been on these forums,' he says. 'There is a lot of talk about rules. Doire seems obsessed with them. Here, look at this message he posted – his manifesto.'

'Well, is it a political statement or a game?' DS King asks, her tone terse.

Mark Black knows that to Doire, who promised to 'go big or go home', it is both. And he regards Elzbieta and Nell, and any other poor woman who may come under his notice, to be of no more value than playing pieces in a game.

'This isn't a mentally stable individual,' Mark says and he hears DS King snort as if he has just won gold in the stating-the-obvious Olympics. He ignores it. He knows there is nothing he can say or do to excuse his behaviour. All he can try and do to quiet Eve King is to get to the bottom of this as quickly as possible.

'Let me message him,' he says. 'It might work. If I play to his ego.'

He notices the glance between his two superior officers. He wonders if they are trying to figure out whether it's a good idea to let him anywhere near a computer when he has admitted what he's done online. He wants to impress upon them that there is no time for thinking things through. The video says the livestream is that evening. It's already gone three. In less than five hours that bastard will be using Nell as live bait for every sick bastard in the world. 'If you want to get her back, then I have to try,' he says. 'And you guys have to do whatever you can to contain this because the bigger the audience the bigger the gesture he will be prepared to make. Numbers of views of Nell's video are already climbing.'

And they are. The view counter is ticking round at an increasing rate. The forum is in meltdown with an increasing number of men with suspect usernames whipping themselves into a frenzy about what might be coming.

'*He burned that last bitch,*' one wrote, with a laughing face emoji. '*They needed dental records to identify her. Let that be a warning. I'll not cry any tears for her.*'

Another wrote: *'We've been telling them. Warning them for months but they haven't taken us seriously. They'll have to now! They won't underestimate us. I'll be watching tonight. I'll be looking for ideas. No reason why we can't all play our own game too.'*

'Jesus Christ,' DI Bradley says. 'Okay, okay. You message him. Don't dare let him know you're PSNI. He mustn't know we are anywhere near this forum. Eve, you sit there with him – check everything he writes. I'm going to take this to the higher-ups. This is bigger than we can manage.'

Feeling worse about himself than he ever has done before, he vows he will do whatever it takes to make this right. No matter the cost.

Chapter Thirty-Six

Marian

Thursday, November 4

Missing seven days

The house is quiet. It seems absurd that it is so still. I'm reclining on the sofa, a soft woollen throw over me, cushions plumped under my head. The curtains remain pulled, and Harry Styles lies in the crook of my legs, behind my knees. He purrs gently, as if all is right in his world. I suppose it is. He is fed. He has a clean litter tray and a safe place to sleep. If he senses the tension in the house, the feeling of impending doom, he shows no outward signs of it.

They've given me some more Diazepam. Just a wee one. Enough to take the edge off but not enough to knock me out. I don't want to be here – existing in this moment – but I can't disappear. I have to watch the clock. The wall clock that I have always hated and that I have always found incredibly ugly is ticking loudly. So loudly it hurts my head.

The police have all their best people working to track down my daughter. I'm told everything is being done to trace the source of the video. It is being analysed for any and all clues.

No, they've said, it's not advisable I watch it. Just like the posts on the forum this video is 'likely to be very distressing'. Nor will they let me know where the livestream will be posted – they are afraid that I'll go online and unleash fury on the sick bastard who has her. I'm told that might just 'feed his energy' and that was enough to make my stomach turn again.

They did show me a screen shot of Nell. It was both a kindness and a cruelty. Her face was tear-stained and her hair unwashed. She looks so tired and so scared. As soon as I saw it I wished I hadn't. It's not an image I want in my head. I can't help but ask myself what if this is the last picture of her alive that I ever see?

'We're trying to come up with the best strategy to find her,' DI Bradley had said as he got up to leave, but I noticed he looked even more uncomfortable than he had earlier. 'We need to get the team together and believe me, we'll keep you informed every step of the way.'

'What time is the livestream?' I'd asked him.

He'd shifted uncomfortably. 'Eight,' he'd said. 'So we really do have to go and get on top of this. Heather will stay here, of course. If anyone gets in touch with you, she'll deal with it. She'll have uniform back-up outside.'

With that, and with a million questions still running around in my head, DI Bradley left and I tried my best to process what I had just been told. I may have become a little hysterical and that was when I was given the Diazepam. I welcomed the numbing around the edges but I don't think there's a dose of any tranquilliser on this earth that could numb the pain that comes with knowing your child is in mortal danger.

As my breathing returned to normal Heather told me to try to sleep again. That, and making endless cups of tea, are her key skills, it seems. She tried to persuade me to go upstairs and lie down properly but that's not going to happen. The look I gave her quickly told her to revert to tea making and leave me alone. Stephen hasn't re-emerged from our room after he stormed out earlier. Heather made her way upstairs and informed him of the video and the escalation of the investigation. She hasn't reported back to me what he said, if anything.

She just crept back into the living room, as I lay on the sofa, my eyes closed tight like a child trying to convince their mammy they are fast asleep when sleep is the last thing possible. How on earth can I drift off, even for five minutes? I don't want her to tell me again that I need to save my strength. I don't need to save my strength. I need to use my strength to find my daughter. But I am tired and my limbs have taken on a leaden quality. I will rest for a moment. I need to.

I will ignore Heather padding through the living room into the kitchen, and very gently closing the door, leaving me here to lie in this darkened room and fight the demons in my head.

Every now and again I hear the low ring of her phone, the soft mumble of her voice – the words unintelligible from where I lie. I strain to try and hear them but I can't make out any of it. So I try to ascertain her mood from those low mumbles. Does she sound more urgent than before? More defeated? Could it be she's only talking to her husband about how he'll have to get his own dinner tonight? She has her own life outside of all this. When everything is said and done, no matter what happens, there will be a time when she leaves our home and goes back to her life. To her family – her husband, her children. She has two boys, she has revealed. Teenagers. Thirteen and Fifteen. She hasn't shared their names. I don't blame her. I'd want to keep my family out of this as much as possible too. I wouldn't even want their names aired in this house.

I imagine she has to keep a professional distance to be able to do the job, but I also know she will go home tonight and regardless of what happens here she will see her boys, probably kiss them goodnight and know they are safe.

At the very thought of tonight my stomach tightens, my muscles now aching with tension. My whole body is stiff and sore and desperate for sleep, but my mind screams that I must stay awake. For Nell. The majority of the press have disappeared from our door. I don't blame them. It's a cold and miserable night – rain is coming down in sheets. They don't know what is happening in here. They don't know about the livestream. They don't know because the police are doing everything they can to keep the upload quiet.

In the search for a story, a better, more emotional story, I imagine they might even have gone to meet the Kowalskis, who hadn't called round to see us after all. I'm told they were too distressed after identifying Elzbieta's emerald ring, and too tired from their journey. I imagine the police may also have decided to keep them away due to the fact our daughter is now under a direct threat. And I'm sure that Stephen and I having had a huge bust-up and can't even stand to be in the same room as each other may have factored in that decision.

I imagine they're also terrified that we might just tell the Kowalskis that one of their own officers has a place on the wrong side of this investigation and is currently 'helping them with their inquiries'.

And yet we are still supposed to trust that everything that can be done is being done to help Nell. What if it isn't just one officer? What if more of his colleagues are in on it? They could be sabotaging the investigation at every turn. My head hurts as I try to make sense of it all.

The sound of a helicopter overhead attracts my attention. It's more than likely the coastguard or the police. My first thoughts are that some poor creature must have gone into the river, or maybe there is a security alert. Those are the things that normally get the helicopter up. It's with a growing sense of unease mixed with hope that I realise they are probably looking for Nell. Or making a good show of pretending to look for her. Paranoia nips at me. I feel my nerve endings prickle and ache.

Even if they are doing their job properly, I wonder how on earth they think they will be able to pick her out from the sky. She's inside somewhere. How will they see her? And even if they did – even if by some miracle she is out in the open – how could they possibly know that one of the ant-like figures on the ground below them is the girl they are searching for? They don't know her. It has grown dark. She's just an ordinary girl. She won't stand out to them.

She stands out to me though.

The darkness makes it worse. All I can think of is the darkness of the room in which it seems Nell is being kept. Is it a basement, or a shed, or a bunker? It's impossible to tell. How can they know where to start looking?

I'm not a spiritual person, not by a long shot, but I close my eyes and I will some of my strength and love to her. I will that she knows that if I could be there with her I would be. That I will do everything in my power to get her home.

The helicopter is louder as it passes overhead, the *thump thump* of the spinning blades drowning out the ticking of the clock.

'Please find her,' I beg. 'Please. I cannot be without her.'

I don't realise I'm speaking out loud until Heather's head pops in through the door.

'Are you okay?' she asks and the most inappropriate urge washes over me to laugh. It's a ridiculous question. At least she has the good grace to look embarrassed for having asked it. 'Well, you know what I mean . . .' she adds.

237

I don't answer. I just shrug and haul myself up to sitting. My head hurts. I know I need to eat something or drink something. At the very least I know I need some caffeine and a couple of paracetamol to ease the tight band around my head.

I know I could benefit from some fresh air but I have been advised to stay in. Things may move fast. Or the press may ambush me. Or some madman might run up behind me and scare me senseless just to get a few likes on social media.

I think I'd feel guilty existing in the outside world too, while Nell is not. While she is stuck in some kind of hell. My phone is on the sofa beside me. It blinks with notifications but I don't want to look at it. I can't talk to anyone. We've been asked to stay absolutely silent about tonight's livestream. Not even to tell friends or family. How on earth am I supposed to have anything approaching a normal conversation in these circumstances?

Heather crosses to the window and peeks through the curtain. A police car sits outside, two of her colleagues on duty keeping an eye on things. I'm not sure what they expect to happen.

'You can invite them in for a cup of tea or coffee,' I say, my own throat dry. 'I'm going to make a pot of coffee. Distract myself.' I say it as if its remotely possible that I will be able to distract myself.

'That's very kind of you,' Heather says. 'But they will be fine where they are. Those guys don't go short of cups of takeaway coffee. They're better fed than most.' She smiles, but it doesn't reach her eyes.

I know she is saying, as politely as she can, that the officers can't leave their post in case something awful happens.

She's about to pull the curtain closed again when she must spot something because she does a quick double take and mutters, 'Oh for God's sake,' under her breath. I've only heard her speak that way once before and it was when that Ingrid Devlin arrived yesterday. There is a ring of our doorbell.

'I'm sorry about this,' she says. 'The guys in the car clearly have taken their don't leave your post instructions too literally. I'll string them up. Let me deal with this – I'll get rid of her.'

'Who?' I ask, looking to confirm my suspicions.

'Ingrid Devlin.' She says the journalist's name as if it leaves a bad taste in her mouth. 'I should've known that she would show up after the others went home. She's like a dog with a bone.'

'Maybe that's what we need right now,' I say. I don't care what the police think of Ingrid; I only care that she might be able to uncover something the police can't. Like, for example, the fact that one of their own is part of this group of sick individuals stalking women. That one of their own might've been able to stop this a few days ago. Maybe even before Elzbieta was killed.

Heather doesn't answer me but instead walks to the door where she begins a conversation with Ingrid. I have to admire the young journalist's confidence in the face of such obvious animosity.

'Heather, come on. You know I'm just doing my job and I might be able to help. We're all hoping to get the same result here. Nell Sweeney back home with her family.'

'There is nothing more to say that hasn't already been said in this afternoon's press statement, which I assume you received a copy of from the media office?'

From the sofa, I look out through the living room door to see Ingrid on the doorstep, her blonde bob getting lashed to her face. The weather doesn't seem to bother her. Heather stands in such a way as to block any chance of letting the woman in.

'I did get the press release,' Ingrid replies, her tone polite. Perhaps overly so. 'But there's more going on in the background, isn't there? I just went to try and speak to the Kowalskis; I couldn't get access. That chopper hasn't left the sky for an hour and I can't get any operational details on why it's up. Some of your guys are very on edge indeed. No sign of Bradley, or King, or even Black for that matter.'

At the mention of these three names something inside me clicks. It could just be a gut instinct but it would certainly make sense. That DC Black. The tall, gangly, awkward cop who always looked as if he was a few inches to the left of where he should be. He has been with King every day since this began. This afternoon, when DI Bradley and DS King came back, there was no sign of him. An image of the expression on his face as I cried earlier flashes before me.

DI Bradley had said: 'Our officer is co-operating fully with the investigation.' The words ring in my ears. Surely it's not DC Black they are talking about? Surely not that long string of piss? Surely he wouldn't be so brazen as to sit opposite me in my own house and offer me tea and sympathy while knowing what was happening all the time.

'It's him, isn't it?' I blurt out, my voice finding its strength again.

Both Heather and Ingrid look in my direction. Heather is doing her very best to hide a look of horror on her face, but she is failing miserably. Ingrid Devlin looks between the two of us, her journalistic radar clearly on high alert.

'Mrs Sweeney,' she says. 'I'm so sorry for your ongoing nightmare. We met briefly yesterday, before the press conference. Can I ask what you mean by "it's him, isn't it"?'

'Ingrid!' Heather says forcefully. 'You have been told to go through the press office for this. Now is not the time to be harassing this poor family. Do you not follow the Editors' Code of Practice? We can put in a complaint.'

Heather's words, although I know she means well, rankle. *They* can put in a complaint? They who have a stalker in their midst want to put in a complaint against a journalist who by

240

her own admission is simply trying to find my daughter. That's enough to get me on my feet and walking towards the door.

'What I mean,' I say, my voice shaking, 'is that a member of the PSNI has been involved in these kidnappings.'

'That's not quite accurate,' Heather blusters. The look on her face is one of a person imploring another to stop talking. She can't say it out loud of course. Can't do anything that would confirm that I'm speaking the truth. They are already planning their cover-up, I see.

'Are you saying your superior officers were lying when they told me one of their own was being questioned about all of this?' I ask, my voice icy. I can see Ingrid Devlin is hooked. She does her best to look very concerned, but I'm not a stupid woman – no matter what Stephen might say from time to time. I know for her, the biggest thrill will be the headline. But I don't care. If it will bring Nell back I'll sell my soul to the media.

Heather tries to convince me we should finish this discussion inside. Away from prying eyes. She is on a fool's errand if she thinks it's going to be that easy. I ignore her. 'Mark Black,' I say. 'He hasn't been back since this latest development came out. It's him, isn't it?'

Chapter Thirty-Seven

Nell

Thursday, November 4

Missing seven days
5 p.m.

It's dark outside. I think. There is no light slipping in under the door but I think I've lost all sense of time passing now. I can't tell the difference between five minutes and five hours. He didn't bring me food this morning and I'm weak with hunger. It's bitterly cold and I hear wind whistle through the minuscule gaps in the mortar. I think every ounce of energy I have has gone into trying to keep warm, and just to keep existing. I should be ready for him by now. I should have made myself presentable. I barely have the energy to move – and my very joints ache from the cold.

But I've done the best I can. I focused on how nice it felt to change into dry clothes. Yes, the dress still has a musty smell to it but compared to my own musty smell it is almost pleasant. I fell asleep after the exertion of trying to wash in ice-cold water and change. I have no idea how long I slept for – but I know I found it hard to wake up. I am so very tired.

While I slept I dreamt I was at home, at my parents' house. I was lying on the sofa, my head on my mother's lap – just how I had liked to lie as a child. She was playing with the strands of my hair, smoothing it and caressing it and telling me how much she loved me. I was wrapped in a blanket of security and unconditional love. Those were the good times, I've realised. The last couple of months – my quest to get out there and find adventure outside of my comfort zone – wasn't what I really wanted. I'd been happy with my life. I'd felt settled but then this little voice had started to creep in telling me settled was boring. Telling me that settled might end up making me feel trapped. I thought of my mother and how the vibrancy I knew that bubbled under the surface never got the chance to shine. Her light was dimmed by my father but she was too afraid to rock the boat and leave.

Now, all I want is to be with her again. For us to sit on the sofa and know that we did whatever we could to save each other. There's so much more we can do together. Things we talked about but never quite got round to. A shopping trip to London – 'just us girls'. Joining a book club. Such minor things, but things that sound so blissful now. I'd give anything for that life now. Anything for time with Clodagh again. Anything to be able to enjoy the small pleasures I have taken for granted. I push those thoughts away – because the grief of knowing I may never be able to do any of these things will overwhelm me.

Eddie has given me no indication of what will happen when he arrives. I have no idea what his plans are, apart from making me famous, of course. I wonder will he take this chain off me. If he takes me out of this place, like he did Elzbieta, then maybe, just maybe I have a chance of getting away. If I'm careful and keep focused I might just find that one time he slips up and I can make the most of it. You see, the one thing I know with absolute certainty is that if I stay here, chained to this floor, in a cell with no exits, I am a dead woman. And it will be too late for both my mother and me. We will be beyond saving.

I'm shivering now and I know it is more than cold. I'm scared. I would give anything I have to be somewhere else. I'm not a religious person. I've never really believed in God, not even as a child, but I've prayed today.

And I've asked Elzbieta to watch over me and help me if she can. If she has any influence at all up there then I hope she can forgive me for not being able to help her, but can also do something to help me.

The whir of helicopter blades attracts my attention. They're quiet at first and I wonder if I'm hearing things. Everything has taken on a fairly surreal air. But as it gets closer I know I'm not imagining it. I know it's near, so near it could almost be overhead and I scream and shout as loud as I can even though I know I shouldn't. Even though I know that Eddie might be listening in and this is most definitely against the rules. Even though I know I could be making things so much worse for myself. But what have I really got to lose at this stage? I can only see this ending one way and it's not good.

I wonder does the helicopter have a heat sensor, or some sort of long-distance microphone? They have those things, don't they? I'm sure I've read that somewhere. Maybe they can pick me up in this hell-hole and they will come and get me. I have to hope because the alternative is unthinkable.

Tears smart in my eyes as I hear the sound of the blades fade again. It's moving on. Maybe it was never looking for me in the first place. Maybe, despite what the papers say, there is no big effort to find me. Or they are chasing the wrong leads. Or something . . .

I can't allow my brain to go there. Even as hope disappears,

I have to try and hang on to it. I have to believe I'll be okay. I scream once more at the very top of my lungs – so loudly that I'm sure I can feel the muscles tear in my throat and my chest hurts, but still it gets quieter.

And all I can do is wait for Eddie to come back.

Chapter Thirty-Eight

Him

Thursday, November 4

5.30 p.m.

Mark Black is on edge. He has tried to find the perfect thing to say to Doire to try and at least get a line of communication open between them. But he has to do it without revealing he is a member of the PSNI, and without revealing that police are on to this website and to the posts.

He knows the best chance he has is to flatter Doire's ego. To elevate Doire to the role of alpha male. To dig deep into his darkest thoughts – to find that anger and pain he had felt when this had all started, and channel that towards getting Doire to open up to him.

And he has to do all that while Eve King stands over his shoulder, watching his every move. She doesn't trust him any more, not that he blames her. There is no way she is going to let him do things his way. She keeps making suggestions as to what he should say and while he knows it is in his best interest to be resolutely apologetic and humble in every way, it is starting to annoy him.

He is under enough pressure without King standing over him as if she knows this world he has been a part of better than he does. Maybe that's always been the problem with her – she always held an air of superiority over him. She never took him seriously. For the briefest of moments the thought that she is certainly taking him seriously now runs through his head.

He'd revel in it, he thinks, if he wasn't up against the clock in a bid to try to save a woman's life. Nell Sweeney, as far as he knows, never looked down on anyone. Anyone he has spoken to during the course of this investigation has said how she was just one of the good people. That she was great at her job. Quiet. Conscientious. Had maybe made a few questionable choices recently but nothing at all to indicate she deserved anything that was happening to her.

He shakes his head. Reminds himself he has to think that no woman deserves what is happening to Nell Sweeney. Not even King and her ever-present sanctimony.

'You have to trust me to write this in a way that gets his attention,' he says. 'I know how these guys think.'

'We're well aware of that,' King replies. 'We've seen your posts, Mark. We know exactly what you think of women.'

He's about to try to explain it to her when he realises now is not the time for this discussion. The clock is ticking. He can see from the forum that it is clear the notification of the live-stream has been shared – and widely. Things like this don't stay quiet for long when it comes to the incel community. So far it seems as if it hasn't spread onto mainstream social media. If it does it will be impossible to shut it down.

'Eve,' he says, his voice sharper than he intends. 'You can rip me to shreds after this, if it makes you feel better, but now is not the time.'

He can see she has no comeback. He can see the frustration in her eyes. It's a hollow victory.

'Okay,' he says and reads over the draft of the message he has been composing.

Hey, lad. Look I know I have pissed you off in the past and you know what, you were right to cut me off. I was jealous. I'm man enough to admit it. There was me trying to start something – to make a name for myself – and you come in and smash it. Your name is going to go down in the history books, my friend. Those girls will be a warning story to other women who think they are better than us. If they want to play with fire, they have to be prepared to get burned.

Look, I'm coming to you as a pal now. A brother of sorts. At the start of this you asked me if I wanted in on the action and I know you can tell me to fuck off, but look, this is going to be epic. Let me help you. Not that you need help, but please. Can I be a part of it? I'd love to be there to see the look on that bitch's face when you get started! You might need someone to hold the camera – you don't want to miss anything with this.

You're a legend, lad.

He feels sick looking at what he has written, knowing that his colleagues will read it and know there is a part of him that has found some comfort amongst this community. He can't wait any longer though. He hits send, and sits back, his stomach twisting, wondering if and when he might hear back. He can only hope it's not too late and his words are enough.

'Fingers crossed,' he says to the room but there is a distinct lack of camaraderie and support. He has already been extricated from the team in every meaningful sense. He's here trying to show he's not a complete bastard, but the damage is done and it is utterly irreparable.

Natalia can't even look at him. He saw disappointment in her eyes when he went to get a cup of coffee earlier, and any easiness and flirtation between them has gone. It wasn't so much that she had blanked him, it was that she kept her distance, standing as far away from him as physically possible. He'd love to tell her that the person in those posts is not the real him. That she was the person who changed his mind and made him think differently. That she has been the person to save him. He wants to thank her for that, but he guesses it is too late and things have gone too far. It's not just that she will believe she is better than him, it's that she knows now, without a shadow of a doubt, that she is better than him.

It's hard not to feel wretched, but the adrenaline of waiting for Doire to respond – hoping with all his heart that he does – is what is keeping him going. God knows how many private messages Doire has received today. He hopes he takes the time to read through them, especially as he's not been able to use his original username. He's used one that might get some attention though – BrandywellBoy – using the name of the playing grounds of Derry City FC. It should signal that he's local. He hopes it will be enough to prick Doire's interest.

'Has the chopper picked anything up?' he hears Bradley ask.

'No. But perhaps now that it's dark any unusual movement around new builds will be easier to spot. We've had uniform search planning applications for private new builds that we wouldn't necessarily be aware of. The chopper will do a fly over some of those sites now,' King tells him. 'They're going to use thermal imaging – see if it flags up any bodies in empty properties.'

'Make sure to tell them to keep circulating. Especially after seven. Let's make him nervous,' Mark says. 'Although he'll definitely enjoy any attention. Good or bad.'

No one responds to him and he starts to feel edgy. There must be something else he can do.

'Has anything been flagged on the criminal record checks

on hospital staff et cetera?' he asks, knowing people can't ignore a direct question.

'It's a pretty big pool of people,' King says, 'but we're making our way through it.'

'Have you narrowed the field to look specifically for people who may have a history of domestic violence, sexual assault or the like?' he asks.

'We're told no one with any offence like that would have been offered employment. It's a non-starter,' Natalia says, her voice small and shaky. He can't miss the sadness and disappointment in her voice and it physically hurts him.

'There has to be something more we can do,' he says, to himself as much as anyone.

'It's a pity you didn't think that sooner,' Natalia says as she walks away and he feels his mood slip further than he thought possible. It's only the flashing of a notification on his phone – a private message reply from Doire – that distracts him. With his heart in his throat, he clicks it open.

Chapter Thirty-Nine

Him

Thursday, November 4

6 p.m.

'He's replied,' Mark says, prompting both King and Bradley to speed to his desk. He can feel his hands shaking as he waits for the page to load, a cool sweat breaking on his brow. If this hasn't worked he has no idea what he can do next and there are only two hours until Doire plans to go live.

His eyes blur as he starts to read, his heart thudding loudly in his chest – so loudly he is sure everyone in the room must be able to hear it too.

I was wondering if and when you'd come crawling out of the woodwork. I knew you had to be still watching despite the block. Can't laugh at you for it – I did it myself after you blocked me. I guess we're more alike than you wanted to believe at first.

Perhaps now you realise you're no better than me. You're in no position to look down on me. Your name won't even be a

*part of this when it's all done. It's me who'll be remembered,
lad. Going down in a blaze of glory, as that song says.*

*But here, I'm not one to hold grudges and I appreciate your
apology. I admire a person who can admit they're wrong. Tonight
is going to be a belter. I totally get why you want to be in on
the action and if I'm honest, it wouldn't do me any harm to
have back-up. If you have the stomach for it.*

*Do you? Do you have the stomach for what might happen?
Because if your comfort zone ends at walking up behind women
and shouting 'boo!' then you have no place here. This isn't an
episode of Scooby-Doo, this is the big leagues.*

*It gets messy, you know. The whole process. But the high?
You only think you've seen fear looking back at you but you
haven't. Not until that moment when hope is gone from their
eyes. That's fear. That's power. That's the best fucking high there
is.*

*But it takes balls — and I'm not sure you have balls big
enough. Or are you some cuck boy who will lose his cool and
go running to the cops when it gets real? When she starts pleading
for you to stop, will you let the bitch win?*

*How do I know I can trust you? It's a big ask, mucker. I
don't even know your name.*

*I can't fuck this up. Have you seen the numbers? The number
of people who will be watching? And there's two hours to go.
The more it spreads, the higher those numbers grow. I have to
leave soon, so tell me, if you have the stomach for it, if you want
to be a part of something they will be talking about for years
and if you promise I can trust you — if you are willing to prove
to me that I can trust you — then reply to this. I want a picture,
your name, your address. Photo ID. I am going to assure you
that if you jeopardise this in any way I will destroy you. Don't
think I won't.*

You have five minutes to come back to me.

Mark's first thought is 'fuck'. If he gives this madman his details – his name, his address, his picture – there's a high chance that a quick Google search will reveal to Doire that he is a member of the police. It will be game over for him, before it has even begun.

Had he more time he would get the guys in tech to photoshop a licence with a different name. Throw together a plausible persona for him to pass off as his own. But the clock is ticking.

'What do I do?' he asks.

'Send him your picture,' Bradley replies. 'I don't see that we have a choice. We have to hope that Mark Black is such a generic name an internet search won't flag up that you're a cop.'

'Have you had any pictures taken for the press?' King adds. 'Any in which you have been named as a PSNI officer?'

Mark has to think fast. He doesn't think so. There's something in the back of his mind, but he can't quite reach it. He has to make a judgement call. Extra tight security measures with PSNI staff mean very few have been publicly identified. It's not something many people know about him. There are people he went to school with or grew up alongside who have no idea he's in the police. He even has family members who have no idea he's a cop. It's not something people advertise about themselves. It would be like sticking a target on his own back. Some of the uniforms, in community policing, may have their photos taken but they won't be living within their own communities. Life is extra complicated for Northern Irish police but his low public profile might just get him through this mess.

Bradley, he realises, is right. He has no choice but to take a risk. 'Right,' he says as he fumbles in his pocket for his wallet to extract his driving licence. 'I can do this.'

'I want all units on standby,' Bradley says. 'This is a major incident and we'll need to think smart and think fast.'

A bead of sweat rolls down between Mark's shoulder blades as he snaps a picture of his driving licence, and then pulls off his jacket and tie, messes his hair a little, tries to look less official before snapping a selfie. On the first go, he notices there is some paperwork with the PSNI logo in the background of the snap and he has to quickly retake the picture making sure his background is as innocuous as possible.

He uploads the images and hits send. There is silence in the incident room as all eyes focus on Mark Black, waiting for his phone to light up with a notification. Only then can they get this rescue mission underway. As long as Doire isn't able to link Mark to the ongoing investigation.

It's only then that the thing that has been nagging at him for these last few minutes, which he's been unable or unwilling to bring into focus, clears itself in his mind.

There had been a picture of him, with his name, uploaded onto *The Chronicle* website. They'd had an inexperienced press photographer working for them yesterday – how on earth was it only yesterday – when the press conference had taken place. A photographer who clearly didn't know the protocols around identifying members of the PSNI.

He'd been meaning to contact Ingrid Devlin all day and have her take it down, but time had got away from him and it was too late now.

As his phone screen lights up, he fears he might actually throw up.

The message is simple. Just two words. *'You're on.'*

Chapter Forty

Marian

Thursday, November 4

6 p.m.

'Officers have made contact with the man who has Nell.'
Heather is sitting opposite me at the kitchen table. Stephen is
beside her – his face drawn tight with unspoken anger at me
for speaking up against him earlier. How he has the energy to
maintain his angry stance – that look in his eye of 'we will talk
about this later' – is beyond me. I have no energy for anything
but hanging on to hope. And this latest news from Heather has
to be good news. The net is closing in.

'How? Do they know who he is?' I ask but Heather is already
speaking, making sure to dampen my hope before it has the
chance to take hold.

'I'm sure you can appreciate this is a very delicate process,
but one that's moving at an extreme pace. I can't tell you much
more – not because I don't want to but because it would more
than likely be out of date already,' Heather adds.

'But how have they made contact?' Stephen asks. 'What has

he said? Or is this some bluff to make you all look better? Has one of your boys just gone and had a chat with that Mark Black fellah who's been involved in all this from the start?'

Heather swallows. Stephen's tone is aggressive but I understand it in this instance. It is justified. In answer to Ingrid Devlin's question earlier, Heather had confirmed that DC Mark Black was helping police with their investigations – that ridiculous phrase that doesn't quite say 'he is a suspect'. The police, Heather told her, are satisfied that he had nothing to do with Nell's kidnap. Not directly anyway. Then again, they're not likely to admit it if he did. There will be some code of silence or similar, which they will have enacted.

Ingrid Devlin had looked as if she might faint. 'Are you sure?' she asked. 'Mark Black? He hardly strikes me as any kind of a criminal mastermind.'

Both Heather and I had turned to look at her at the exact same moment. Who was this strange woman, sneaking her way into my house and then, it seemed, defending the man who had admitted his involvement in this viral video trend?

While it is true that Mark Black doesn't look like he could be a threat to anyone, there's no reason why he would lie about it and land himself in a whole world of trouble.

'Ingrid, I'm asking you, very nicely. In fact, I'm begging you, please keep this under your hat. For now at least,' Heather said.

'You know you can't ask me to sit on information like this,' Ingrid said.

'You don't have to sit on it forever, but please,' Heather said, her voice pleading, 'for tonight. I promise you that if you keep it to yourself for now I will make sure that DI Bradley speaks to you first on this.'

'An exclusive?' the journalist asked as a fat, round raindrop rolled off the end of her hair and landed with an unceremonious *plop* on my carpet. I could hardly believe they were talking exclusives when there was a much bigger picture that needed to be looked at.

'I can't say that,' Heather told her. 'But I will give you a head-start.'

'And you, Mrs Sweeney,' Ingrid said, turning her attention to me. 'Can I count on you to talk to me after . . .' Her sentence trailed off. None of us knew what after would look like. How could I possibly be expected to answer that question? I could see by the look on her face that Ingrid knew she had gone too far and she opened her mouth to speak, possibly to apologise, but I didn't want to hear it.

'I think you'd better leave,' I told her. 'Now.' I hadn't anticipated my voice sounding as harsh as it did but I wasn't sorry about it. I just wanted this woman out of my house before I physically pushed her through my front door. Despite her words she had no interest in getting Nell home. She doesn't care what the outcome is as long as she gets a headline.

'Look, I'm sorry . . .' she began.

'Just go. Heather, make her go,' I said and turned and walked back into the living room, slamming the door as hard as I could behind me. So hard in fact that Harry Styles jumped from where he had curled on the chair and bolted for the kitchen. I heard the swing of the cat flap as he ran out, and I thought that he'd be gone for a while.

He's still gone now, I realise as Stephen snipes at Heather and I wonder what exact headline Ingrid Devlin is going to end up with. I close my eyes tight and imagine my daughter walking back into this house, into my arms and me apologising for ever letting her go. Positive visualisation works, doesn't it? It can't hurt. I have to try everything. Grab on to every helpful thing and run with it.

I open my eyes again as Stephen says he wants to 'see this Mark Black fellah' and gets irate when Heather tells him that simply isn't possible, and that DC Black is a little bit busy just now helping with the investigation.

'How do you know you can trust him?' Stephen rages, and I notice how unkempt he is. Tired, drawn. He looks old, saggy, broken. I imagine I look the same. I imagine he spent his time upstairs staring at the walls instead of sleeping. We are running on empty now but we have so much more to endure. 'He could be leading you all down a dead-end street.'

'I can assure you that every single move he makes is being watched,' Heather says but I can tell by her expression that the same thoughts have flitted through her mind too. She continues, 'His own tech equipment has been seized and he has no access to any other communication means. DI Bradley wants me to tell you that. He says he knows it's a big ask, but so far DC Black is co-operating. He could be the key to this.'

'Big whoop whoop for him,' Stephen says, sarcasm dripping from his words. 'Great of him to try now, when the clock's ticking . . . Why didn't he speak up before? That's what I don't understand.' His voice cracks, and I wonder if I should reach out and take his hand. In truth I'm too afraid he will pull away from me, humiliating me further in front of Heather. It's not so much that I'm walking on eggshells with him right now – it's that I'm so used to living on them I know it can take the smallest of stresses for him to snap.

'Can we not go to the station?' I ask. 'If it's moving, maybe if we're there we can help. Maybe we could talk to this guy. If we make contact with him then he might think twice. If he knows how much we love her . . .'

Stephen gives a derisory snort. 'Oh for God's sake, Marian. You really think this bastard has a softer side you can appeal to? You're even more stupid than I took you for.'

Tears prick at my eyes – which are so red and sore that the fresh trickle of saltwater burns. I swallow my humiliation at how Stephen has spoken to me and keep my gaze on Heather, pleading with her to let us do something to help.

Heather looks at me, and only me, and shakes her head slowly. 'I wish I could let you, Marian, but I can't. The man who has Nell doesn't know he's talking to a policeman. If he did, I wouldn't want to think about what he could do. We have to keep up the pretence that he's talking to an ordinary person – someone who wants to help him.'

'Help him?' I ask. 'In what way? Surely not for this livestream he has planned?'

'I don't know,' she says. 'I really don't have all the facts and that's the truth. I can only assure you we're doing everything in our power to locate Nell before ...' She doesn't finish her sentence. She doesn't need to. We all know where this could end.

'Fuck this,' Stephen shouts, standing up so quickly that his chair falls back and hits the floor with a bang. 'You can't expect us to just sit here and behave ourselves,' he says. 'We can't just sit here and wait for them to tell us if she's alive or not. This is torture.'

'I know how hard it must be,' Heather says as she stands up and wordlessly rights the chair. 'But this is where Nell needs you to be now. Do you understand that?'

'How the fuck would you know what Nell needs?' he says. His mask has slipped entirely now. This is angry Stephen. Snide and sneering Stephen. The Stephen who pushed all the love I used to have for my husband away. My face blazes with embarrassment, and shame. I know he is in pain. I know he is scared. But I also know he is a bully.

'We're just supposed to sit here like passive little sheep and trust your lot – who didn't even spot they'd a fucking psycho in their midst – to save our child. Christ, give me strength.'

Each word is spat out, his tone and his body language aggressive. I can see Heather tense up, then straighten her back. 'Mr Sweeney, please try and calm down.'

'Stephen, please,' I plead, but I'm unable to meet his eyes. I don't want to see the hate and disappointment in them. Everything between us is shattered, I realise. It has been for some time but it's as if I'm only seeing that clearly now.

My phone rings and I jump. Every ring and every notification jolts through me like an EpiPen driving adrenaline directly into my arm. Stephen's face is twisted and sour. He rolls his eyes. I know what he is thinking – vapid little me still attached to my phone, even now. I break his stare and look at the screen only to see it's a withheld number. 'Who is it?' he barks. 'If it's Julie-Anne you can tell her to give us peace to deal with this.'

'It's not Julie-Anne,' I say, flashing the screen in his direction. 'It's withheld. Probably just PPI or something. I'll let it go to voicemail.'

'No!' Heather says. 'Answer it. Put it on speaker.' She's fumbling with her own phone.

I do as I'm told even though I'm not sure why she'd be interested in this marketing call.

'Hello,' I say as Stephen walks to the kitchen counter and leans on it, his head bowed.

There is a crackle and a fizz. I wait for a recorded message to start – one asking me if I've been involved in an accident recently or taken out an unwanted loan. The silence continues.

'Hello,' I repeat to the same white noise. I shake my head and am about to tap the end-call button when I hear it. Small, quiet. But I know it instantly. I'd know it anywhere in the world.

'Mum. Mum, are you there?'

My child. My eyes meet Stephen's, and I'm vaguely aware of Heather doing something but I cannot hear anything but my child's voice. It is the most beautiful sound and the most painful sound all at once.

'Nell,' I croak before I repeat her name again. 'I'm here, baby.

I'm here and we're looking for you, darling. Where are you? Are you free? Has he let you go? Nell, tell us where to get you.'

'Mum,' she repeats and her voice is shaky. 'You don't need to look for me. I'm okay. I'm where I am meant to be, with a good man who treats me just as I deserve.'

Her words buzz around my ears, not making any sense. This can't be real. I want to tell her what we know, that we have seen a video of her scared and dirty, but Heather thrusts a piece of paper under my nose.

'Say nothing about the police. You know NOTHING.'

My eyes fill with tears as I speak. 'You are happy?' I ask her, pain searing through me because I sense I am being played as part of a game.

'Yes, Mammy. I'm happy. He's a good man. You don't need to look for me. We saw the paper and we don't want you to be scared. Or worried. But let me go, please. I need to do this for me.'

I know instantly she is lying. Even if I'd never seen the screenshot from the video or had been talking to the police I would know she is lying. She never calls me 'Mammy'. Ever. Even as a child it was always 'Mummy'. Her friends used to tease her that she was snobby.

'He is looking after you?' I ask as my entire body shakes with the effort of not sobbing and screaming down the phone.

'He is, Mammy. We're even having fish and chips for tea tonight – my favourite. Just like we used to share on a Thursday. You'd like him,' she says and I can hear the same effort in her voice. Nell has never liked fish and chips. Not since she choked on a fishbone as a child. I know she is telling me that she is not okay.

I feel sick to my core at the thought she might believe what I'm saying to her, but I have no choice.

'Okay, sweetie Yes, I remember how much you loved them. They were always your favourite. Funny, I was just talking about that to the policewoman who's here with us.' I don't know if that's the right thing to say but I just need her to know we have the police here. We are looking. I understand what she is doing and I understand she needs help. I want to tell her that we'll find her. That we are all looking but I can't and it kills me that I can't offer her that reassurance when she needs it most of all.

I hear her sniff and I push away the thought that this might be the last time I talk to her. This might be the last time I hear her beautiful voice. It's as if every version of her I've ever known is standing beside me now and I'm supposed to find a way to let them go. My baby, my girl, my headstrong teenager, my best friend . . .

'We'll have to get some when you get home,' I tell her. 'Or maybe go out together. All of us. You can choose.' My voice is shaking and I know this is inane conversation but I have to keep talking to her. I have to keep her with me for as long as I can.

'That would be lovely, Mammy,' she says and I hear her voice crack. Oh dear Jesus, how I wish I could reach through this phone and haul her back to me.

'Your Dad is here, pet,' I say, aware that Stephen is looking at me, his eyes pleading. He wants to talk to her. Of course he does. 'Do you want to talk to him?'

There's a pause, the phone is muffled and when she speaks again I know she is crying. 'No. It's okay. We were just getting ready for dinner and really, I'd better get on with it.'

She's going. This is the moment she says goodbye. I want to scream at the unfairness of it but this man she is with — this animal — he is dangerous. I can't shout. I have to play along with his game.

'Thank you for getting in touch,' I tell her. 'I'll let everyone know you're fine. Hopefully we'll see you soon, darling, okay? I love you so very, very much. More than you could know.'

My voice breaks and I have to hold the phone at a distance in case she hears the sobs that are racking through my body.

'I love you too, Mammy,' she says, 'to the moon and back.'

Stephen grabs for the phone and his chance to speak to her too. He gets as far as calling her name then the line cuts out.

She is gone.

Chapter Forty-One

Nell

Thursday, November 4

6.30 p.m.

'Good girl,' Eddie tells me as he pulls the phone away and hangs up. 'You're quite good at this game, Nell. You seem to be getting the hang of the rules quickly.'

He arrived about ten minutes ago. I don't know what time it is, but he seems extra jumpy. As if he has taken something. Even in the dim light I can see a gleam of sweat on his brow and it is most certainly not warm.

'Don't worry,' he'd said as he'd walked in. 'It's not showtime yet. Now be a good girl and stand up and give me a twirl. I want to see how that dress looks on you.'

I'd clambered to my feet, which was no easy task. My ankle is increasingly painful from the rubbing of the chain and the skin is broken, swollen. Oozing a clear liquid, but I don't imagine it will be long until infection sets in. It's not as if I can clean it adequately. Of course, I'd thought as it rubbed again, keeping it clean might not matter anyway. Not if I'm going to end up like Elzbieta.

I'd stood, my hands at my sides, and looked at him.

'You look very unhappy,' he'd said. 'I mean here you are, in a nice new dress, about to become famous and you have a face on you that would curdle milk. I think that might be your first rule infringement of the night,' he'd said, almost gleefully, as if he wasn't the one making up the rules as he went along.

'I'm sorry,' I'd muttered and plastered a fake smile on my face. 'I'll try harder.'

He'd looked me up and down, assessing me, then asked me to turn around. I almost told him that it would hurt to do so, but I'd guessed complaining was another rule infringement. I'd stayed quiet and slowly turned, holding in the grimace of discomfort at my chafed and torn ankles until my head faced away from him. I'd dropped my smile momentarily, managing to fake it again by the time I was facing him again.

'You look so much prettier when you smile,' he'd said. 'And I like that dress very much. It's demure. Not slutty. I don't want other people seeing you half-naked. I don't understand why you women like to wander around dressed in next to nothing, flashing your body, anyway. There's no dignity in it. No self-respect.'

He'd crossed the room towards me and I'd breathed in, vowed to myself to keep calm. He'd raised his hand and taken hold of my face, grabbing my chin and twisting my head this way and that. His hands, calloused and rough, smelled vaguely of petrol. My stomach had lurched.

'And you look so much better without make-up. Less whore-like. You know.' He'd laughed. 'Not that I mind a bit of whorish behaviour, but it should be confined to the bedroom. To pleasing your man.'

His grip had been so tight I was sure I could feel my skin bruise at his touch.

'Don't you agree?' he'd asked, before pulling his hand away. I instinctively knew better than to reach up and rub at my sore face.

'Yes,' I'd told him. 'I couldn't agree more.'

He'd nodded, paced the room, muttering to himself. And that's when he had pulled the phone from his pocket and thrust it at me.

I hadn't known what to do, how to react. Was that a test too? To see if I took it? Surely he wasn't letting me go. He wasn't letting me call for help.

Seeing the hesitation in my eyes he'd gestured for me to take it. 'Go on. It's not a trap. Take the phone.' My hand had trembled as I took it from him, my eyes not leaving his.

'I have programmed one number and one number alone into that phone,' he'd said. 'Your next of kin details from work. I believe it's your mother.'

My heart had been thumping by then. Was my mother really only the push of a button away?

'I'm not a complete bastard,' he'd said. 'I think that's something that not everyone has ever understood about me. That's the problem, you see. Men make one mistake and they're branded for life. No one cares what happened to provoke it, you know. No one looks at the big picture.'

All I could do was nod and grasp the phone, unsure what he wanted me to do with it.

'I know about the big picture – that's why we're here. This isn't about me, Nell. Not at all. This is about what you've done to us all. It's your fault. You've left us with no choice.'

I'd wanted so much to scream at him: 'What have I done?' because I didn't understand. I have never intentionally hurt anyone in my life. I never would.

'We're just a joke to you all. Men. Here to be laughed at. To be put down. To be mocked. To be labelled. Even if women provoke us to anger.' The more he'd ranted the more I could see rage build in him. I didn't know if I was allowed to speak but I feared if I didn't at least try to reach him, he would spiral into a place where he had to physically lash out to release tension.

'I know,' I'd said. 'It's not right. It has all gone too far.'

That got his attention and he'd stopped pacing, blinked and looked at me. 'It *has* gone too far,' he'd said. 'And the only chance we have to stop it is to make people take notice. We have to go big. You understand that, don't you, Nell? It's not about you as much as it is about making people pay attention. You're just . . . what's that phrase again . . . collateral damage.'

I'd nodded as if I'd understood. As if I didn't feel like I was going to faint with fear.

'Call your mother,' he'd said as he rummaged in his trouser pocket and pulled out a crinkled sheet of paper. 'That chopper has been up all afternoon. It's making me edgy. We need to get them to back off.'

He'd handed me the paper, which was covered in his scrawling handwriting. I could barely read it in the dark. I'd blinked at him and apologised. 'I can't read it,' I'd said. 'It's too dark.'

He'd sworn under his breath but pulled a small torch from his pocket and pointed the beam at the paper. It seemed to be a script of sorts.

'Stick to that and nothing more. I mean edit it a bit so she knows it's genuine. Your favourite takeaway . . . I didn't know what you ate.'

'This is fine,' I'd said with another fake smile. 'I'll stick to this.'

'You have to get her to believe in you. Believe you're happy. That you've gone somewhere of your own free choice. Nell, you know that there will be consequences – swift consequences – if you try anything.'

I'd nodded, then hand shaking I'd pressed the button on the phone and waited for the call to connect.

I did my best to please him even though I despise him. But

it had been so hard. It hurt me to hear the heartache in her voice. When he had given his head a shake and fired me a warning glance to let me know I was not to speak to my father, I'd had to stifle a sob. He would've hated it if I cried, despite the fact he must've known he was being cruel beyond measure.

I wonder if Mum believed me. If she now thinks I'm happy and able to walk away from her and my life without looking back. If she picked up on the language cues. I'm so tired and my head so fuzzy, I can't even be sure of what I said any more.

I feel desolate. I want her. I want my mum.

My expression must betray my feelings. 'Don't be sad,' Eddie says. 'She thinks you're happy. She'll be happy too. It's all good.' He is grinning now. He snatches the phone back from me, pulls out the SIM card and flushes it down the toilet. 'I don't want them to get any notions that they might be able to find us,' he says. 'I've seen on TV sometimes, them flushing these things down the toilet. Do you like shows like that? Crime shows? *CSI* and the like. I love them – all that information just out there for us to learn.'

'Yes. They're good,' I say. Is it a rule that I have to agree with him? I'm not sure so I just play it safe.

'Right, well, this is good. It's all good. Not long now,' he says, his eyes darting madly around the room and then back at me. 'You look lovely. Really lovely. And you're very photogenic, Nell. One of the beautiful ones. That was important. The beautiful ones get the headlines.'

I mutter a thank you even though I'm shaking with fear. He is unhinged. He is nothing like the Eddie who talked to me occasionally on the ward. That Eddie was shy, awkward. Harmless.

Or I'd thought he was harmless.

He stands for a moment, silent, staring at me. I'm not sure what I'm meant to say or do, if anything. I notice he's not really looking at me. Not properly. He is looking beyond me. I'm just another thing in this room. An object or belonging. He isn't acknowledging my humanity at all. I don't know how to reach him. Normally I'd pride myself on being able to get people to open up and chat. It was one of the things my tutors at college had commented on again and again. My great bedside manner. It won't count for anything here though. He is beyond me and I fear any attempt to reach him will just end really badly.

'Right!' he says, clapping his hands together so loudly that the slap of skin on skin makes me jump. 'I have to go and see a man about a dog,' he says, using the old idiom for leaving to carry out some secret task. He taps the side of his nose and makes to leave, stopping briefly at the door before turning to face me.

'I was thinking I'd pick up a bottle of wine. Would you prefer white or red?'

It's such an unexpected, weird question that it floors me. I stare at him. I want to scream: 'Are you actually fucking mad?' but I know I daren't – and yet I feel it. A spark of anger. One almost strong enough to overcome the fear. It passes almost as quickly as it arrives but it leaves me with the knowledge that it exists within me.

'White,' I tell him. 'A dry white would be my preference. Thank you.'

'Anything the lady wants,' he says with a lascivious leer. Then he leaves, and I am alone with my heady mix of fear and suppressed anger, not knowing when he will be back.

Chapter Forty-Two

Him

Thursday, November 4
6.45 p.m.

He should've known Doire wasn't going to make it easy. Even though as far as he is aware Doire has no reason to suspect that Mark is a police officer, he knew there was still no way he was going to be trusted with enough information to get Nell out of whatever hell-hole she was in without too much drama.

Of course he'd hoped that Doire would drop the ball. Would give the address of where to meet him, preferably at the site where Nell was being held. He could get a full tactical response in place to get her out. They'd be able to block any outgoing broadcast or mobile service. It would be swift and sharp.

But that, of course, is not what happens. A further reply arrives from Doire and his hands are shaking as he opens it.

Mark,

Go to Ebrington then to the bus stop on the Limavady Road. A car will pick you up. Don't worry about identifying it. The driver will know you. That's all that matters.

You will be collected at 7.

If you are late, you miss out.

If you bring anyone with you, you will become a target.

If you contact the police, you will be considered a traitor to your gender and will be dealt with accordingly. Don't think I won't do it.

I have people watching. Any sign at all of funny business and you'll get a starring role in tonight's games too.

Do you still have the balls for that?

'Do you think he really has people watching?' King asks.

Mark shrugs. Doire has always come across as a lone-ranger type of person before now. He has never mentioned anyone else, but that was before this started to grow.

'I'm not sure it's worth taking the chance,' he says. 'We have to assume that he's telling the truth.'

'It was too much to expect him to ask to meet you wherever Nell is,' King says with a note of disappointment. 'We'll just have to tail the car. Or get the chopper to do it.'

'He says I'll suffer if he's followed,' Mark says, his skin prickling with a mix of adrenaline and fear. He knows he has fifteen minutes to make it to the pick-up site. That's just about enough and he has no time at all to sit and try to plan the best strategy.

'We can't let you go there with no back-up,' Bradley says. 'We just have to play it careful. If we can get the car registration we can hopefully track it some of the way through ANPR. Then we can get the chopper to keep a safe distance until we know for sure you are both inside.'

271

'Take your gun and take your phone with you. Keep your location settings on,' King says and he wants to roll his eyes. Does she not think he has brains enough in his head to think of that? And does she really think Doire won't have thought of it either? He imagines he and his phone will be parted pretty quickly. Doire might not know to look for a gun, but can he take that risk? Then again, it's a bigger risk to walk into this horror show without any form of self-defence. He'll have to chance it – he has no choice. He slips his gun into the inner pocket of his jacket, the weight of it comforting him.

'I need someone to take me there. Now. I can't risk being late,' he says.

'I don't think we can risk dropping you off in a police car, marked or unmarked,' Bradley says and looks around the incident room. 'We need a civilian driver to drop Mark off,' he says. 'Natalia, could you do it?'

Of all the people in this room, of course he had to pick her. It hurts Mark's heart to see the look of utter revulsion on Natalia's face at the thought of being close to him. But she's a conscientious employee, and despite her revulsion wants to make a good impression on the boss. She has hopes that one day she can join the PSNI herself and not just work as a civilian investigator. 'Of course,' she replies to DI Bradley, but her tone is dry.

Mark doesn't have time to worry about her tone. He just has to go.

'Let's go then,' he says and stands up.

'Right,' Bradley says. 'Get onto the City Centre Initiative, or anyone with CCTV in that area. The City Council will have cameras all over Ebrington, surely?'

King nods and Mark watches as she lifts the phone and starts making calls. He has to hope that Bradley is right. Ebrington is a community space – a former British Army barracks now redeveloped to house offices, cafés, and host large-scale outdoor concerts. Hundreds of people use it each day on their way to and from the pedestrian Peace Bridge over to the city centre.

Natalia silently leads the way to her car – a red Mini that he knows he will look ridiculous trying to fold himself into it. She doesn't smile or make a joke about his height as she might have done yesterday or the day before. She just opens the door and climbs in herself.

'The bus stop at the top of Ebrington?' she asks as she starts the engine and switches on her windscreen wipers.

'Yes, please. Thank you,' he says, but he is met only with silence. They set off and he wishes so much that he could say all the things he wants to say. That he could cram a lifetime of 'sorry' into the next ten minutes. But he knows she is in no place to hear it and he can't allow his mind to slip into self-pity. He must focus. He has no idea what he is walking in on, or even if he will walk back out of it.

He stays quiet, as they drive through the streets, over the bottom deck of the Craigavon Bridge and up the link road towards Ebrington. The only sounds to be heard are the swish of the windscreen wipers and the thumping of his own heart. He knows he can't fuck this up.

'Turn up here,' he says, pointing to one of the streets off the Limavady Road. 'I don't want him to see your car dropping me off at the lay-by. I don't want to put you at any risk.'

He knows his act of gallantry is a case of too little, too late, but it's something. He has to try something. Natalia nods, indicates to the right and crosses the line of traffic until she is driving up one of the narrow side streets lined with terraced houses. As she stops, Mark pulls up the lapels of his jacket in a pathetic attempt to shield him from the heavy rain. She may not want to talk to him, but he turns to look at her anyway. He needs to see her face, even if it is set in a scowl.

'For whatever it's worth,' he says. 'I am sorry.'

'Not half as sorry as I am,' she says coldly and he steps out of the car, into the rain, and walks towards the pick-up point. There is no turning back now.

Chapter Forty-Three

Marian

Thursday, November 4
7.30 p.m.

I have barely been able to breathe since Nell called. This is hell and I am in it. To hear my daughter trying to sound so brave when I know she is terrified has broken me. I'm trying not to think about what that man might have done or said to make her say all those things to me. I wonder what his motivation was. Was he trying to get the police off his back, or was he just extraordinarily cruel? Did he revel in hearing both Nell and I in such distress?

Has he thought at all about Stephen? Is it another level of his cruelty that he intentionally did not let her speak to him? He didn't react how I'd expected. There was no shouting or screaming – no acting the big man in front of Heather and I.

He had just cried. Sobbed, his shoulders heaving. In that moment I felt sorry for him, but his softer side would never be enough to repair us. Not now.

Heather had cried as she got straight on the phone to her

superior officers to ask for advice. She had recorded the loud-speaker conversation on her phone and sent the call through to the incident room. We're told they will try to trace the call, but the chances of finding it are minute. They've sent someone round though – a tubby older man who barely speaks and just sets up his equipment on the kitchen table. In case they call again.

I instinctively know that they won't and if the police don't find Nell that will have been the last time I will ever have spoken to her. The memory of my last conversation with her will be of one where her voice trembled, where she tried to drop clues to let me know she was not okay.

I wonder what he has told her. From what she said, she must know we are looking for her. I hope she does. I hope she doesn't think we could ever just move on. But does she know about Elzbieta? Did she see what happened to her? Is she scared it will happen to her too?

I know he is keeping her somewhere dark and she is not being looked after. The screenshot showed her dirty face, her hair in need of a shampoo, wearing grubby clothes I didn't recognise. I wonder does she know that he posted that video online. The thought that she might think the world is not bothered about her is painful.

'DC Mark Black has been picked up by a man driving a black Ford Focus,' Heather tells us. 'We believe this is the kidnapper. ANPR will be trying to track that car and see where it ends up. The police helicopter will be maintaining a distance, but if necessary it will move in.'

'ANPR?' I ask.

'Automatic Number Plate Recognition,' Heather says. 'One of our civilian officers was close by and was able to get the car registration and flag it on the system.'

'So, Mark Black, the same Mark Black who started making

videos because he got a kick out of scaring women is now someone we're supposed to trust?' Stephen asks.

Heather blushes and shrugs. 'Look, I know it sounds all wrong but he had made previous contact with the kidnapper – a man going by the username of Doire69. This Doire character had, it seems, been trying to find an ally in Mark but then went rogue. Mark has managed to persuade him to let him help out with tonight's . . . erm . . . event.'

I ponder on the word 'event' – as if it is something to be looked forward to. Something to be anticipated. I can see she looks pained at having used the word, but I can't bring myself to say anything. There is no acceptable way to describe it.

'And are we to trust that he will actually do what he can to help her and not this Doire character instead? He isn't someone I think we should be asked to put our trust in,' Stephen says, and I notice the anger is gone from him. It has been replaced by desperation and I think that is probably worse than seeing him angry. I'm used to angry. I'm not used to this. Desperation is painfully close to giving up.

'Obviously I don't have all the information at this time, but I know DI Bradley wouldn't have sent him without believing it's the right thing to do,' Heather says.

'What you mean is that we're all out of options and the clock is ticking?' Stephen asks and even hearing those words is physically painful.

'Yes,' Heather says. 'I could lie to you, but yes. The team are still doing everything they can to trace Nell and get her out of there. They won't give up, but at this stage our options are limited.'

I think I go to a different place. I feel as if I am no longer weighted to my chair with anxiety and fear. I am floating above it. I want to stay here. I want to take every Diazepam I can find and I don't want to go back.

Chapter Forty-Four

Him

Thursday, November 4
7.30 p.m.

The man in the car beside Mark hasn't spoken since he pulled up at the lay-by and gestured that he was to get in.

Mark has been almost too scared to look at him directly. He knew this was going to be serious and messy but he didn't expect that he would feel so sick with nerves.

He assumes the man driving is Doire, but he doesn't know for sure. All he knows, from what he can see, is that the man beside him is wearing a T-shirt despite the time of year and the bitter cold weather. He has a tattoo, some sort of Celtic symbol on his forearm. Mark is trained to try and take in as many details as possible so his eyes dart around him. The car is spotless. There is nothing to give any clues as to this man's identity or his habits. No empty takeaway coffee cups. No receipts crammed into the cup-holder. There is no phone, no sat nav, no GoPro and the radio is off. There is nothing to read here.

The silence is unsettling and it becomes even more so when the car pulls over into a lay-by at the end of the Foyle Bridge.

'Do you have a phone?' the man asks.

Mark nods, giving himself a moment to steady his voice. 'I do.'

'Hand it over then, lad,' the man says, his accent local and his voice gruff. On hearing it, Mark knows this is the man he has come to know as Doire. He recognises the raspy tones from the video he watched that morning. Reaching into his pocket he takes out his personal phone and hands it over.

'And that's your only phone?' Doire asks. 'Or do I have to frisk you?'

Swearing internally, knowing he has to stay in control and do whatever he can to make sure Doire doesn't find his gun, Mark reaches into his pocket again and takes out his work-issue phone. An older model, functional but lacking in any street cred.

Doire laughs as he takes it from him. 'Jesus, 2001 called. They want their phone back,' he says before he rolls down his window and throws both of the phones into the bushes.

Mark gives a half-hearted protest – because he thinks that's what the average person would do.

'This is my night,' Doire says. 'I've to make sure no one else is recording it and passing it off as their own. Ye know.'

'Of course,' Mark says. 'It makes sense.'

Doire taps the side of his nose, then takes a box of cigarettes from his shirt pocket and lights one. 'It also makes it really hard for anyone to track us. We really can't have that happening,' he says, blowing smoke out of the window before offering Mark a drag.

'I'm good,' Mark says, with bravado. 'But here, do you not trust me or something? Who the fuck do you think would be tracking me? The only person who wants to know where I am is my landlord. I still owe him fifty quid from this month's rent.' He fakes a laugh and hopes he hasn't sounded as if he is trying too hard.

'Just being careful,' Doire says, with a rueful grin. 'I don't know you from Adam. You're very lucky to be here, you know. Loads of people would love to be here right now.'

'I've no doubt,' Mark says. 'I appreciate it. You just tell me what you want me to do when we get there. You're the boss.'

Doire takes a final drag from his cigarette before he unclips his seatbelt.

'Get out of the car,' he says.

Mark has looked around enough to know there's no nearby site that matches the images in this morning's video. 'We here already?' he asks.

'Naw, mate,' Doire says as he opens his door. 'Just taking precautions ye know.'

Mark gets out of the car, glancing up at the CCTV camera on the streetlight overhead. He hopes it can pick up the lay-by, although he thinks it's more than likely trained on the four lanes of traffic traversing the bridge.

'We've an audience waiting,' Doire says and Mark follows him to where a dark green Nissan Qashqai is parked. With the touch of a button the car unlocks. 'In you jump,' Doire says. 'We've a wee bit to go yet.'

Mark can't afford to show even a moment's hesitation. He has to look as if he is all in, even though he is worried. ANPR has been tracking the first car. There's no guarantee it will pick up the change of vehicle. With his phones static, and the car they were travelling in abandoned in the lay-by, chances are all resources will be focused on that area. He has no doubt his colleagues will work out they've been wrong-footed, but it will take time and that is one thing they simply don't have at the moment.

He plasters on a smile, gets in the car and smiles wider when Doire gets in, starts the engine and switches on the radio. 'Mr Brightside' by The Killers blares out and Mark is back in the moment when all this started. That first night, when he hadn't even intended to scare that woman. And look now, in just a few weeks, it has turned into this. One woman dead. Another in jeopardy. His career in tatters. He doesn't feel like singing along at the top of his lungs tonight but as Doire thumps the steering wheel and launches into the chorus loudly and tune-lessly, he forces himself to join in. He has never felt so powerless in his entire existence.

'Let's fucking do this!' he shouts as they speed off.

Chapter Forty-Five

Nell

Thursday, November 4

7.55 p.m.

I read a book once where the main character, who believed he was on his way to meet his death, mentally went through a list of his family members and loved ones and said his good-byes to them. I have been trying to do that for the last twenty minutes, but it's no good. I can't get past my mother and father without becoming so overwhelmed with fear and pain that I can't go on.

I don't want to say goodbye to them. I don't want to give up. I don't want to end up unrecognisable like Elzbieta. I wonder if she was alive when he set her on fire and then as quickly as I ask myself that question, I push it away as bile rises in my throat. No, surely he wouldn't be that barbaric?

I try to curl up as small as I can, the metal of the chain tearing again at the edges of the broken skin around my ankle. I'm aware that all I have now is this hell where I am being kept in darkness. With only the bare minimum of supplies. With no heat. No warm or dry clothes. Chained like an animal. Everything hurts. I'm pretty sure an infection is setting in on one of my fingers, injured while I tried to scrape the mortar from the walls. My ankle is weeping. I can't see what lies beneath the chain, but I can feel it. Last night I dreamt that it was crawling with maggots.

It was a relief to find that it wasn't, but the relief was short-lived when I realised I was still chained to the floor in a dank room and maggots were probably the least of my worries.

It's quiet now, bar the sound of wind and rain outside. A dripping somewhere, which has been here since the day I arrived, and at times comforts me and at other times makes me want to scream. Lying on the ground, I am staring at the dark space where the light comes in through the door. With the left side of my face on the cold, gritty concrete, a cold draught crawls in over me. Watching for movement, for any difference in the shade and light to indicate someone is approaching. Listening out for footsteps, of the sounds of an approaching car – the purr of an engine, the screech of tyres on gravel, the crack and snap of footsteps on sticks and leaves, stones and rubble.

I want to hear it, to have whatever will come begin and end. I am tired of waiting. Tired of being scared. Tired of imagining how awful it will be. A calmness descends, momentarily. I can't change this. I have to endure it. I have told the family of patients that before. Those who have been told their loved one is now only receiving palliative care. 'Unfortunately, no one can walk this journey for you or your family but you. We can just be here to support you.'

Who is here is support me? I have to think that even if they aren't beside me, that my parents are with me. That Clodagh is with me. That my friends and my family are with me. A part of me needs to believe that Elzbieta is with me too. If I can hold them in my heart, I can be brave. I can try to be brave.

Then there is the distant sound of a car engine and the hairs on the back of my neck stand up. Wherever we are, no cars pass us. The only time I have heard an engine is just before he has arrived, or after he leaves. This is it, I think, as the noise grows closer. Louder. The draught under the door seems to grow colder.

I look around again, take in this room one more time.

The engine is silenced and I hear a car door open, followed by a second. There are mumbled voices. Definitely more than one. I sit up, push my hair back in the vain hope it will somehow make me able to hear better. Clearer.

Footsteps, heavy. For a moment I think maybe it's not Eddie at all. It's someone else – the police maybe, come to save me. But my hope dies as the voices grow closer. That's definitely Eddie. He's laughing. Sounds excited. The key is in the lock.

'This is going to be wild. It's going to be wild. You just keep it rolling, okay? Keep it streaming. It's all set up,' Eddie says.

As the door creaks open, there is a muffled response from the second person and then I am blinded by the brightest of lights and I instinctively shuffle backwards and lift my arm to cover my eyes.

'Honey,' Eddie calls. 'I'm home!'

Chapter Forty-Six

Him

Thursday, November 4

8 p.m.

The smell hits him first. Damp, cold, mouldy. He'd guess this house hasn't been worked on in a long time. Probably from before the first Covid lockdown. The land outside is a mess of mud and weeds trying to reclaim their rightful place. It is bleak and depressing – more so because Mark can see what it could have been. A beautiful home in a picturesque, secluded setting close to the Donegal border. It could've been a peaceful haven – instead it is dark, foreboding and the dampness is already clinging to him and catching his throat.

Doire is shining a supersized LED torch directly at the figure on the ground, who he has seen scuttle backwards in a reflex response to fear and pain. It takes a moment for his eyes to be able to focus properly on her and even though he knows the woman will be Nell, even though this place is obviously the same place from this morning's video, it still feels surreal. This scene is macabre in a way he's not seen before.

This is not just a room in a house, this is a torture chamber. The walls are rough, the floor just bare concrete. It is pitch-dark – the windows boarded up and in the centre there is this thing – this woman, barely more than a girl, in an old-fashioned dress, her skin dirty, her expression haunted, a heavy chain around her bare ankle. She is shivering, as much from fear he thinks as from the biting cold.

It goes against every single one of his instincts not to remove his coat and wrap it around her. Doire has let go of any pretence of normal behaviour and is buzzing around as if he's high or drunk or simply mad. Everything about Nell's countenance, how she flinches with his every word, shows just how scared she is to put a foot wrong. Mark watches as she pulls herself to standing and brushes dust and dirt from her dress and pushes her hair behind her ears.

'Good girl,' Doire says. 'You know the rules. I'm impressed.'

She nods but she does not meet his gaze. Her head remains bowed. Mark guesses this is another one of the rules. Speak only when given permission. Be submissive at all times. Things other posters on the incel boards advocate.

'I brought a friend to play,' Doire says. 'Be a good girl and say hello.'

Blinking, Nell glances up at Mark, her eyes narrowing against the bright light for a moment. He wonders does she remember him, but then guesses she probably can't even see him properly in this light.

'It's nice to meet you,' she says, reaching out her hand for Mark to shake. He can see it is bruised and scraped, but he shakes it, trying his best to be gentle. He is afraid of hurting her.

'You too,' he mumbles, disgusted at how pathetic that sounds.

'You have met before though,' Doire says. 'It was Mark here who gave me the idea to take you.'

Nell blinks and looks at him again, raises her hand to shield her eyes from the worst of the light. He feels the urge to look away but knows he has to front this out. He has to appear as ballsy as Doire does. He has to be the person he was in the forum. Who ranted about how men were hard done by and women had too much power. He has to show her the same disdain he did that night when they first met. When he scared her and filmed it – then posted it online as if she were nothing but a punchline. As if his actions were empowering not inherently wrong.

He smirks at her as she narrows her eyes, trying to see him properly.

'Ah, do you not recognise your co-star?' Doire says. 'I was a fan of his work anyway, but then he shared that video of you – you know where he scared the life out of you – and I knew you were perfect for my game. Just think, if it wasn't for that video I'd have gone for one of the other girls. One of those bitches who used to laugh at me. I'll give you this much, Nell. You never laughed at me. You were nice but it was just so enticing. That look on your face. The fear. It made me feel alive.'

Mark feels a chill run right through him. This was never really about feeling hard done by as a man at all. Doire had most likely always been unhinged.

Nell smiles. It's so obviously one she knows she must give or she will be breaking another one of Doire's rules. 'Yes, I remember. It's nice to see you again,' she says, her gaze turning to Mark.

'I didn't expect for our paths to cross again,' Mark says, doing his best to sound cocky and over-confident. 'But I'm happy they have. And tonight of all nights.'

'Isn't this a nice surprise?' Doire asks.

'It is,' Nell says, 'thank you.'

He doesn't know if they are livestreaming yet. Doire has told him there are a number of cameras in the room, hidden in places Nell can't see. He hopes there are because that means the police are watching as well as the users of the forum.

'So,' Mark says. 'You two knew each other before all this began?' He is hoping he can feed as much information as possible back to the rest of the team in the incident room. He doesn't know if Doire has more people watching or if he really is a lone operator.

He sees Nell open her mouth to speak but before she can, Doire has raised his hand. 'Careful now,' he says. 'You know better than that, Nell. But I'll give you that one for free. That's your last chance, though.'

She nods.

'You can speak,' he says, with the pomposity of a Roman emperor. Mark feels his disgust and hatred grow.

'Thank you,' Nell says, before she turns to me. 'Eddie and I worked together.'

She has barely finished her sentence when she is knocked to the floor by the force of a full fist punch to the face. Mark feels his stomach turn as her sees her spit blood from her mouth and muffle a sob.

'You used my name,' Doire shouts. 'You broke the biggest rule of them all.'

Before Mark can intervene, Doire or Eddie or whatever the hell he is called, follows up his punch with a swift kick directly to Nell's stomach while she lies on the floor. She crumples around his foot, a noise somewhere between a scream and a growl escaping from his throat.

'Whoa!' Mark says, his voice trembling. 'Go easy. You want to enjoy this. Another kick like that and you'll have nothing to work with.'

'True. True,' Doire says, turning away. 'Just got a little excited there. Big night, you know.' He sounds almost euphoric. He is buzzing on adrenaline, and possibly something illegal. Mark glances back down to Nell and sees her looking directly at him. There is more than just fear on her face now. Her eyes are filled with absolute hatred for him. It cuts through him but he has to remind himself, she doesn't know who he is. She has no reason to think of him as anything more than that madman who chased her just to scare her and who has now showed up with her tormentor.

After a pause, he turns back to Doire. 'You brought wine, didn't you? Let's have a drink.'

'Beer too,' Doire says and turns his phone on himself. 'Hey all,' he says as he reaches into a bag and pulls out a bottle of beer, which he slams off the side of a small table in the corner to open. He takes a long, cool drink. 'If any of you want to get in on some sweet sponsorship action, hit me up.'

As Doire talks to his viewers, Mark takes a step closer to Nell, who shuffles further back. Even in the darkness he sees her eyes are filled with tears. He crouches down, wonders if he can risk whispering something to her.

She lies, completely impassively, as he reaches out and curls her hair back behind her ear telling Doire he made a good choice.

'Course I did!' Doire says as he crouches down beside them. 'I'm not stupid. You have it all, don't you, Nell? Everything you need to make people do whatever you want them to. A wee flutter of those eyelashes and I could see how all the porters would fall over themselves to help you. You used that to your advantage.'

'I didn't,' Nell sobs and Doire pushes him roughly. His hands scrape against the concrete floor as he tries to right himself, watching as Doire twists the hair from behind Nell's ear and pulls it tight. 'I told you, no talking!' he hisses. 'You're bringing this on yourself!'

She falls silent. Mark watches as Doire lets go of her hair and runs his hands down the length of her body, groping her breast and grinning at the camera while he does so.

'Right,' Doire says. 'Let's get this evening started. Nell, it has to be fair,' he says. He tells her to stand up and Mark watches as he runs his hand up her inside leg, her face crumpling the higher he goes. He could reach into his jacket and draw his gun now, he thinks. Order Doire to stop, to move away. But Doire is unpredictable. He wouldn't be surprised if that only made things worse for Nell and he can't risk that. Whatever happens now, he knows he cannot make things any worse for her. They are bad enough.

And he will carry the look on her face right now – scared that she will be violated – with him for the rest of his life.

He watches as she closes her eyes in anticipation of what will come, but he's surprised when Doire stops, rocks back on his heels and unlocks the chain from around her ankle.

Chapter Forty-Seven

Nell

Thursday, November 4

I open my eyes and look down, seeing Eddie pull the chain away from my ankle and stand up. His friend, this bastard who filmed me a few weeks ago, is gawping at me as if he has never seen a woman before. From the moment he arrived he has been assessing me, staring me down, getting too close. I wonder if he has been in on it all along. Did Elzbieta meet him when Eddie took her from here?

'There's more beer in that bag. And wine too,' Eddie says. 'Be a dear and please pour our friend here a beer. Or would you like wine, Mark?'

'Wine would be good,' tall, awkward, awful Mark replies as he stares intensely at me.

'You can have a glass of wine too if you like,' Eddie says. 'I brought some of those plastic cups. Nothing but the best, eh?' He laughs, a small brittle laugh and I know that to play this game I must greet this as if it were the funniest joke I've ever heard. I laugh and tell him of course I'll pour the drinks but all I can think is that I'm free. My ankle is free. I could run.

He didn't lock the door behind him when he came in, if I can get past him, past them both and out the door, then maybe I can get out of here. I'll just keep running, I don't care how sore my ankle is. I'll run on broken glass if I have to. If only I can get past him, across the room and to that blasted door.

As I pull the bottle of wine from the bag, I wonder if I could just smash it now, against the wall, use the broken end as a weapon.

But there are two of them, and only one of me. And I'm weak, and tired and they look as if they wouldn't think twice about turning a broken bottle back on me and tearing at my skin with it.

Everything aches. I'm pretty sure he has broken my cheek-bone. I'm dizzy and my jaw hurts. I can feel pressure building in my eye. I dare not touch it to assess the damage. I'm no match for them, I realise my heart sinking.

Maybe I should just tear at my own skin with the bottle, I think. I could be the master of my own destiny here. The cool glass of the bottle feels heavy in my hands. I think of all the nights I'd open a bottle of this exact wine with Clodagh and we'd put the world to rights, or I'd open a bottle of wine over Sunday dinner with Mum and Dad. A fresh wave of grief washes over me.

My hands are shaking as I unscrew the lid and pour a measure into one of the plastic beakers he has brought and I hand it to Mark, my hand brushing against his as I do. I pour another measure and bring it to my lips, the tang of the wine stinging against my cut lip. I do my best to hold in my grimace.

'Slainte!' Eddie says, holding his beer bottle aloft. I raise my cup and say 'Cheers'. Mark raises his cup silently. I place my cup on the table and notice a set of keys – car keys – poking out from under the bag. Could they be his keys? To the car outside, maybe? Could they act as a weapon?

'I think we should make this place more homely, don't you?' Eddie says, slapping his hand heavily on my shoulder and making me jump. 'It's a bit cold. Maybe we should put the heating on.'

He turns me towards him, away from the drink and away from the keys and leads me towards the centre of the room.

'Pity we don't have anywhere to light an open fire,' Eddie adds, before turning to look at me, then to the phone in his hand. 'Not yet anyway!' He gives an exaggerated wink to the screen and I feel what little is left of my courage leave me.

My legs buckle but before I hit the floor I feel arms grab me. I'm pulled to standing. 'You're okay,' Mark says and I want to scream at him.

I want to shout: 'Are you actually fucking out of your mind?' but again, I'm pretty sure that would be against the rules and I can't face another kick to the stomach or punch to the face.

'Thank you,' I mumble and pull myself from his grasp. The feel of him touching me makes my skin crawl. 'Will I put the gas heater on?' I ask, unsure if this is rule-breaking or not. I have spoken before being given permission but I also know I'm supposed to take care of 'household tasks'.

'Good girl,' Eddie says and he sits down on the edge of the bed, his camera still pointed at himself.

'You see, the thing you need to know – the thing we have forgotten in all of these liberal, equality-driven days – is that women need routine. They need to have a defined role. If we, as men, don't set limits and boundaries we end up with the mess we have now. We might as well just hand women the scissors to cut our balls off with. It takes bravery to keep a woman in line – to make them remember that they are the weaker sex. That they are here to play a supporting role. We didn't have this bullshit – men being emasculated and humiliated – when women knew their place. We've become too lax. We have to take responsibility for it, but I'm telling you, we have the power to change things. Isn't that right, Mark? We have the power!' Eddie laughs, turns the camera to Mark who gives a thumbs up while I crouch at the gas heater and do my best to bring it to life.

'Fear is an uncanny motivator,' Eddie says. 'It can make even the more rabid of bitches compliant. Being able to instil a healthy dose of fear gives us men the upper hand. We were always meant to have this power. We were always meant to use this power. God made us this way. Stronger in body and mind. It is what He willed.'

It's then, as I crouch by the heater, and listen to him, that there may be a way to do this. To incapacitate them and give me the smallest chance to get past them.

It's a risky move. I may not walk away from it. God knows, if Eddie finds out what I'm doing I *won't* walk away from it. But I want to prove to him that he doesn't have the power after all.

He never did and he never will.

I fumble with the gas settings, turn them as high as I can and start to mumble about it not igniting. I don't turn the gas supply down or off though, even though the sickening smell is already washing over me – a mixture of it and the pain in my head making me dizzy and the world go a little fuzzy.

He is still ranting into the camera and I keep playing at trying to make it work, hoping he won't notice it hasn't actually lit yet. I'm relying on his ego to distract him and I can only pray it does. When I glance around I notice Mark is staring directly at me, but if he has caught on to what I'm doing he's saying nothing about it.

I look back to the heater, continue with my false attempts at lighting it. The sweet smell of the butane is filling my nostrils, and nausea ramps up until I feel I might be sick. I step up and backwards, swaying a little as my head swims. I glance again at Mark who's giving me a curious look. He opens his mouth to speak and I know this is the moment when he rats me out. He knows exactly what I've done and he's not going to let me get away with it. This is a man just like Eddie who gets off on fear – he must be in ecstasy now, knowing what will come. This is too big a rule-break for just a punch or a slap.

I am determined not to plead with him. I am determined to be brave. I won't cower. No man will make me cower.

But he doesn't talk. Instead he raises his hand to his mouth, gestures with one finger that I'm to keep quiet while he slides the other hand inside his jacket. There's something on his face that I can't read, but he glances towards the door and the keys on the table. He jerks his head slightly as if to say: 'There you go, there's your chance. Run for it. I know you've seen the keys. Get them and go.'

I don't know whether to trust him or not. In fact I'm pretty sure I shouldn't trust him. Maybe he wants me to run so he can run after me. He likes the chase, after all. I think of that night and the sound of his footsteps behind me, growing ever closer. And these guys like the drama. They have created a show. I don't know who Eddie is talking to over his phone but I do know people are watching. People are watching and none of them are helping me. No one is coming to save me.

I'm running out of time and out of options. I have no choice but to trust Mark. There is no alternative. There are no white knights about to arrive and rescue me.

I realise I need to move. Now. There is no more time to waste. Eddie is still lost in his epic declaration on male dominance, distracted by his own ego. But then he stops talking mid-sentence, sniffs, looks up at me and then at the fire.

'Did I not tell you to light that?' he says, and he's on his feet, walking towards me and I realise time has run out.

'I couldn't get it to catch, I'm sorry,' I say, head bowed down, awaiting a punch but not knowing which direction to expect it from. I should've made a break for it. I should've just started to run and not stopped.

'Stupid bitch,' he mutters but to my shock and surprise, I feel him walk past me. 'Never ask a woman to do something when you can do it yourself quicker and better,' he rants, crouching down in front of the heater.

I take a step back, glancing quickly at Mark to see if he is reacting. His hand is still in the front of his jacket and he gestures with his eyes again towards the door, his expression more animated. There is no mistaking that he wants me to go.

So I take another step, and then another, and then another. Backwards towards the door. Towards the keys. Towards freedom. Slowly at first, not quite believing that I can do it and for some illogical reason worried that I am only going to make things worse for myself. If Eddie sees me move towards the door . . . I can't think of it. I take another step, my heart beating faster and louder the closer that I get to the door. I keep expecting Mark to speak – to rat me out. Or to launch himself on me.

Eddie meanwhile is reaching his out hand towards the ignition switch on the heater and I have no idea what kind of blast it will emit, but I only need it to disorientate him long enough so I get to the door and get it open. I hope it hurts him. He deserves all the pain. He deserves every nerve ending of his to scream. I am almost there as he crouches down and I know this is my last chance. I don't have time to look to Mark. I don't have time think. I just have to get out.

'Fuck's sake!' Eddie shouts, pulling his hand back from the heater. 'Have you left this fucking gas running? Are you trying to kill us?' I'm almost at the door and I expect him to call me out on that. Adrenaline is now coursing through my veins and my heart is pounding so hard and so loud now that I can barely hear him.

'No, I swear. It's had a leak for a while. You know that. That's probably what you're smelling.'

In a beat he is up and coming towards me. Not thinking, I stumble back, reaching out behind me, grasping for the keys on the table.

'Are you telling me I'm stupid or something?' he snarls. 'You're the one who can't get it to work. You useless bitch!' He is gaining on me now, I've nowhere else to go but out of the room.

I feel the cold metal of the keys in my hand and grab onto them, relishing the feel of the crooked edges jagging at my skin. I must not pause.

I keep moving. I'm stumbling backwards as he comes towards me, eyes angry slits. I see Mark move, starting in my direction. Was he lying to me after all? Both of them will be on me soon and if they reach me I know I'll have no chance at all. I'm sore and weak but adrenaline is keeping me moving and I'm not going to make this easy for them.

'What the fuck are you doing with my keys?' Eddie snarls.

I can feel the grit, dirt and stones from the cold floor dig into the skin of my feet. I can feel blood, wet and warm, trickling from my ankle. I breathe in and my ribs hurt and my head is pounding and they are almost, almost on top of me. A few steps is all it will take. Time is speeding up and slowing down and I don't know if these are my last moments in this life. I turn and reach for the door that has kept me here for much too long. This cell door.

Taking my eyes off them is the scariest moment of all but the door is heavier than I expected and I have to use all my strength to try to haul it open, letting out an involuntary sob as it sticks – the weight of it pushing my bruised, tired arms to their limits. I'm expecting to feel a hand on my shoulder at any moment; to feel the crack of a bottle over my head, or a knife in my back or . . . or . . . .

The door gives and I don't, can't look back. I stumble through it, into the blackness of the night and a hallway I've no memory of seeing before.

I'm dizzy and I stumble, cracking my shoulder against the wall. I barely register the pain. I don't have time. I hear footsteps, heavy breathing. 'Oh no, you fucking don't,' Eddie sneers and I can feel him grow closer, the heat of him behind me and God, I don't want him to touch me ever again. Wind is whistling behind me. I can almost smell the rain and the fresh air and even though I can't see where I'm going, I can sense my way out of here. 'Please!' I plead to myself, to God, to anyone or any entity that might be listening for help. I can't get this far only to fail now. My eyes adjust and now I can see the doorway that leads outside, I can feel the dampness of the rain blowing into the shell of this building and I think I've done it. I'm getting out.

But then, soft as a feather but sharp as a knife, I feel the brush of a hand on my back and I know it's all too late.

Maybe I was stupid to think I stood a chance.

'Fucking bitch,' I hear Eddie snarl and feel him grip the back of my dress. The feeling of his hand brushing against my back is like a burn and still I try to run, to pull away but there are two of them and only one of me.

I pull forward, desperate to feel the fresh air on my skin just one more time and I'm not expecting it, but suddenly he has let go and I fall forward away from him, stumbling out of the door and slamming face first into the damp, cold ground.

The car keys fly from my hand and I scramble forward, feeling around in the cold and the dark to find them. I've no idea what is happening, or where he is. All I know is that he is not pulling at my dress, but he doesn't strike me as the kind of person to give up easily. I can't stop. I can't try and pull the air that has been knocked from my lungs back into me. Gasping, spluttering, my dress now wet, my knees bruised, my entire self broken, I try to find purchase on the slippery ground. My bare feet sliding in the mud, the cold and the damp are like vinegar on the cuts around my ankle. I am sobbing now, and then I feel the cool metal of the keys below my hands and I manage to stand up.

It's quiet around me, save for the wind and the rain and I glance around. I see Eddie's car but I can't see him or Mark. Where are they? Are they hiding in wait? Will they crawl out from under the car? Are they waiting in the back seat, ready to strangle me? I lose control of my bladder, as my body shudders in fear and confusion.

My hands shaking, I squeeze at the buttons on the fob until there is a flash of the indicators and the car unlocks. I'm almost there, but it's wet and dark, and my hand is slippery with my own blood. I'm shaking so hard that the keys slide from my grasp again.

Dropping to my knees, my eyes now darting between the ground and the skeleton of a house. I hear shouting. I think it's coming from inside but I don't know. I can't tell what is real and what isn't. I don't have time to think about it. Fishing in the mud, I put my hand once again to the metal of the keys and a sob of relief escapes from my mouth. Quickly, I haul myself to standing, open the door and climb in. I don't have time to think, I just stab at the ignition crying out again when the key slips in.

Just as the key turns and the engine roars to life I see, for the briefest of moments, the night sky light up giving me a glimpse of the house where I have been a prisoner. My mind is trying to make sense of what I'm seeing when a deep, low rumble builds in mere moments to a deafening boom – one that shakes every bone in my body, that pulls cell from cell.

The heat and the noise push me backwards, coming at me

in a giant wave, slamming my head off the head rest, crushing my chest and pushing the air from my body as a spray of broken glass glitters in front of me for just a moment before forcing its way into my face, my hands, my arms.

I'd been so close. I'd almost done it. The pain which is so intense, so brutal and violent, gives way to darkness as I slip out of consciousness.

Chapter Forty-Eight

Marian

Thursday, November 4

The city of Derry is built on a hill. On two hills in fact. One on each side of the river Foyle. The result of which is that it has the quality of a natural amphitheatre, and sound travels much further than you'd think possible, amplified on the water flowing out towards the Atlantic.

We're sitting in our living room, the room lit only by the dullest of lamps, afraid to talk. The only noises are the ticking of the clock and the gentle purr of Harry Styles who is sleeping peacefully beside me.

And then, it is there. Noise carrying on the air. The growing swell of sirens. More than the one or two that might be heard at any given time of the night or day.

The thump thump of the police helicopter blades.

They say that a mother knows, instinctively, when her child is gone. I wasn't sure I believed that but with the noise comes a change in the air. There is a fizz of energy, of power, of electricity. I know, in my heart, that it is over.

I do not fall to the floor. I do not scream and shout. I just sit, frozen, listening to the sounds around me mixed with the thud of my own heart. How dare my own heart continue to beat.

I don't know how long I sit like that. It may be five seconds, or five minutes. But I am caught in the moment until I glance to the clock on the wall and a voice inside me whispers, 'Time of death . . .'

Stephen mutters and I look at him, the link between us severed. He has his head buried in his hands, just as he has done this past half hour. I don't have the strength to feel sorry for him. I have room for nothing more than my own feelings.

I look to Heather, who it is obvious, even in this poor lighting, has gone very pale. The tubby older policeman I can see through the kitchen door is staring directly at his computer screen.

I stand up. This is enough to break Stephen from his head-burying stupor.

'Marian?' he says and I'm not sure what response, if any, he expects me to give.

Silently, I climb the stairs and walk to what was Nell's bedroom. It has a view over the city, down into the valley, and from her window I can see the traffic snake along the top deck of the Craigavon Bridge. Two fire engines. An ambulance. Two police cars.

I sit on the edge of the bed and I close my eyes. From this moment on, everything is changed.

Chapter Forty-Nine

Him

Thursday, November 4

This had happened too fast. There was no way the police would get here in time. They had driven along a dark private road, into a clearing surrounded by trees next to the house. Even if he could hear the helicopter overhead, which he couldn't, there was very little chance back-up would arrive before this was all over.

So he'd known before he drew his gun that this wasn't going to end well. He'd never shot anyone before. It's different in training. Targets. Dummies. Not people. Not flesh-and-blood human beings who bleed and tear and splinter. Who scream and cry and call for their mothers.

But he'd known that he did not want to listen to Nell Sweeney cry for her mother. He didn't want to see her face contort in fear. He thought of Marian Sweeney, the woman who had cried and buckled with grief in front of him earlier that day.

He'd known quite a few Marian Sweeneys in his time. Good women. Loving women. Good mothers who would do anything for their children but who put themselves last in a long line of people they believed deserved protecting.

He could feel her love for her daughter radiate from her, just as he could see how the presence of the arrogant, insensitive man she was married to made her smaller than she deserved to be. Just as his own mother had been.

Both were women who were compliant, just as Doire or Eddie thought all women should be. Maybe not out of fear in their cases, but out of responsibility. Out of a feeling of what a woman should be.

Marian Sweeney wasn't a broken woman, but she wasn't a woman who adored her life. She was a woman who had been hurt and losing her daughter would break her in two.

No, he wasn't prepared to let Eddie do that to Marian Sweeney.

And he sure as hell wasn't going to let Eddie hurt Nell again. The bruising had already bloomed deep and purple on her cheek. He couldn't help but notice the mottled, discoloured and torn skin around her ankle. He dreaded to think of all the bruises, and all the hidden trauma, that he couldn't see.

When Eddie had taken the chain from Nell, he'd started planning how to get her out of there. If he could just get her towards the door, put enough of a distance between her and Eddie that he could pull his gun without fear that Eddie would use her as a human shield, he could do this.

Maybe he did have people close by, watching them. People other than those ghouls tuned in through their computers. But he'd deal with that if he needed to. Nell Sweeney had looked up at him while she tried to light the gas fire. She'd such hatred in her eyes, he knew he'd already lost the battle. It was the same look Natalia had given him earlier. It wasn't fear that he and Eddie and their like were fostering in women, it was hate. They were proving all women's worst fears to be accurate.

He'd been impressed when he saw Nell switch the gas on to high and pretend it wouldn't light. He'd tried to signal to her that he was one of the good guys, and her secret was safe with him, but he could see in her eyes that she hadn't believed him.

He supposed he deserved that.

All he could do, when Eddie realised what she had done, was try to keep him from getting to her. It wasn't easy. Eddie was a wiry wee bastard, quick on his feet. The only thing slowing him down was the alcohol he had been pinning since they arrived at the house.

His heart had been in his mouth as Nell Sweeney managed to open the door and run from the room but Eddie was after her and he could see that with every step, he grew just that little bit closer. And then he had her. He watched as Eddie pulled at Nell's dress, trying to drag her backwards into this hell. He had to get him off her, he had to give her the chance to get away. He knew she'd lifted the keys from the table. If he could buy her some time, even seconds, she could be in the car and away.

His long, skinny legs finally came into their own, enabling him to catch up with Eddie in two steps and grab him from behind, immobilising his arms, before dragging him back towards the room where Nell had been kept.

'Let her go,' he said, his voice shaking. 'She's not worth it. There will be others.'

He'd thrown Eddie to the floor. 'She's not the one,' he'd said. 'She doesn't deserve to be famous.' He was still trying to mollify him, hoping that he could win enough time for them all to walk out of here.

But Eddie was on his feet again in seconds and was barrelling towards the open door using all his strength to knock Mark to the ground – both of them watching as his gun skittered across the room as he fell. 'You fucking bastard,' Eddie had hissed before righting himself and making for the door again. 'I fucking knew it!'

Mark realised in that instant that if Eddie made it out the door he would catch her and he would be merciless. He had moments to make a decision. He dragged himself towards the gun, realising he could aim at a moving target in the hope of felling it or . . . he could just take aim at the gas canister, still leaking its sickly smell into the room . . .

He had nothing to lose but he could, perhaps, redeem himself in those final seconds.

Without hesitation he raised his weapon and fired at the butane gas cylinder. The room erupted in an explosion of blue, orange and red, and Mark Black's gun fell to the floor.

Epilogue

Nell

Six weeks later

Harry Styles purrs contentedly on my lap. I am curled up on the armchair in the living room of my parents' house and I am watching the lights on the Christmas tree slowly fade in and out.

I know I will be safe here, with my mother to fuss over me. Although she has accused me of fussing too much over her, I glance across the room to where she is dozing on the other armchair, her legs curled up tightly on the seat, a cushion propping up her head.

It's astounding the transformation in her. When I saw her that night, she looked so old and as if all the colour had been washed from her. She was a shadow, an echo of herself. Then again, I don't think I was looking my best either.

Some time after the blackness had enveloped me, I had heard a voice say my name over and over, pulling me into consciousness. I forced my eyes open, fighting against my body's urge to stay in the darkness. I hadn't made it. I hadn't got away. I knew it was Eddie or Mark who was saying my name, and it was only a matter of time before they hauled me from the car and finished what they had started.

Still dazed, I had slammed my foot on the accelerator but the car had just bunny hopped forward, then stalled and the door beside me opened, scattering glass everywhere. I had nowhere to run and no ability to run anyway.

'Nell. It's okay. It's Sam, the paramedic,' a woman's voice registered with me. 'We've met at the hospital before. You've been hurt, but we're here and we're going to help you. You're safe now.'

Sam was a paramedic I knew well, but I could hardly believe that it was her beside me when I opened my eyes. I blinked, still trying to find my bearings.

'What hurts? Are you okay?' I swivelled my head round towards her voice, my ears still ringing, my skin burning, my chest tight. I hurt everywhere. Her eyes widened, just a little at the sight of me and then she was back in professional mode. As she asked more questions, I realised she was probably expecting me to answer them, but I was so frozen with shock I couldn't speak.

The scene around me was just coming into focus. I could pick out new sounds and sensations. Slowly, I became aware of the flashing blue lights around me. The clump and crunch of firemen's boots through the mud and sticks. The buzzing of radios. The shouts of men and women doing their jobs. Fear coursed through me. Was he out there? Eddie. Was he hiding among them? And Mark? Did they know who they were looking for?

I tried to speak, but the words wouldn't come and Jesus, but my jaw ached and clicked.

The fear must've been evident in my eyes.

'It's okay,' Sam soothed. 'They're gone. They're both gone.'

Blackness slid in over me again.

*　　*　　*

I woke in the hospital to see the ghostly appearance of my parents, standing on either side of my bed. Each held one of my hands as gently as they could, trying not to exacerbate my bruising or dislodge the cannulas that had been inserted.

'You're back,' my mother said, her voice a balm to my heart. 'You're back and you're safe.' I felt a tear run down my cheek, tearing at my red-raw skin.

Through his own tears, my father explained to me there had been an explosion, ignited by the spark of a gun firing. Mark Black's gun. Detective Constable Mark Black. No one can say for certain what happened but from footage caught at just the right angle, it looks as though Mark Black had deliberately fired at the canister. Whatever the truth of it, his actions had stopped Eddie in his tracks and had undoubtedly saved me.

He who had started it all that night when he followed me as I walked along the Dungiven Road, had helped save me. He had sacrificed himself for me. I can't stop thinking of that look on his face as I knelt by the gas heater. That signal to keep quiet, to move towards the door. The way he reached into his coat.

For his gun.

I couldn't read it then. I was too scared. My ability to see the good in people had been annihilated.

Some have hailed him a hero. My feelings are more complicated than that. He started this after all. And I can still see the hatred in his eyes that first night as he scared me for internet likes. There was a contempt in him that ran deep but even with that I don't think he deserved to die. Elzbieta's death was already one death too many.

Eddie and Mark won't have the chance to hurt any more women, but I am also acutely aware they will never face true justice. It's a hollow victory for me. I would've liked to have seen Eddie torn to shreds in court. I would've loved to see him rot in a cell for the rest of his life.

To some of his followers, Eddie is a martyr now. That sickens me the most. To them, he is a hero. I think that was probably his intention all along. He must've known he was never getting out of it unscathed. He wanted to be famous – well, he got his wish. He'll just never see it.

I can't allow myself to think about it all too much. I can't allow myself to play those memories over and over again, or play the 'what if' game. But I can allow myself to say that Mark Black was not the person who saved me. I saved me. I fought and clawed my way out of there. He has no ownership of that.

I hold onto that when pain and fear wash over me again. That week haunts me enough, every time I close my eyes or hear a key turn in a lock. I wonder will that feeling ever leave. It seems as much a part of me now as the tens of tiny scars on my arms and face from the shards of glass that cut me in the explosion.

Every time I wake up, it takes a minute or two to realise where I am. That I am safe. That I am warm. That I have survived. I dread going to sleep knowing that panic will come at some stage during the night. But I have my mum, sleeping beside me, holding my hand. Reassuring me.

I've not moved back in with Clodagh yet, but I will. As soon as I feel able. We are mending our relationship. I will never take her for granted again. I will never wish for more than contentment. She has been to visit regularly. There's something lovely about drinking tea at my mum's kitchen table, gossiping just like we did when we were teenagers. There is still love there, even if it has been bruised.

But for now I need to be close to my mother, and she needs to be close to me.

She has told me that she realised over the days I was gone, when I could so easily have been murdered, that she'd had enough.

She'd made a solemn promise to herself that whether or not I ever walked back through her door she was calling time on her marriage. The thought, she said, of him being all she had left was unbearable.

My father didn't argue with her. He cut a sad figure as he left, but she is so much happier. The colour is coming back into her life. I'm only now realising how long his bad behaviour really had gone on for. I'm only now realising how much she hid from me. How much of her day-to-day life was an act. I had seen her as weak when in truth it took a remarkable strength to keep going all those years, supporting a man who could only ever love himself.

We are healing together, slowly but surely.

Harry Styles stretches, blinks up at me before snuggling back down and starting to purr again. I exhale.

Author's Note

On the day I submitted the first draft of this novel to my editor, the body of missing marketing executive Sarah Everard was discovered in woodlands near Ashford in Kent, in England.

The 33-year-old was kidnapped and murdered as she walked home from a friend's house in March of 2021.

In September 2021, former police officer Wayne Couzens received a whole life sentence for her kidnap, rape and murder.

Sarah Everard was sadly not the first, and nor will she be the last, woman not to make it home. Her death sparked a major outpouring of grief and anger, but it also acted as the catalyst for women to speak out about all the times they have felt threatened or unsafe simply for being women. Women spoke up about all the times they carried their keys in their hands as makeshift weapons. About the times they have been cat-called. About the fear that we as women experience simply walking the streets on our own at night.

Institutional and systemic misogyny is real and in March of 2021, it felt more exposed than ever before.

As part of the wider discussion on misogyny, the spotlight

inevitably fell on the growing popularity of the incel (involuntarily celibate) movement.

I first heard about incels around seven years ago – when in 2014 Elliot Rodger killed six people and injured a further 14 before killing himself in California. Rodger had self-identified as an incel and was active on incel message boards. He posted videos on YouTube detailing his beliefs and left a 137 page Manifesto. To many in the incel community he is seen as a martyr and has been elevated to hero status. His name, and his actions, have been referenced in subsequent discussions and attacks and the movement has grown. The growth has been despite a crackdown on incel discussion forums and message boards.

Reddit had once hosted multiple incel discussions, with 41000 users registered to their incel sub-reddit boards. These discussions were banned in 2017, but many examples or screenshots of archived threads are still accessible with the help of a good search engine, a strong stomach and a lot of patience.

When researching this novel I read some truly horrific discussions. But there is also a lot of discussion from men, particularly young men, who feel lost, useless and worthless in a world that is redefining what it is to be a man.

It's not hard to see how vulnerable and angry men can find themselves caught up in these boards, and how insidious the incel philosophy can be.

Here we have men who consider themselves unattractive berate themselves, describe their shortcomings and at the same time express extreme anger that they are being overlooked by female partners. They find people who empathise with their frustration and allow them a place to voice their anger.

They find a place when men idealise the 'good old days' – times when roles were very clearly defined. Men were the breadwinners, women were subservient, and often dependent on their husbands.

In the incel community, blame is laid very firmly at the door of feminism for stripping men of their worth. In these communities, men outline their ideas for a 'fairer' world – believing that they have a biological need for sex and that being denied this most basic of all rights dehumanises them.

In the course of my research I found suggestions that women who have had multiple sexual partners should be made available to have sex with incels as they clearly have loose morals. The most disturbing thing I read was a suggestion that women could be used simply as warm bodies for men to have sex with. There was a suggestion that women who have been declared as legally brain-dead should be kept alive artificially for just this purpose.

There was much to read that horrified me. Many of the usernames that I have used in this book are genuine ones from boards I have seen. They illustrate the way in which women are viewed. They also highlight the very toxic masculinity that surrounds this culture.

The incel movement has been identified in multiple mass shootings around the world, resulting in in excess of sixty deaths by August 2021. The latest, at the time of going to print, was the murder of five people in Plymouth England by self-identified incel Jake Davison (22) in July, 2021. That incident occurred on the day I began the final edit of this novel.

The incel movement is one we should all be concerned about. Not simply because of the graphic and violent nature of some of its rhetoric but because in the years since I first became aware of it, I have watched it grow and take hold on an exponential level.

The lack of a public online space to discuss incel ideology has pushed the discussion to the darkest recesses of the internet, where no moderation takes place and extremism thrives.

But incel beliefs are making their way into mainstream society

– as the social media reaction to the Plymouth Shooting high-lighted.

The level of vitriol against women online grows on a daily basis. Many of the women I know with an active Twitter presence have been threatened with rape, murder and even the rape of their children. Unsolicited dick pics – an act of aggression and intimidation – are a reality for most women online. Disagreeing with a man's opinion or rejecting a man's advances can often lead to a slew of misogynistic abuse. While sex is weaponised against women, there can never been true equality.

This book was written because I have seen how pervasive this ideology has become and how quickly it can spread. I also wanted to examine how someone could become indoctrinated into this cult like community without even realising it. How validation of their fear and anger is addictive.

I fear we are closer to a world where Margaret Attwood's Gilead could be a reality than we have ever been in the past. That's something we should all be scared of.

Claire Allan
2021

Every family has its secrets...

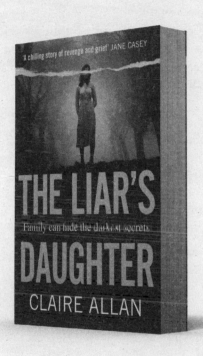

A gripping suspense novel about deadly secrets and lies.

Available in all good bookshops now.

I disappeared on a Tuesday afternoon.

They've never found my body...

A unputdownable serial killer thriller with a
breath-taking twist.

Available in all good bookshops now.

Just how far is a mother willing to go?

A gripping psychological thriller from the *USA Today* bestseller.

Available in all good bookshops now.

You watched her die.

And her death has created a vacancy...

A gripping thriller that will have you hooked.

Available in all good bookshops now.

Not all secrets are meant to come out...

A twisty crime thriller from the
bestselling author Claire Allan.

Available in all good bookshops now.